Praise for *Falling for You Again*

"Kerry Lonsdale's *Falling for You Again* takes the classic 'fake date' romance we all love and gives it a sparkling, fresh twist that delighted me from the first page. I really connected with Meli, who is strong, ambitious, and unwilling to make unreasonable compromises in her personal and professional life. And Aaron . . . what can I say about Aaron, except why did Meli have to sit next to him that day on the plane instead of me? This is a wonderfully warm, relatable love story where the stakes are realistic and the swoon-value is stratospheric. I loved it!"

—Carol Mason, bestselling author of *Second Chance Romance*

"Can you be partners in business and in life? Kerry Lonsdale's latest, *Falling for You Again*, asks the question, and readers will fall hard for the answer. Hands down, Aaron and Meli are Lonsdale's sexiest couple yet. I flipped through this playful rom-com and held my breath through the layered, emotional parts. You will never hear the words *husband* and *wife* the same way again as these characters fall again and again in this delightful romp. Lonsdale's fans are in for a big treat. A complete joy to read—utterly charming and the perfect escape!"

—Rochelle Weinstein, bestselling author of *This Is Not How It Ends*

"In this captivating tale of a gifted artisan who makes an impromptu decision that may forever change her future, Kerry Lonsdale again proves that she's the queen of women's fiction—but isn't afraid to bring a fresh spin to her storytelling. *Falling for You Again* will delight readers seeking a layered romance brimming with family drama."

—Camille Pagán, bestselling author of *Good for You*

Praise for *Find Me in California*

"Kerry Lonsdale is back with another heartfelt, romantic story about love, loss, and second chances. *Find Me in California* is a wonderful novel that beautifully weaves the past and the present. Full of passion, grief, and devastating generational secrets, this perfect story also has the perfect ending. Not to be missed!"

—Hannah Mary McKinnon, bestselling author of *Only One Survives*

"Wow. Kerry Lonsdale has done it again. *Find Me in California* is pitch perfect. A touch of mystery, a hot dose of romance, the glamorous film world, and a deeply rooted family connection. Lonsdale weaves a brilliantly crafted novel of loss and redemption, forgiveness and hope. Poignant and unputdownable."

—Rochelle B. Weinstein, bestselling author of *What You Do to Me*

"When family secrets from past generations surface, there's a second chance for forgiveness and hope for a new generation. Past and present interweave to unravel a story brimming with secrets and surprises. *Find Me in California* is an emotional ride from beginning to end. I enjoyed every moment of it."

—Annie Cathryn, author of *The Friendship Breakup*

"This gripping and unexpected love story is truly one of Kerry Lonsdale's best. With a beautifully crafted dual timeline and the perfect sprinkle of magical realism, *Find Me in California* hits all the right notes."

—Camille Pagán, bestselling author of *Good for You*

"Kerry Lonsdale does it again! A poignant, warm, absorbing story of family bonds, secrets, betrayal, and forgiveness."

—A. J. Banner, #1 Kindle, *USA Today*, and *Publishers Weekly* bestselling author

"I found myself totally invested in both Julia's and Matt's stories. I loved the themes of family and found family, and choked up with tears at several parts."

—Meredith Schorr, author of *Someone Just Like You*

"*Find Me in California* brims with star-crossed lovers, poor decisions, loss, abandonment, and numerous secrets . . . This touching novel is about opening up to love and facing not just the past but also the future with an open mind and heart."

—Bookreporter

"[Lonsdale] packs quite the emotional punch [in *Find Me in California*]. If you enjoy angst—and I do mean a whole boatload of angst—this is the book for you. My emotions were fully engaged from start to finish. What a ride."

—The Romance Dish

Praise for *No More Words*

"Lonsdale expertly maintains suspense throughout. Psychological-thriller fans will be well satisfied."

—*Publishers Weekly*

"A perfect summer read."

—Red Carpet Crash

"[A] mesmerizing first installment in her newest No More series . . . *No More Words* simmers with drama and secrets, sure to dazzle readers as an unmissable summer read."

—The Nerd Daily

"Lonsdale's first book in a new trilogy about love, betrayal, and the secrets families keep. Read in one sitting!"

—Frolic

"[Lonsdale] creates stories that readers will want to read again and again."

—*Write-Read-Life*

"Lonsdale is at her best with this multilayered story about three dysfunctional siblings and the secrets they keep. What a ride. I'm still a little breathless. This one was an addictive page-turner—impossible to put down. Fans of domestic suspense will EAT THIS UP."

—Sally Hepworth, bestselling author of *The Good Sister* and *The Mother-in-Law*

"Kerry Lonsdale is back and better than ever with this multilayered tale about three siblings torn apart by a series of tragic events. Nuanced and smart, filled with characters with real emotion and depth, *No More Words* is everything you've come to love from the master of domestic drama. A mesmerizing beginning to a new trilogy that will have you one-clicking the next in the series."

—Kimberly Belle, internationally bestselling author of *Stranger in the Lake*

"Full of suspense, romance, and drama, *No More Words* is a powerful story about what it means to be a family. Emotional and honest, it tells the story of three siblings, each dealing with demons from the past. I fell in love with all three Carson children and look forward to the second and third installments of this series. Kerry Lonsdale is a master storyteller of family drama, and this is Lonsdale at her best."

—Suzanne Redfearn, #1 Amazon bestselling author of *In an Instant*

Falling
for
You
Again

ALSO BY KERRY LONSDALE

THE EVERYTHING SERIES

Everything We Keep

Everything We Left Behind

Everything We Give

STAND-ALONE NOVELS

All the Breaking Waves

Last Summer

Side Trip

Find Me in California

THE NO MORE SERIES

No More Words

No More Lies

No More Secrets

Falling for You Again

A Novel

Kerry Lonsdale

LAKE UNION
PUBLISHING

Text copyright © 2025 by Kerry Lonsdale Inc.
All rights reserved.

Published by Lake Union Publishing, Seattle

www.apub.com

Amazon, the Amazon logo, and Lake Union Publishing are trademarks of Amazon. com, Inc., or its affiliates.

EU product safety contact:
Amazon Media EU S. à r.l.
38, avenue John F. Kennedy, L-1855 Luxembourg
amazonpublishing-gpsr@amazon.com

ISBN-13: 9781662525285 (paperback)
ISBN-13: 9781662525292 (digital)

Cover design by Ploy Siripant
Cover image: © Jon Bilous / Alamy; © sakkmesterke, © New Africa / Shutterstock

Printed in the United States of America

For anyone who believes love is worth fighting for

THE GREATEST LOVE STORY

"Love is too fickle, Meli, to waste it on someone who will leave you," Uncle Bear once said to me when I'd asked why he wasn't married. He was bent over a plank of white maple, planing the surface.

I stopped sweeping under his workbench and leaned on the broom handle. I was twelve at the time and just opening my eyes to the world of boys and middle school romances. "Do you think I shouldn't get married?"

"I don't think. What I *know* is wood, and wood is constant." He waved a small cut of maple between us before tossing it over to me. "Wood will always be there for you. If you nurture anything, make sure it's your craft, not a relationship."

I felt the rough grains on the edge and added the piece to the slowly growing pile on the floor. I understood wood. Boys, I didn't. But I'd watched *The Princess Bride* and I'd read *The Baby-Sitters Club* and some of the Sweet Valley High books. There was a cute boy in class who my friend said had a crush on me.

"Then why are there so many stories about love? What if I can't help it and love just happens to me?" I'd never been in love so I didn't know whether I could stop myself from feeling it.

"Meli." His voice took on a serious note. "If there was ever a great love story, it's between an artist and their creation, and nothing else. Best you remember that."

At the time, I was apprenticing for Uncle Bear at Artisant Designs, the high-end wood-furniture studio he'd inherited from his father, my grandpa Walt. The shop I would one day inherit from Uncle Bear. Every afternoon since I'd turned ten and he unexpectedly found himself my legal guardian, I'd joined him at the shop after school. While I swept sawdust in the dappled sunlight leaking through the high, dusty windows of the old warehouse in South Boston that had been in our family for generations, he enlightened me with his Bearisms, witty pieces of advice. And he had plenty of them, such as, "Commitment is like a fresh coat of varnish: it is beautiful at first but cracks with time."

Or, "Love isn't just fickle; it's also a thief. Love steals your time, energy, and focus. It will steal your art if you don't pay attention."

"Love fades, but a well-built table lasts for decades."

"Balance is an illusion" was another Bearism. He taught me that I can't equally love this shop and everything it holds dear for our family and be in love with someone else. One always wins over the other, so I'd better make a choice ahead of time.

Then there's the Bearism he made me swear to never forget as he handed me the planer for the first time, as I felt the tool's vibration up my arms, the motor jarring my bones: "If you ever do fall in love, Meli, heaven forbid it's someone you work with. Splitting creative control is like splitting wood with a butter knife: it's not only impossible but will also leave you cold and lonely and resentful in the end."

I never understood why Uncle Bear was so jaded about love. Who had hurt him so badly? He refused to explain when I'd asked why he wasn't married or didn't date. What I did need to understand, according to him, was that if I wanted to inherit the shop one day—which I did—I needed to love my craft more than anything or anyone else in the world. The shop was our family's legacy. It would always come first.

Until the day came that it didn't.

CHAPTER 1

HOME AWAY FROM HOME

Shortly before 8:00 a.m., I give Blueberry, my adopted, one-eyed senior Russian blue cat, a kiss goodbye, just as I do every morning before leaving for the shop. I scratch him in his favorite spot under his chin while he lounges in a square patch of sunlight on the couch. "See you tonight," I coo, already missing him. I don't like leaving him for the day, but the shop isn't a place for a cat, not with the noise and heavy machinery, and with people constantly coming and going.

Blueberry watches me leave with his permanent wink, stretching his legs and spreading his toe beans. He yawns deeply as I close the door and will happily nap for most of the day.

Across the hallway, I knock on my best friend Emi's door. She lives in a one-bedroom apartment that matches mine, our floor plans flipped. We met at trade school, and I begged her to come work with me at Artisant when we graduated nine years ago. But she's made a successful career at Stone & Bloom, an upscale kitchen and bathroom showroom, designing gourmet kitchens for restaurants and town houses.

"Coffee?" She greets me with a smile as bright as the sunlight in my apartment when her door swings open. Always stylish compared with my daily uniform of coveralls and steel-toe work boots, she's wearing butter-and-wisteria-striped palazzo pants with a white ribbed tank top under a softly woven white cardigan and camel leather flats. A wide gold headband holds back the curly cherry-brown hair I've always envied. My rose-gold-tipped brunette hair is flat and lifeless in comparison. Soft freckles dust her tawny nose and high cheekbones.

"Yes," I agree, even though I already drank two espressos before my shower. I have a long, laborious day ahead.

"How's Isadora's table coming along?" Emi asks as we make our way along the Charles riverfront toward Bean There, Done That, the coffee shop we frequent in our Cambridge neighborhood.

Emi referred Isadora de Medici to me after she'd completed the kitchen remodel. Isadora is a lovely woman with four ex-husbands and two Italian greyhounds named Sophia and Loren she claims are more loyal than any man has been to her. She wears a sapphire on her right ring finger that is as large and blue as an ocean, a promise ring to never remarry, which she purchased after her fourth divorce. I've designed a custom table for her that will fit her kitchen's new dimensions.

"Almost done," I say of the 92-inch American walnut table. "Once I sand and stain, it's finished. It'll take another week, two at the most."

Emi's amber eyes glitter with excitement. "Excellent." She rubs her hands together. "Let me know when it's delivered. I'll send Shae over. I want a photo with your table for my portfolio."

"Will do." I open the coffee shop's door for her.

Bean There, Done That is bustling. We wait in line to place our orders and chat about the new cookbook Emi bought last night at Codfish & Chapters, a bookstore near Stone & Bloom's showroom. She wants to cook a succulent artichoke-stuffed beef tenderloin for me and her coworkers Shae and Tam, one of the happiest married couples I know. I don't think Emi would be thrilled to learn Uncle Bear and I have a bet on how long they'll last since they live and work together. He's giving them three years. My money is on five. Neither of us believe they'll successfully balance work with their marriage. One of these days, something will give.

The barista shouts our names, and after we collect our coffees, we walk to the T as Emi plans a dinner party for Saturday night and I offer to bring the wine and dessert. We ride the Green Line together until she gets off at her station, then I switch to the Red Line, heading toward the waterfront and Artisan Designs.

Today is delivery day, and Uncle Bear keeps the rear roll door open to receive our lumber orders throughout the morning. It's late spring, the temperature mild with the promise of a warm afternoon. The shop will get hot, and it already feels that way as I enter the brightly lit, cavernous space. Artisan Designs, as usual, is alive with activity. Brick walls support ancient, stained timber beams overhead. Underfoot, cracks vein the concrete floor. Mom is at the coffee bar, wearing her favorite purple puffer vest she keeps zipped to her chin no matter the temperature. It coordinates brilliantly with her silver-threaded brunette bob and purple Nike running shoes that support her weak arches. She manages the shop's accounts and oversees customer service, and usually greets me at the front desk with a smile. But this morning, her usual buoyancy is replaced with a sour scowl. No doubt Dad did something to irritate her. He's probably late with an order again.

My parents have proven that my uncle's Bearisms are solid pieces of advice. Business and love don't mix. As much as I enjoy that we all work here—the studio is the only place where, other than Uncle Bear's apartment to celebrate holidays and birthdays, my family willingly spends time together—Artisan Designs has strained their marriage. Dad is incapable of pleasing Mom, and Mom constantly nags Dad. They haven't been happy since they returned when I was sixteen, six years after they left us, and that was thirteen years ago. Honestly, I'm shocked they're still married. They really should spend more time apart.

Dad is at the table saw. He guides a white oak plank through a blade that whines like a buzzing mosquito amplified a thousand times over. The earthy musk of freshly sawed wood infuses the air. Toward the back, Uncle Bear and Kidder, a lanky intern from the same trade school I attended, sort through this morning's first of four deliveries, organizing the wood by type and cut.

"Want a cup?" Mom hollers at me with a lift of her mug.

"Just had one, thanks," I yell back, opening my locker. I swap my backpack for gloves, safety goggles, and noise-canceling headphones.

Dad pauses the blade and pulls a headphone cover off an ear. "I'll take a cup."

"You got legs. Get it yourself." Mom drinks deeply from her mug, giving Dad her back as she returns to her workstation.

Ah, love. Mom and Dad have their own special way of showing it.

I head over to Isadora's table and sink on my heels, peering at the surface as I study the natural beauty of the live edge for imperfections. My fingers coast over the wood I started sanding yesterday, and, feeling a rough spot, I mark where I'll begin working today.

I pull on my gloves.

Uncle Bear gestures for Dad to turn off the table saw. "I think they shorted us," he says of the lumber.

"Want me to recount?" I offer.

"Grab the invoice. It's on my desk." Uncle Bear flaps his gloves at the old metal desk he found beside a dumpster some forty-odd years ago when he and Dad started working full time at Grandpa Walt's shop.

I leave my gloves on Isadora's table and approach my uncle's desk. Not an inch of surface is visible under the heaps of furniture catalogs and haphazard piles of graph paper marked up with design sketches. Old invoices are mixed in with yellowing receipts, everything strewn about. Uncle Bear evidently missed the memo that the twenty-first century has gone paperless and we're in a climate crisis. He prints his emails along with their attachments to read them, and that's only when he gets around to checking his inbox, which isn't often.

"What am I looking for?" I holler over the saw Dad has turned on again. We source lumber from four different mills. I leaf through a stack of invoices, nothing jumping out at me.

"Jackson's. It's on top," Uncle Bear shouts.

"I don't see it." I flip through papers, fanning corners, searching for Jackson's lumberman logo, only to stop cold at a printed email dated a few weeks back. "What's this?" I mumble to myself, picking up the paper.

TO: bearwoodMA@aol.com
FROM: swright@thesavanthouse.com

SUBJECT: Letter of Intent Regarding Potential Acquisition of Artisant Designs

Dear Mr. Bernard Hynes,

Thank you for informing the Savant House, Inc. of your desire to sell Artisant Designs, LLC. This letter serves as the preliminary expression of our company's interest in acquiring Artisant Designs. We are impressed . . .

I stop reading as a hollow, sinking sensation forms inside me. As if each printed word carves away a little piece of my dream. The paper shakes in my hand. I'm supposed to inherit the shop. Uncle Bear promised it would go to me.

"Are you selling the shop?"

Mom spins around in her office chair at my stunned shout. Dad turns off the saw, the blade's whine petering out. Kidder, who was helping himself to a fresh coffee, freezes with the mug halfway to his mouth. Everyone looks at my uncle, but I seem to be the only one shocked by this news.

Uncle Bear rubs the side of his neck. "Aw, Meli, you weren't supposed to have seen that." He sounds genuinely disgruntled.

"You promised me the shop when you retire."

Uncle Bear drags a hand down his cheek. "You don't want it. It's too much trouble. The cost of lumber these days, the machinery upkeep . . ." He shakes his head.

"That's why you're selling?" It doesn't make sense. The shop has had its share of bumps and bruises over the years—recessions, pandemic lockdowns, competition, supply shortages—and we've dealt with them. We usually come out stronger on the other end of a crisis. Customers always return because of our expert craftsmanship and the way we embrace our materials' imperfections and aesthetic resonance. These days, you can't easily find the quality we produce.

"Told you she wasn't going to like this," Dad says.

"Exactly why we didn't want her to know, Dean," Uncle Bear snaps at his younger brother. "Not yet. It's too soon," he says, confirming everyone knew but me.

"Did you know?" I ask Kidder in disbelief.

He vigorously shakes his head. "I didn't know."

Okay, then. Everyone except me and the intern.

Kidder does his best to look small over by the coffee bar, which isn't easy for such a tall, lanky guy. His eyes dart about the shop as if he's looking for an escape hatch.

That's one disadvantage of working for a family business. You can get caught in the middle of their family squabbles.

Speaking of families, what will happen to mine if we don't have Artisant Designs to hold us together? I always figured my parents would continue to work with me after Uncle Bear retired. He might be ten years older than Dad, but I didn't expect him to retire for another five to eight years. Grandpa Walt had worked until his late sixties.

I read more of the letter. The Savant House will acquire all assets, tangible and intangible, that are owned by the seller.

"My designs." They are copyrighted under Artisant. I'll lose years of work. "How could you do this to me?" I feel violated.

"We did it *for* you. You'll be happier at Savant."

I gape at Dad. "Excuse me?"

"Damn you, Dean." Uncle Bear smacks his gloves against the lumber pile. "We talked about this."

My stomach churns with dread. "Talked about what?"

"He didn't want to tell you until the deal is signed," Mom explains. "We know how much your heart has been set on taking over the shop."

"Unbelievable." Uncle Bear tosses up his hands, fed up with my parents.

Dad rubs the side of his nose, fixing eyes a shade lighter than my brown ones on the floor. Kidder retreats until the counter bites into his back. Watching us warily, he sets down his mug like a rabbit ready to bolt.

Mom gives me a fleeting smile. "The Savant House is creating a position for you. They want you to oversee a team of artisans and design an exclusive furniture line for them."

"You didn't think to include me in these conversations?" Not only are they selling off my future but they're also negotiating a new one for me—without my consent.

Uncle Bear sucks in his bottom lip, his brows disappearing into his thinning hairline. "They'll pay you well, Meli. Benefits too. Things I haven't been able to provide you here. You'll have a solid career path with them."

"If I wanted to work for a large corporation, I wouldn't have been working here since I was ten." This is where my family is.

Uncle Bear averts his face, which makes me think he's trying to hide his guilt.

"Why *are* you selling?" I want real reasons, not lame excuses about unreliable suppliers and faulty equipment.

"We're tired." Dad answers too quickly.

I fix him with a skeptical stare. If it were that simple, Uncle Bear would gradually transition the business to me like we discussed, allowing me time to grow accustomed to running the shop on my own. This sale is sudden.

Kidder wipes his palms over his hips. "Does this mean my internship is over?"

"Not yet," Uncle Bear says.

"How long, then?" I demand.

"I'm not going back on this, Meli," Uncle Bear says, knowing how my mind works.

I want to know how long I have to change *his* mind. And if I can't do that, how long do I have to apply for a business loan and make an alternative offer? Though if it's money Uncle Bear wants, I doubt I can match what the Savant House can pay. There must be a way I can stop the sale.

I return the letter to the desk and pick up a card with fancy, gold-embossed lettering. It's an invitation to the Savant House's annual fundraising gala, scheduled for tomorrow night at the Park Plaza. We've received their invites for years, but Uncle Bear and my parents always decline attending. They aren't ones for fancy soirees. I, on the other hand, have had my own reasons for avoiding their functions. Reasons my parents and uncle don't know about. But as a memory comes to mind an idea coalesces. I pocket the invitation and grab my backpack from the locker.

"Where are you going?" Uncle Bear asks as I head for the exit.

"Out."

"Don't get any funny ideas, Meli. We've already started negotiating."

That might be so, but it isn't going to stop me from shopping for a dress. He doesn't know it yet, but I have a date with my ex-husband.

CHAPTER 2

RUNAWAY BRIDE

After my parents, I'm the second reason that proves my uncle's Bearisms have merit: balancing the work I'm passionate about with a relationship is impossible for me. So I made a choice, albeit almost too late.

It happened five years ago. I met Paul through his mom, Cheryl, a former client of mine, when I delivered a matching set of side tables I designed and built for her. She'd remodeled her home, a lovely estate just outside the city, and Paul had been there when I arrived. He helped us move the living room furniture to make room for the new tables.

I don't date often, and I'd never dated anyone long term because of Uncle Bear's advice. I figured it best to take it to heart rather than deal with the heartache of a failed relationship. But at twenty-three, I had been young, naive, and rash, and Paul had been charming—his family even more so. Since I wasn't close to my parents, I craved what he had and what he could offer me, and deep down, I desired to feel loved. He was the first person who wanted me all to himself, and I fell for him easily. I let him sweep me away, and before I realized it, almost a year had passed and we were engaged.

But finding Paul hadn't helped me find myself; it had made me feel more lost. And I'd been in denial that our relationship wasn't right for me until the moment my best friend and maid of honor, Emi, proceeded up the aisle before me. In the vestibule of the church, I turned to my uncle, who was escorting me into my new life—a life I'd just realized I didn't want—and he took one look at my stricken expression.

"Oh, Melisaurus," he'd said with a touch of compassion, reverting to the childhood nickname he'd used when I first came to live with him, and my walls of denial came crashing down.

"I should have listened to you. I can't marry him. I shouldn't marry anyone," I said, getting slightly hysterical in my panicked state.

"Sh-shh. There, there." He rubbed my bare arms below the ginormous poufed shoulders of my wedding dress—my "something borrowed" from Paul's mom. "Are you sure this isn't just nerves?"

"No." I shook my head hard, feeling tears rise. "It's more than that," I said and quickly shared with him what had happened several nights prior.

I'd been working on a chair for a client at Artisant, trying to complete the project before I left on our honeymoon. With all the wedding festivities and obligations Paul's family had been demanding of me, I'd already missed my client's deadline. It hadn't been intentional, but I'd lost track of time and forgotten that Paul had offered to give me a lift to my apartment so I could get ready for dinner with his parents. I was bent over the partially assembled chair with a chisel when Paul stepped into the workshop.

"Hey, Meli. Ready to go?" His voice carried a hint of impatience.

I glanced up. "Almost. Give me a minute."

"We're already running late." He glanced at his watch and approached the workbench. "I thought we agreed on the time tonight. You also said you were cutting back on your hours here."

"I know, it's just . . ." I sighed, my heart aching over a promise I regretted making as I wiped sweat from my brow. "This piece is special and I want it to be perfect. I'm almost done. Promise."

His gaze lingered on the chair, his mouth set in a firm line and a slight frown drawing his brows together, conveying his displeasure and frustration, when a flicker of envy passed over his face. "Do you realize you always put work before everything else?"

I hesitated, my hand clenching the chisel. Paul had once admired my passion for my craft, but lately he'd treated it like competition for my attention. A competition he was losing.

Whether or not he intended to make me feel guilty, his words had that effect on me. "I'm sorry. I don't mean to." I was going to make us late, but I couldn't make myself stop working on the chair. It wasn't that I yearned for the satisfaction of a completed project or was chasing a deadline—I sought my parents' praise, something I was too ashamed to admit out loud to Paul, or even to myself. Because I sought praise they'd never give. They just didn't think to do so anymore. That, or they didn't care.

Paul sat on a nearby stool, his gaze lingering on my hands as I tried to finish my work so we could get out of there. "You know I'd never ask you to give this up, but . . . ," he said after a few moments of heavy silence.

Alarmed, my gaze snapped to his. "But what?"

"Nothing," he muttered, standing. "Let's go. My parents are waiting."

"He did ask me," I said to Uncle Bear as we stood at the entrance of the church where I didn't want to be. Paul had asked me later that night when he walked me to my apartment door. He'd asked me to give up woodworking. "I can't do that."

"And you shouldn't," Uncle Bear said. He clasped my hands with palms calloused from years of hard work. "Woodworking is as much a part of you as your left arm."

I knew he'd understand. "What am I supposed to do?"

"Whatever you choose. I'll support you."

Whatever I choose . . .

The music inside the church surged, and I glanced in that direction, knowing Paul was waiting for me at the end of the aisle. He had asked me to make a choice, and I'd made the wrong one. I felt that in my soul.

I couldn't give up my craft, and I couldn't spend my life with a man who expected me to be something less than myself.

I regretted that it had taken me until that moment to realize it. And I anguished over abandoning Paul at the altar. But I couldn't go through with our wedding.

"I have to get out of here," I said with mounting panic.

"Where will you go?"

I knew Uncle Bear was worried about me, but I didn't have an answer for him. "I don't know. I'll call you, though." I just had to go. Go, go, go.

I started vibrating with nervous energy, the instinct to flee nipping at my slingback heels.

He seemed satisfied with my response for the moment, because he slipped his credit card into the beaded clutch that matched my wedding dress, also a loaner from Cheryl. She'd worn the dress for her 1985 marriage to Paul's dad. "For emergencies," he said of the card.

Without wasting a second more, without a backward glance at the church, where I'm sure the guests had grown restless, I ran.

Uncle Bear whooped. He chased me down the front steps and hailed a taxi, hauling open the door when one came to an abrupt stop at the curb. I crawled headfirst into the back seat because Cheryl's dress was massive; everything had been big in the eighties. Uncle Bear scooped up the yards of gossamer as I ordered the driver to take me to the airport. *This* was an emergency.

"That's my girl." Uncle Bear handed me the dress train and shut the door.

I put down the window. "I'll text when I get to wherever." My gaze nervously veered to the church behind us.

"I'll talk to them. Get out of here." He smacked his palm on the roof.

"I love you!" I shouted as the taxi shot into Boston traffic.

I hadn't planned to be a runaway bride. I also hadn't planned to fly to Las Vegas. But I was distraught, and on the taxi ride to the airport, I booked the first flight out with available seating. The next thing I knew, I was racing through Logan International in a wedding dress.

I arrived at the gate winded and with only sixty seconds to spare, and I thrust my boarding pass at the attendant. I was flying business class for the first time ever. An expensive ticket, but the last one left.

"You're one lucky woman, Melissa Hynes. Just in the nick of time." The attendant scanned my boarding pass, barely glancing at my gown and veil. I gave her a big, relieved smile. I'd saved myself from getting hitched.

With the gown's train tossed over my arm, I yanked up the front hem to keep from tripping and ran through the jet bridge. Someone else was gaining on me from behind. The bridge shook under our weight, the sound echoing through the metal tunnel.

I leaped onto the plane and abruptly stopped before I ran into a flight attendant, catching the guy behind me off guard. He rammed right into me, pitching me forward. I shrieked, grasping for the flight attendant's arms as I stumbled.

"Sorry!" The guy behind me grabbed my shoulder and hauled me upright into a cloud of cologne. He smelled too nice for his own good.

"Are you all right?" The flight attendant picked up the beaded clutch that had popped out of my grasp.

"I'm fine. *Fine*," I snapped at the guy over my shoulder who was pawing at my dress. My veil was stuck to his sweaty face. I peeled it off him and snagged my clutch from the patient attendant before flopping into my seat in the second row. I just wanted to melt into the cushions and try not to think of how angry Paul must be with me right now. But I sat on the veil, and the combs tugged hard on my hair, pulling at my scalp.

"Ow." I yanked out the combs, along with the pins in my updo, and shook out the dramatically cut shoulder-length bob I'd dyed a dark-strawberry ombre two days prior. Cheryl hadn't been pleased. Paul had left it at "No comment." But the glow in his eyes had dulled. This was after he'd asked me to give up my craft. Maybe he sensed I just hadn't been that into our relationship anymore.

I gave my scalp a good scratch and balled up the mesh tulle, stuffing the veil into the seat pocket as the guy who'd boarded after me dragged his luggage down the aisle, scoping out overhead bin space. I was hot and scratchy, and I had to pee.

Inside the clutch purse, my phone incessantly vibrated. By now, the wedding would have been called off, and Paul was either terribly distraught or planning to commit murder should he find me. I took out the phone to text Uncle Bear where I was off to, only to wish I hadn't seen the screen. Text notifications steadily appeared. The shit has hit the fan, read one from Uncle Bear. Another arrived from Emi: Proud of you! She'd pressed me earlier about how committed I was to going through with my marriage. Uncle Bear hadn't been the only one to notice my heart hadn't been in it.

I deserved the text from Paul, but it still stung: Mom said you weren't marriage material. I should have listened to her.

"Congratulations! Champagne?"

I didn't correct the bubbly flight attendant pushing two champagne flutes on me as I shoved my phone back inside the clutch. There wasn't anything to celebrate. "Yes, please." I took a glass.

"Would your husband like one?" He tipped his head toward the guy in the suit making his way toward the rear of the plane in search of overhead bin space, the same guy who'd barreled into me.

"He's not my husband." Not yet, anyway. But he was assigned to the seat next to mine.

His name is Aaron Borland, and at the time, he was the Savant House's director of acquisitions. And we were on our way to Vegas.

CHAPTER 3

GLITTER, GALAS, AND GIRLFRIENDS

I text Emi as soon as I leave Artisant Designs, begging her to meet. I don't want to discuss this crisis through a string of texts. I need to talk out what happened and tell her what I'm planning to do, because I want her to come along. I tell myself it's for moral support. Which is true. But I also don't want to show up at the gala without a plus-one. I'm breaking my promise to Aaron just by going.

Emi texts back that she can't meet until lunch, so I take the T to my apartment, feeling outraged and hurt. I can't believe Uncle Bear went behind my back after promising me Artisant. I've been looking forward most of my life to owning the shop. So I focus on a new plan now while changing out of my coveralls and into loose jean shorts with lace-trimmed hems and a slouchy off-white, long-sleeve shirt, wrangling my hair into a floppy bun at my nape. Then I take the T downtown and impatiently wait for Emi to join me at Lettuce Entertain You, a soup-and-salad café near Stone & Bloom. I'm two macchiatos in when she arrives, and with the amount of caffeine I've consumed even before I got here, I'm buzzing.

Emi enters the café like a spring breeze and immediately spots me seated at a two-top along the far wall. I wave at her, my knee bouncing.

"What's going on? Everything all right?" she asks, picking up on my agitated fervor. She hooks her purse on the chairback and settles into the seat across from me.

"Bear's selling the shop," I announce, outraged.

Emi's face lights up. "That's wonderful!"

"He's not selling to me." Emi slow-blinks, and I flap my hands for her to catch up. "He's selling to the Savant House."

"The furniture catalog?"

"Yes." The Savant House is an upscale home-furnishings company headquartered in the heart of Boston. Their catalog is only one aspect of the business. They sell merchandise online, through their fourteen design galleries located along the Eastern Seaboard, and in their retail shops in Nashville and Chicago. The company was founded over forty years ago as a vintage hardware-and-fixtures thrift shop less than a mile from Artisant Designs. While they are still privately held, Savant received an influx of capital a few decades ago and quickly expanded, buying out woodshops to acquire their talent and copyrighted designs. If I can't stop the sale of Artisant, Uncle Bear will get his way and I'll be Savant's next prize.

"Why would he do that?" Emi asks.

"I don't know." I clap my hands on the table, my knee still bouncing.

Emi peeks inside my coffee cup. "How many of these have you had?"

I grimace. "Including the espressos I drank before we went to coffee this morning?"

She *tsks*. "Let's get some food in you before you short-circuit. Then tell me everything."

We split a pulled-pork sandwich on a ciabatta roll with cups of chili on the side. As we eat, I tell her about the email I found and the deal Uncle Bear is apparently negotiating on my behalf.

"I can't believe he didn't ask you first," Emi says when I finish. "Seems presumptuous, even for him." She knows Uncle Bear. I lived with him when Emi and I met at trade school. She sees him around the apartment building. He lives on the floor above us, while my parents live in an apartment on the floor below us. Bizarre, I know. But that's my family. God forbid my parents socialize with me outside work hours, but we'll live a floor apart from each other.

"I don't know what's worse: Uncle Bear selling or he and my parents conspiring against me."

"Why is he selling?"

"He gave me some lame excuse about the cost of lumber and machinery upkeep. Two things, mind you, we deal with all the time—it's nothing new. But get this: Dad said they're selling because 'they're tired.'" I air-quote with my fingers. "He and Mom are only in their fifties. They're too young to retire. Something else is going on with them."

"Did you ask Bear if he'd sell to you instead?"

"His mind is made up. He's already started negotiating with Savant."

"Nothing is signed yet, though?"

"Not that I know of."

"Then you still have time."

"That's what I'm hoping." I scrape my teeth over my lower lip, and Emi squints at me.

"You have a plan."

"I do." With a racing heart, I show her the invite. "We're going to Savant's gala."

Emi leans back, perplexed. "I'm always up for a party, but how does this help you?"

"I know someone I think can help me."

"Who?"

"What are you doing this afternoon?" I ask, purposefully avoiding her question.

"Wrapping up a proposal." She glances at her calendar. "It's not due until Monday. Why? What do you have in mind?"

"You and I are going dress shopping." I haven't seen my ex-husband in five years, and I want to make an impression.

CHAPTER 4

THE LIST

I haven't seen or spoken to Aaron since we amicably parted ways at Logan International six days after we'd met on the plane. We said goodbye right after he gave me the most soul-scorching kiss I've ever experienced to this day. While I secretly hoped we'd run into each other again—and even considered deliberately throwing myself in his path only to change my mind because pining over him and what could have been was torture—I've been fine with our decision. We agreed: no contact. What had happened in Vegas would stay in Vegas.

So far, we've honored our agreement, which we came up with over several glasses of champagne for me, some bourbon on the rocks for him, and a frenzied trip to the lavatory where I'd wrangled him to help me out of my wedding dress. I was already drunk at that point since I hadn't eaten all day, and I had to pee. I couldn't fit into the lavatory because of the yards of tulle in Cheryl's dress. And it turns out, I was much more comfortable wearing just the white slip underneath, which became the perfect clubbing outfit in Vegas.

But more on that later.

I stuffed Cheryl's dress in an overhead bin under the watchful gazes, raised eyebrows, and little smirks of nearby passengers who'd just witnessed my undressing before Aaron and I collapsed in our seats with mortified giggles. "That's the first time I've been undressed by a stranger," I said. I couldn't believe I'd talked him into undoing thirty-three tiny buttons, or that he'd actually done it. This guy would make some woman very happy one day.

He laughed. "It's a safe bet I've never had a day like yours, and I don't even know what happened."

"Jilting grooms at the altar isn't your thing?"

"Ouch. Marriage isn't my thing. I'm Aaron, by the way. I probably should have introduced myself before I undressed you."

"Meli." I took his hand, noticing how smooth his palm felt compared with mine, which was riddled with calluses. I'd also noticed how thick and dark his hair was, appreciating how it flopped over his forehead when he'd bent his head to peer at the buttons on my back. I'd sneaked a peek over my shoulder. And his eyes . . . They were a cool steel gray that glinted with blue flecks in a certain light.

"Is it short for Melissa?" When I looked surprised, he said, "I overheard the woman checking our boarding passes." He rolled up the sleeves of his lavender dress shirt, revealing corded muscle beneath sun-kissed skin and a tattoo on his right forearm. I could barely make out the silhouette of two intertwined branches, one broken with an incomplete bird in flight, before his sleeve slipped down a little, covering the image that sparked a dull ache within me. The silent story etched on his arm seemed both powerful and sad.

"Nobody calls me Melissa, not even my mom," I told him. "Thanks for your help. I was dying to get out of that dress."

"The least I could do after plowing into you. Sorry about that."

"It's all good." I brush off our run-in. We'd both been in a rush to board the plane. "How about that drink I promised you for helping me? Looks like I owe you dinner too." I inspected the chicken meal that had gone cold while we dealt with the monstrous dress. The broccoli florets looked soggy.

"You also owe me an explanation. I'm curious why you bailed. If you want to talk about it."

"Only if you tell me why marriage isn't your thing." Apparently, it wasn't mine either since I'd proved Uncle Bear was right—balancing my craft with a relationship was impossible—and my interest was piqued. I wondered what else we had in common.

"Deal." He rubbed his hands together and flagged the flight attendant.

After our drinks had been replenished and we'd snacked on chicken salad sandwiches brought up from Economy, I asked Aaron about his stance on marriage. "Is it because you haven't met the right person yet? Is that why it's not your thing?"

"No, nothing like that. My parents have opinions about everything I do. I guess not marrying is my way of having some control over my life."

"Look at you, you rebel."

A shadow darkened his face before he cracked a smile. "I wish."

"Are your parents married?"

"Divorced. They work together, which is fine. They've always had a great working relationship. But somewhere between raising me and my sister and running a business they forgot why they'd married in the first place."

"That's because it's impossible to work with the person you love. Those relationships rarely work out." When you fight over work at work, you'll fight over work at home.

"Exactly. What about you? Your parents married?"

"Yes, and they shouldn't be. They also work together but they bicker constantly." I left it at that without explaining further. Conversations about my parents inevitably circled back to our weird living arrangement and why my uncle had to raise me.

"Cheers to questionable role models." Aaron toasted his bourbon to my champagne. "What about you? What compels a bride to run from her own wedding?"

"A groom who asked her to give up a job she loved."

"Oof." Aaron grunted.

"I should have said something to him earlier, but I sort of freaked out when I got to the church. Took me long enough, but I finally remembered why I promised myself I'd never marry. Which is fine. My fiancé just now texted I wasn't marriage material. Okay, that hurt.

But we never would have worked out. Oh, gosh." I startled, realizing something. "I guess Paul isn't my fiancé anymore."

Aaron made a short noise that sounded like a deflating balloon. "Screw Paul. What makes someone marriage material anyway? Someone who doesn't snort when they laugh?"

I did exactly that and playfully shoved his arm. "Stop."

He laughed, leaning into me, and I caught a hint of bourbon on his breath and pine on his skin. I sank farther into my seat, relishing his scent, and tucked a leg under me as I angled to face him more fully. "People put such ridiculous conditions on relationships. No wonder more marriages fail than succeed. What makes someone marriage material is someone you want to wake up with every morning. Their smile is the first thing you want to see each day. Simple as that."

His head tilted as he studied me with a newfound intensity. "That's really nice."

I felt a warm flutter in my stomach and yearned to impress him further. "Another thing, he'll prioritize us and our time together over friends and family. Paul didn't do that. His family always came first. Like him asking me to give up my work because it interfered with his mom's weekly family dinners."

Aaron's mouth turned down in a show of empathy, and he added his own thoughts. "She'll love to dance with me. My ex-girlfriend didn't."

"Who doesn't love to dance? He'll sing his favorite songs with me."

"Even if he can't sing?"

"Even if she can't dance?"

"Yes," we said in unison, laughing at ourselves.

We were being spontaneous and random, and despite the circumstances that had brought me to him, I was enjoying myself. Talking with him was helping me forget why I'd ended up on the plane with him. I wanted to remember everything we were talking about. "We need to write these down." I swiped his cocktail napkin. "Got a pen?"

He dug one out of his backpack just as my ears popped with the plane's descent.

I tapped the pen against my lips. "He'll understand the importance of 'me time' and that it doesn't mean I don't want to be with him."

"She won't say 'I love you' like it's a salutation."

I frowned at him. "What do you mean?"

"People get complacent. They say it out of habit without feeling. 'Love you, bye.'" He mimicked being on a call.

"That's the worst." My parents never said "I love you" to each other. Or to me, but that's a whole other story. Either way, I don't know which is worse: being complacent or not hearing it at all from your life partner.

"The words lose their meaning. If you're going to say it—"

"Say it from the heart," I chimed in. We shared a smile and something shifted inside me, clicking into place. "He won't be jealous of or resent me for the time I spend at work. I can't help it that I'm passionate about my craft."

"He'll support your passions and interests."

"Darn right, he will. He'll also know how I take my coffee," I added to our list.

"She won't scrunch her nose at pineapple on pizza."

"He won't wear his shoes in the house."

"That's a condition," he pointed out.

"You're right." I frowned, crossing it off, and skimmed the list. "Several of these are." I slashed through more lines. "They should be good qualities or positive traits."

"All right." Aaron drained his drink. He seemed as buzzed and loose-lipped as me. With flushed cheeks, he rubbed his hands, getting serious about our game. "She's adventurous and playful."

"Because boring and serious makes for a dull partner. He's fun."

"She likes to try new things with me."

"Like visits to the bookstore for date night?"

A slow smile played on his lips. "You like to read books? Fallon, my ex, hated reading."

"Immensely, which is why he's cool with me reading while he watches the game."

"Does she read beside him while he's watching?" His gaze held mine. I couldn't look away from his intense gray eyes.

"She can," I whispered.

"What if he wants to read with her?" he asked, and my brows quirked upward.

"Instead of watching the game?"

He did a one-shoulder shrug. "Game could be boring, the book more interesting. Her company more exciting."

"Then I'd say he can read with her."

Turbulence bounced the plane, rattling our glasses, and the spell that had fallen over me broke. I blinked, looking at the napkin on my tray table, unsure of where else to look if I wasn't looking at him. "What else would you put on our list?"

He was quiet for a beat before he said, "She's compassionate and respectful. Kind." I had the impression these were important elements for him.

Just as my next addition to the list was the most important element for me, and not because I planned to be in another long-term relationship. That wouldn't happen again. I'd made my choice. But because I regularly witnessed how my parents treated each other. "He'll stand behind me and he'll stand up for me. He'll also stand up *to* me. He isn't a pushover."

"She'll get me."

"He'll have faith in me."

A voice crackled through the PA system and announced the cabin was being prepared for landing. The flight had gone too quickly and I wasn't ready to say goodbye to my new friend.

Aaron leaned into my shoulder. "That's a good list we've got."

"It is."

"Your ex is wrong," he said as we returned our seats and tray tables to the upright position.

"How so?"

"You're witty, intelligent, and kind. Definitely marriage material."

His compliment hung in the air between us, and my champagne-soaked brain wanted to hear more. I wasn't used to receiving compliments. "Am I compassionate and respectful too?"

"Absolutely."

"Do you really believe that?"

"I do." He punctuated his conviction with a sharp nod.

I studied his beautiful face, chewing on my bottom lip, and an idea blew into my head with such force that my eyes widened and my lip popped from my teeth. I didn't know where the thought had come from or why I didn't stop myself from speaking it out loud. But there it was, appearing out of thin air like an unexpected twist in a bestselling novel.

"Marry me."

"Say what?" Aaron lurched back with a nervous laugh.

I stared at him wide-eyed and in complete shock at myself.

I should have retracted the offer, laughed it off as a joke. Instead, I blinked, determination sharpening my resolve. Call it a temporary escape hatch or drunken bravado. Maybe I just wanted to postpone returning home to face the consequences I'd created. Maybe I desired to do something outrageous and unforgettable. Or maybe I just needed to prove something to myself. I wasn't sure what, but deep down, despite all Uncle Bear's warnings in his Bearisms, I craved a genuine connection with someone. And something with Aaron had sparked to life, like a tiny flame on a delicate piece of flint.

I argued my case. "If you honestly believe I'm marriage material, somebody worth spending a lifetime with, a great catch, if you will— someone you could share a passion with and wouldn't choose work over relationship for but believe it's possible to balance the two—then as soon as we land, marry me for one full day." In that moment, I wholeheartedly believed that if we could be for each other everything described on our list, we could have a relationship that worked. Even if it was for only twenty-four hours.

His gaze narrowed. "Is this a dare?"

I leaned in close until we were nose to nose. "It's Vegas, baby."

He leaned back and studied me. I had no idea what he saw or what was going through his head. Maybe it was our list.

"You did put adventurous and playful on our list," I challenged.

A mischievous glint danced in his eyes, a waggish smirk tugging at his lips. He gave me his hand and the shock of my life. "You're on."

CHAPTER 5

NOT SO FASHIONABLY LATE

The following night, Emi and I arrive at the Park Plaza, glammed up and relatively on time. The gala is lit with a twenty-piece orchestra and cashless bars serving up premium cocktails. Trays of fancy appetizers and champagne-filled coupe glasses float through the glitzy crowd like cruise ships on the ocean's surface. Tuxedos mingle with sparkling gowns as guests browse tables laden with gift baskets and other big-ticket items for the event's silent auction.

I deliberated coming until the last minute, despite my initial determination. Tonight might not be the ideal time and place to confront Aaron. I could have called him, but I didn't want to chance leaving a voicemail that wouldn't be returned. And a text could be ignored. What if he refuses to see me? No, regardless of how nervous I am, I need to ask for his help in person. Even Emi agreed I had to come. He'll remember how important Artisant Designs is to me when he sees me. He'll feel my urgency vibrating off me. Of course, I couldn't explain this to Emi.

She still doesn't know how Aaron and I know each other. Nobody does. We agreed to keep our week together between us. It isn't every day you marry someone you just met, let alone on the same day you jilted someone else. We'd acted rashly, and our behavior would reflect poorly on our families and businesses and ourselves. I imagine if Uncle Bear knew, he'd have all the more reason not to pass down Artisant Designs to me. Last thing he'd want is someone at the helm with a history of acting irrationally and irresponsibly.

I don't like lying to Emi, but as far as she knows, Aaron is an acquaintance, someone who runs in the same industry circles and who I met at the Contemporary Furniture Fair in New York several years back.

Emi's bare arm brushes mine as we take in the festive ballroom. "Do you see him?"

Despite the extra three and a half inches with my slingback heels, I still can't see over the sea of bodies. "Not yet." But I know he's here. The Savant House's gala is one of our industry's premier events. Close to six hundred people attend each year, many eager to wire unseemly amounts of money for the auction that Savant will sink into their foundation for the betterment of the planet. Every executive and board member should be present. But Aaron is the only one who might listen to me.

Uncle Bear taught me to be self-reliant and independent. "A beaver gathers his own wood," he said. "He doesn't sit around waiting for trees to drop their branches."

Ironic that I'm in this situation because of Uncle Bear yet I fall back on one of his Bearisms. Artisant Designs will be mine, and I'm the only person who can manifest the future I desire. The only person who can stand up for what I love most.

"I hope you're right about this guy," Emi says.

I fidget with the bangles on my wrist. "I am." Aaron was the director of acquisitions when we met, but he's since been promoted to chief operations officer. Forty-plus years after starting the Savant House in a small warehouse near our shop, Aaron's dad is now the CEO and his mom is president. Aaron told me he and his sister change positions every six to twelve months, learning the business. When his dad retires, which I'm guessing is soon, his mom will be voted in as his replacement, and Aaron will step into her position as acting president. But as the chief operations officer, the acquisitions department reports to him.

He might be able to convince his team that Artisant Designs is not an attractive investment, assuming I can convince him.

But what I'm really counting on is the promise he made to me in Las Vegas. Would he follow through?

"I know you're nervous about talking to him, but you look beautiful," Emi compliments. "He'd be a fool not to listen to you."

"Thank you."

We found our floor-length dresses on consignment. Emi is a knockout in a red, cowl-necked satin gown. My off-the-shoulder silhouette is adorned with shimmery embellishments and a tulle skirt that flares at my thighs, making the dress easier to walk in. We watched a makeup tutorial to do our faces, and my flat-ironed hair cascades down my back in a gleaming sheet of glossy brown. It's much longer than when Aaron last saw me. And the blush gown not only brings out the rose-gold ends my hairstylist added last week but also highlights the color in my cheeks that I swear has nothing to do with how jittery I feel.

"I'm going to walk around," I say.

"I'll get us something to drink." Emi's gaze follows a passing tray. "Do you want champagne?"

"Yes." I squeeze her fingers. "Off to save my future. Wish me luck."

"You got this. Don't worry about me. I'll come find you."

Emi heads for the nearest bar and I wander the ballroom's perimeter. I complete one loop without seeing Aaron, and I'm about to make another pass when I notice him. My fingers curl into my palms as energy thrums up my arms.

I take a steadying breath and push through the crowd toward the man I never thought I'd see again. Though his arms are crossed, his posture is relaxed, his feet comfortably braced apart as he leans in, listening to an older gentleman dressed in an impressive tailored tuxedo who has him engaged in an animated conversation. I tap Aaron on the shoulder and square my own.

He turns swiftly with a slightly annoyed expression at being interrupted. "Yes?"

Self-preservation has me lurching back. But I smile determinedly and plow forward. "Hello, Aaron."

"Meli?" His face opens in shock, and the sound of his voice floods me with memories.

"Hi." I flutter my fingers in a casual greeting, even though I'm feeling anything but.

"You're here!" he announces like he's been expecting me. Then he smiles, and I'm reminded of a sunflower unfurling in the sunlight. It brightens his disarmingly handsome face that has just a touch of wildness. Everything I adored about him that I've forced myself to forget falls back into place, and we're back in Vegas as if we married only yesterday.

CHAPTER 6

I Do

Hollywood has it wrong. You can't spontaneously get married in Las Vegas, not like they did in *The Hangover*, which Aaron and I quickly discovered. We first needed a marriage license. Also, officiants won't marry you if you're under the influence.

Intoxication wasn't an issue for us. Nothing sobered us faster than Aaron dropping $102 in cash for our license at the Clark County Marriage License Bureau, the only marriage license bureau open from 8:00 a.m. to midnight, seven days a week, including holidays. No exceptions, no appointments needed. Funnily enough, they prefer walk-ins, which worked perfectly for us.

All this valuable information came courtesy of our very knowledgeable, very enthusiastic Uber driver, Calvin, who waited for us during the fifteen minutes it took to procure the license. Calvin also insisted on being our witness. Why pay for one at the chapel when we were already paying him?

Why indeed?

Calvin loved love, and I didn't have the heart to tell him love had nothing to do with our arrangement.

Aaron and I stared at the marriage license when the clerk handed it over. My heart thumped in my throat. He glanced from me to the license in his hands, then back to me. "It's not official until we say 'I do.' There's still time to back out."

Our wedding wasn't until 9:45 p.m. We had over an hour, which gave us plenty of time to change our minds.

"Do you want to back out?" I asked. He'd told me on the ride over that the business meeting he had in Las Vegas was canceled. He didn't find out until after he'd boarded the plane, and by then, it had been too late to get off. He was stuck in Vegas for the night. But as we stood there, I worried that maybe he was now realizing the magnitude of our dare. If we did this and couldn't get an annulment afterward, we'd have to go through a legal divorce.

I was sure he was about to change his mind. I was close to doing so myself. But he smiled, a soft upturn of his lips that was as shy as it was reckless. His first smile since we'd filed for the license. "I won't back out if you don't," he said.

I chewed on my lip, contemplating how gutsy I wanted to be, and his eyes met mine. They were a cool, solid steel in the twilight, an anchor amid our nerves.

"Tell you what, we'll do exactly what you dared us to do: get married for twenty-four hours. We'll stay up all night. I'll buy you dinner, we'll take in a show, do whatever you want. We can walk the Strip, drink giant slushies, gamble, go clubbing. We'll even eat those greasy hot dogs they sell on the street corners. Come morning, we'll enjoy a big buffet breakfast, then fly home, file for an annulment, and go our separate ways. We never have to see each other again."

It would be as if it had never happened.

It was wild and crazy, and I had never been so impulsive . . . except for earlier that morning when I'd ditched my wedding.

Why stop now?

I latched on to the cool confidence reflected in his gaze. "All right. Let's do this."

Aaron pumped a fist. "We're getting married, Meli Hynes." His hand found mine and my heart did a funky little tumble at the contact.

We returned to Calvin's car, and Aaron kept hold of my hand for the drive to the chapel.

We'd ordered the drive-thru wedding package online while the plane taxied to the gate. Our ceremony would be short, and we'd remain in the car. My bouquet was included. I chose yellow roses, and our officiant, a blond woman with Botoxed lips and false eyelashes, passed the flowers through the window after Aaron gave her our marriage license and IDs. I felt a demented urge to ask for a side of fries to go with my flowers.

"Are you ready?" the woman leaning out the window asked. I didn't catch her name, and if I were to ask her what it was, I doubted I could speak if I wanted to. I just smiled tightly, my body trembling as I gripped the bouquet, rustling the flowers, and squeezed Aaron's hand just as hard.

He looked at me for confirmation. "Ready?"

Wide-eyed, I nodded.

"We're ready," Aaron told the woman, not taking his stare off me.

Holy crap, we were really doing this.

"Good, good. Keep looking at each other just like that," the officiant cooed as if she didn't perform forty ceremonies exactly like this every day. Then she began ours. "We are here tonight to celebrate two hearts bonding in the commitment of marriage."

Calvin gleefully clapped, then froze. "Omigosh. We need video."

"Shit, shit, shit," Aaron said through gritted teeth, and I squealed. We were sweating.

Calvin scrambled for his phone and aimed the lens at us. "Now we're ready."

The officiant began again. "We are here tonight to celebrate two hearts bonding in the commitment of marriage. Aaron, you may say your vows."

"What am I supposed to say?" he asked.

"Whatever comes to mind, as long as it's from the heart," she answered.

"Ah, okay." Aaron locked eyes with me. I knew he was trying to think of something impressive. Then he took a measured breath. "Meli, I promise to sing your favorite songs with you, read books with you, and only say 'I love you' when I mean it. I'll support your passions, whatever they are. Whittling, finger painting, clamming."

"Clamming?"

"I don't know. It just came to me. I promise to stand behind you, stand up for you, and stand up *to* you. I'll always have faith in you."

My heart stumbled.

He was reciting our list.

This marriage was fake. It had an expiration date. But it didn't stop me from thinking, *What if Uncle Bear is wrong? What if it's possible to balance the love of my craft with the love of my life? What if I can have a partner in business and in life?* Maybe I was different from my uncle and parents and could manage a delicate balance between the two. Because if there was a partner out there for me who had the qualities I suspected Aaron possessed, maybe, just maybe, there was hope for a life more fulfilling and enriching than I'd let myself imagine.

I could also be getting ahead of myself.

I remembered something else my uncle had taught me. Another Bearism. "A cluttered heart, like a cluttered workshop, leaves no room for creativity to flourish."

I shouldn't be greedy.

But a solitary tear slipped unchecked over my cheek and clung to my jaw. The lonely little girl in me desired connection more than anything else. Dare I say, more than owning Artisant Designs?

Aaron noticed and his face folded with concern.

"I'm fine, I'm fine." I ducked my head, embarrassed and bewildered. I was getting emotional over something that was supposed to be a joke, nothing more than us being fun and adventurous.

Aaron had the audacity to make it more uncomfortable for me. He gently brushed away the tear with his thumb.

Damn. I was going to start bawling.

"Your turn, Melissa," the officiant said.

I took an unsettled breath and gathered my wits and yellow roses. "Aaron, I promise to dance with you, read beside you even when you prefer to watch football over reading with me."

"Baseball." He winked at me.

"Baseball," I corrected with a soggy laugh. "I promise to try new things with you, and when nobody else can, I promise to get you, to understand you better than anyone else."

Aaron's eyes welled, startling me. I wasn't the only one getting emotional. He pinched the inner corners of his eyes with a short, throaty laugh. "Don't mind me."

"Beautiful," our officiant exclaimed. "Are you exchanging rings?"

"Rings?" My eyes widened in surprise as I stared up at Aaron.

"Rings." He patted his thigh as if he might just happen to have a pair of wedding bands. "We forgot rings."

"I got rings. Got 'em right here." Calvin set down the phone and tugged off a dented silver pinkie ring and, from his middle finger, a polished wood band.

"Are you sure?" Aaron closed his fist over the rings Calvin dropped in his palm.

"Absolutely. Just tip me well." Calvin picked up the phone again. "We're rolling."

"Aaron," our officiant began, "do you take Melissa to be your lawfully wedded wife?"

"I do."

Something between a giggle and a gag escaped me as he slid the dented silver ring onto my finger. And another tear fell down my cheek.

Aaron cupped my face. "It's all right," he said in a gentle whisper. I was about to lose it, and he seemed perfectly okay with that.

Damn, this man.

"Do you, Melissa, take Aaron to be your lawfully wedded husband?"

"I do," I said, reminding myself we weren't committing to forever as I pushed the wood band onto his finger. "You're shaking," I murmured, mystified by his display of emotion. He clenched his hand.

"By the power vested in me by the State of Nevada, I now pronounce you husband and wife. Aaron, you may kiss your bride."

My gaze snapped to his beautiful mouth. We hadn't talked about kissing.

Aaron didn't give us the chance to overthink it. He cupped my cheek, locked his eyes on mine, and lowered his head. When our lips met and eyes closed, it felt like our hearts collided, and all I could think was that I wanted him to kiss me. I'd been waiting for this, and for him. It was nothing like I'd felt with Paul, which only reaffirmed how wrong I'd been to accept his proposal and how right I was to not marry him. I wouldn't have made him happy.

But with Aaron . . . It must have been the dare, or our spontaneity. Maybe it was the mystery of the man I was now legally bound to, or the enormity of what we'd done. But something about this and us, what we were doing, heightened everything—my emotions, my senses. My desire. His tongue delved into my mouth, caressed my lips. And I kept thinking over and over, *You, you, you. I've been waiting for you.*

I didn't want him to stop kissing me.

It wasn't until Calvin hooted that Aaron finally lifted his head with a guilty smile. My fingers were in his hair, and my other hand, the bouquet forgotten in my lap, gripped his shirt. Our kiss had been indulgent. Our kiss could have gone on for hours or could have lasted only seconds. I just knew I hadn't experienced anything like it before.

Aaron bit the corner of his lower lip, looking as awestruck as I felt. We stared at each other, at a loss for words.

"Congratulations, Mr. and Mrs. Borland!" Calvin cheered.

Aaron found his voice first. "You okay?" His thumb stroked my cheek. I nodded, dazed. He leaned forward and said by my ear, "We did it."

"We did."

"Twenty-four hours, *wife.*"

"Twenty-four hours, *husband.*" No big deal.

I wasn't breaking my promise to myself about never marrying. I wasn't putting a relationship before my art. We were only being playful and adventurous, exactly what we'd written on our list. And that commingling of excitement and exhilaration buzzing through me? That otherworldly experience of his kiss, as if I'd waited for years to feel exactly that? To feel him? It meant nothing.

I had everything under control.

Goodness, was I naive.

CHAPTER 7

ONE-TWO-THREE

A quirky smile tugs on my lips. "Were you expecting me?" I ask Aaron as a kaleidoscope of emotions dances in his eyes, mirroring the feelings that wash over me—joy, surprise, disbelief, longing. I have so many questions about the past five years. Did he miss me? Did I often cross his mind? Did he ever regret our agreement? There have been many days I wish we kept in touch, because I think of him often. I have missed him.

"Yes. No! No, I wasn't." Aaron finally comes around to answering my question. "I'm glad you came, though. How have you been?"

"Good. Hey, um . . . ," I begin, remembering I came tonight for a reason. My gaze briefly jumps to the man behind him. "I'm sorry to interrupt, but do you have a few moments? We need to talk."

"Aaron?" asks the man with him. "Care to introduce us?"

Aaron moves aside, which brings him closer to me. I catch the faint scent of his cologne, the familiar pine spice warming my nose, and I feel a flutter in my chest. We've barely spoken, and already I know my attraction to him hasn't diminished.

The man joins our circle. "Dad," Aaron politely introduces. "This is Melissa Hynes. She's with Artisant Designs and, in my opinion, their finest craftsman. She's also Bernard Hynes's niece."

My brows lurch upward. If I had any doubts Aaron wasn't at least familiar with the Savant House's interest in acquiring Artisant Designs and the position his company is creating on my behalf, he effectively erased them with the mere mention of my uncle's name. Displeasure courses through me. I can't believe Aaron didn't reach out the moment he learned of my uncle's desire to sell the shop. We have a no-contact agreement, which I'm completely disregarding at this very moment, but still . . . I just arrived and I already feel like he's let me down.

Aaron watches me closely and his brows pull together as my delight over seeing him dims. His smile turns hesitant, wary. "Meli, this is my dad, Graham Borland, our CEO."

"Not for long. I'm waiting for this guy to let me retire." Graham claps Aaron's shoulder. "Lovely to meet you, dear."

I quickly get over my shock at how much older than my uncle Graham is. He must have at least fifteen years on Bear. Aaron is only thirty-two. He wasn't kidding when he told me in Vegas that his dad had kids at an older age.

I take Graham's hand. "Nice to meet you."

"We'll finish this later, son. I'm sure you two have much to discuss." Graham dips his chin at me before plunging into the crowd, where he's quickly swooped up into another conversation.

Aaron and I turn to each other. He leans forward, close to my ear. "Hello, wife."

The fluttering in my chest returns. I'm giddy being near him again. "Husband." My ghost of a smile matches his, hinting at an amusement we can't quite contain.

Technically, Aaron is my ex-husband. When we returned to Boston, we couldn't annul our marriage. That's what happens when you enter into a contract mentally fit, then take off to Maui for five days. But Aaron's attorney was discreet and our separation was quick, uncontested, and quiet. His attorney's office orchestrated the entire process online. Aaron and I didn't even have to speak to each other. We haven't texted, emailed, or spoken since.

But I have googled him—obsessively in those early days. While our time together became just a memory and felt more like a movie I watched only once and didn't plan to see again, Aaron haunts my dreams. He continues to torment my thoughts. Not a day has gone by when my mind doesn't take me back to the week I spent with him.

Aaron slides his hands into his trouser pockets, looking sophisticated and elegant in a tuxedo that clings to him like a second skin. He's a broader version of the man I met on the plane, even more attractive with age. He exudes a quiet magnetism, always drawing my eyes. Gone are his boyish twenties. And his smile . . . It's charming and amusing. Why *is* he smiling?

"What?" I ask with a tentative smile of my own.

"You. You're here."

"In the flesh." I lift my hands as if to say, *Here I am.*

"Are you here with someone?" He glances behind me.

"My friend, Emi. What did your dad mean when he said we have a lot to talk about?"

"Dance with me." His hand opens between us. I look at his palm, then up at his face. He angles his head in challenge, as if daring me. "How can I not ask you to dance when you're wearing a dress like that?"

How indeed?

My smile slowly broadens. I did want to make an impression, but I can't let whatever is happening between us—this buzzing sort of energy—distract me from the reason I came. "Only if we can talk while we dance."

"Of course. Whatever you want." His expression is open, waiting, hopeful, borderline vulnerable as his hand hovers in the space between us.

Tentatively, I slip my hand in his, feeling that electric charge tingle my fingers, as I try to ignore how much I want to pick things up where we left off. He leads us onto the dance floor and turns to me, taking me into his arms. Where I belong. Where I want to be. With a hand at my waist and the other clasping mine, his presence feels both familiar and foreign. Peaceful and unsettling. Almost as if no time has passed, yet years have gone by since we parted ways.

He guides us effortlessly across the floor in a swirling waltz the orchestra enthusiastically plays. His moves aren't even in the same league as those in Las Vegas, which weren't really moves at all. There, for almost two hours at XS, a nightclub at the Wynn, we gyrated to a pulsing bass and sang at the top of our lungs. Hot and sweaty, we clung to each other. It was easily the best night of my life.

Now, though, we're ballroom dancing, which is an entirely different animal. And I, who have never taken a dance lesson in my life, can only clutch on to Aaron as he rotates us to the center of the floor, where he slows his fancy footwork to a gentle sway. His fingers press into my lower back, and I instinctively move closer.

I feel his warm breath in my hair. "You didn't mention you knew how to dance. You're just full of surprises, husband."

"One of many in my arsenal to woo you, wife."

I laugh, drawing glances from the couple beside us. "'Woo'? Who says that anymore?"

His ears turn a shade darker. "That was cringe."

"My inner grandmother just fainted."

A laugh rumbles from him. "Blame my dad. He's ancient. Some of his slang is bound to rub off. Let's start over." His thumb strokes the inside of my wrist. I wonder if he realizes he's doing it. He's close enough for me to notice the small spot on his jaw he missed shaving. "Hello, Meli. I've missed you."

His honesty floors me.

"Aaron, I—" I catch myself before I echo his confession. "We need to talk about—"

"You're more beautiful than I remember." He leans into me and deeply inhales.

"Did you just sniff my hair?"

"Fuck. Sorry, I did."

"You're acting weird."

"I'm nervous."

"Because of me?"

"I thought I'd never see you again."

"We promised we wouldn't seek each other out."

"It wouldn't be the first promise we broke."

I glance away, remembering our sunrise breakfast at Mandalay Bay. We spent the entire night on the Las Vegas Strip doing exactly what Aaron had proposed when we bought our marriage license. We were exhausted and famished, and I was so ready for sleep. But I wasn't ready to say goodbye. I didn't want to leave our bubble. So even though we'd only promised each other twenty-four hours, I dared him to fly to Maui with me. I'd booked and paid for my honeymoon with Paul. It was too late to cancel. I couldn't get a refund. Why waste the trip?

A few hours later, after a quick shopping spree where we purchased matching tropical outfits, we raced through another jet bridge to catch a Southwest flight to Hawaii. Once again, we were the last two to board.

"Aren't you the cutest?" the flight attendant greeted us. "You're matchy-matchy."

"We're newlyweds." I leaned my cheek on Aaron's shoulder, playing it up.

The attendant pouted. "There are only two middle seats left. Afraid you won't be flying together."

"But it's our honeymoon."

I looked up at Aaron. Did he just whine? I bit the inside of my cheek to hold in the laughter.

"Isn't there anything you can do?" He played up the charm. Then he cupped my face and looked directly into my eyes. "I can't bear for us to sit apart."

I could have melted in that gaze. Out of nowhere, envy spiked, and I was instantly jealous of whomever he would marry for real, assuming he ever decided to get married.

"Aww." The attendant pressed a hand to her breast. "You are so adorbs. Give me a sec." She picked up the PA system's receiver. "Aloha, ladies and gentlemen. Welcome to Flight 1585 to Kahului Airport, Maui, Hawaii. We'll be departing shortly, but first, we need to get these newlyweds seated—*together*. Aren't they the cutest?"

"You match!" a passenger in the first row shouted, and I curtsied.

"They're going on their honeymoon," the attendant declared with more enthusiasm than a college cheer squad.

Aaron turned to me, his chest against mine, and did the most expected thing a newly married husband would do: he kissed his bride. I gasped when his mouth landed on mine, shocked at the contact. This kiss didn't feel anything like the one during our wedding that, for a blip, had me feeling like a real bride. I had actually considered that our adventure could unfurl into something meaningful. This kiss was for show.

And show off he did.

His tongue swooped into my mouth. He sucked my bottom lip between his and nibbled at the corners. My knees buckled. I grabbed his arms to brace myself. He kept kissing me and kissing me until the noise registered. Passengers cheered. They whistled and catcalled until one woman hollered, "They can sit here!"

Aaron lifted his head and his thumb stroked my cheek, turning a very public moment in a public place into something private between just us two. The kiss hadn't meant anything, but it left me wanting. Aaron left me wanting.

The flight attendant hung up the receiver. "We have side-by-side seats for you near the back."

I looked down the belly of the plane. A short woman scooted into the aisle, waved at us, and shuffled into the row across from where she'd been sitting. She settled into the middle seat, leaving adjoining middle and window seats for Aaron and me.

In less than twenty-four hours, we broke our promise to marry for only twenty-four hours. We were off to Maui.

The hand on my lower back moves up an inch, drawing my attention back to the gala and to Aaron. "Why are you here, Meli?"

His question makes me think of the gala's invitations. How they started arriving with my name on the envelope alongside Uncle Bear's that same year. Before Aaron and I met, the invites had been addressed just to my uncle. Has Aaron been trying all along to break our promise to quietly go our separate ways and not see each other again, at least not deliberately? We work in similar industries. Even though it hadn't happened prior to meeting on the plane, there was always the chance we'd run into one another down the road.

"You know why. I'm sure it's for the same reason your dad said we have much to discuss."

"Savant's intent to acquire Artisant."

"I learned of it only yesterday."

"That's why I hadn't heard from you."

"About me coming to work for Savant, I didn't agree to that. My uncle has been negotiating without my consent."

"I see." His fingers press harder into my back, and his attention shifts over my shoulder. "Can we talk about this later?"

I stop swaying, confused. His quick dismissal sharpens my tone. "I realize this isn't an ideal time, but I—"

"There you are, darling," comes a lyrical voice behind me.

Aaron's arms fall from me as he steps back. His expression cools as an elegantly dressed woman slides into the space I just filled. She loops a thin arm possessively around Aaron's waist. His hand lifts to rest on her back more from habit than adoration. At least that's how it looks to me.

She smiles pleasantly at me. "Hello. I don't think we've met."

"I'm Meli," I introduce myself, aiming a bewildered look at Aaron. Who is this woman?

"Meli's with Artisant Designs here in Boston," he explains in a guarded tone.

"*The* Artisant Designs?"

Red tinges Aaron's cheeks. He shifts away from the woman. Barely, but enough that I notice. So does she. She leans closer to him. "Aaron talks about your work all the time, and I have to admit, I'm a bit of a fan myself. Don't tell anyone at Savant, but I have a couple of your pieces."

"You do?" I can't help but preen. "And you are?"

"Fallon." She offers her hand. Her name is as unusual as it is memorable, but not as a past client. Aaron spoke of her a few times over the week we spent together, referring to her as his ex-girlfriend, and I would have made the connection if I'd worked with her directly. She must have purchased some stock pieces we keep on hand. Mom would have handled her order. "I'm Aaron's fiancée. Such a pleasure to meet you in person, Meli."

"You too." My eyes snap to Aaron. So much for marriage not being his thing. He doesn't meet my gaze.

Fallon pokes his chest. "Your mom is looking for you. The auction's starting. She wants you onstage."

"All right if I call you Monday?" Aaron asks me.

"How about I find you later?" My tone is clipped as I chastise myself for secretly pining after him when, all this time, he'd gotten back together with Fallon. This is why I've sworn off relationships. They're too distracting and only lead to disappointment. Once again, I have to remind myself of Uncle Bear's advice.

Aaron's mouth pulls up into a strained side smile, and he walks away with Fallon. I watch his retreating back, Fallon's hand resting possessively between his shoulder blades.

CHAPTER 8

BURGERS, BEER, AND BAGPIPES

I don't get the chance to speak with Aaron again. Between the auction and an endless parade of guests competing for his attention, he remains otherwise occupied. The gala winds down and Emi convinces me to text him about meeting over coffee tomorrow morning. Surely he will be agreeable.

"I saw the way he was looking at you. If I didn't know any better, I'd swear you two were close. He's not going to pass up an opportunity to see you again."

Guilt twists my stomach while we wait at the curb for our rides. I'll have to be more careful around Aaron when she's near or she'll press for the truth.

Emi is meeting up with Shae and Tam for drinks at Beacon, a jazz and cocktail club, but I don't want to stay out late if I'm going to get up early to meet Aaron, assuming he returns my text. He hasn't yet.

"Are you sure you don't want to come?" Emi asks, her face pinched as she stares at her phone. "Unless I can't get a ride. It's still searching for a driver."

We aren't the only ones waiting for rides. People crowd the sidewalk. Everyone left the gala at once.

"I'm sure. I'm going to get some sleep."

A cab pulls curbside right in front of us. "Kismet," Emi exclaims. She opens the passenger door before anyone else claims the ride. "Text when you get home?"

"Have fun!"

She blows me a kiss through the window while I continue to wait for a driver to claim my ride, glancing from my phone to the street and back. People crowd me, doing the same. Cars pull up, passengers load, and cars drive off. Down the sidewalk, I notice Aaron assisting Fallon into a waiting black Escalade. My heart does a little jump upon seeing him. He doesn't get into the SUV with her, and after the vehicle leaves, he turns around and sees me watching him. He strolls over with a lingering smile.

Aaron knows about the acquisition, and he never reached out to me. He swore he didn't want to marry, and here he is engaged. We spent one night in Las Vegas and five in Maui. We kissed a few times— our wedding, on the flight to Hawaii, and at Logan when we said goodbye—but nothing more than that. Instead we talked, and the trip felt more like a retreat, a mental cleanse. A regroup and reevaluation of the decisions we'd made that got us to where we were then. For six days, we were each other's confidants. I returned to Boston regretting that I'd hurt Paul and his family while at the same time, feeling more at peace with who I was and what I wanted from life. But do I really know Aaron? Can I trust him with my dilemma?

I don't have answers, not yet. But that doesn't stop me from returning his smile or the confession that slips out when he joins me on the sidewalk. "You were right, Aaron."

The corner of his mouth quirks, deepening his laugh lines. "About what?"

"I never stopped thinking about you."

Upon our return to Boston, Aaron and I stood outside baggage claim waiting for our rides. I felt sad I wouldn't see him again, but I knew that for me, especially after what I'd just gone through with Paul, it was for the best.

My ride arrived first and I turned to him to say a final goodbye. But his hands clasped my face and he kissed me. This kiss was stripped of the nerves and wildness of our first kiss, and the boldness of our second kiss. This one was tender and sweet, so wistful and full of longing that I couldn't discern whether he was projecting on me or if it was what I'd been feeling. He ended the kiss as suddenly as he'd started and pressed his forehead to mine.

I inhaled a deep, shuddering breath. "That was unexpected."

"Everything about you, Meli, has been unexpected. Thank you."

"For what?"

"For listening to me this week. For being a friend." Aaron had mostly confided his frustrations toward his parents and how unsatisfied he was with his career. He planned to make some changes. We both agreed we'd reached a point in our lives where we only wanted to pursue what made us happy. We wanted to control our own destinies and not have them dictated by others.

I hugged him hard and stepped back. "Goodbye, Aaron."

"Take care of yourself, Meli."

I opened the car door.

"Hey, Meli."

I turned back to Aaron.

"You're never going to stop thinking about me."

"I'm not?" I scoffed at his confidence. "And how do you know that?"

His smirk was a dare, oozing self-assuredness and a hint of mischief. "Because I'm not going to stop thinking about you."

I gave him a sly smile. "You sound pretty sure of yourself. Hey, what are we going to do about that piece of paper between us?"

A wicked grin spread across his face. "You'll hear from my lawyers." Then he got into the car that had pulled up behind mine. It was the last time I saw him. Until tonight.

Aaron's tongue now swirls over his teeth, his mouth pursing in a poor attempt to stop his grin. Hands in his pockets, he tips his head back and looks at the dark sky. "Nice night."

"It is," I say, my stare fixed on him.

He offers his elbow. "How about a walk instead?"

"Instead of what?"

"Coffee in the morning. Unless you want to do both."

His tone is teasing. Daring.

Suddenly, I no longer feel tired. "I'd love to," I answer, unsure what I'm saying yes to. Perhaps it's both, a nighttime walk and an early-morning coffee. I'm just eager for the time with him in between.

I cancel my ride request and take his elbow.

We weave through the bustle of guests clamoring to get home. A few people call out to Aaron. He waves to one man, shakes another's hand, thanks them for coming. But he doesn't let anyone waylay us. We round a corner and we still haven't said anything to each other. We just keep looking at one another like we can't believe we're here, together. I clear my throat. "You're quiet."

"Thinking."

"About?"

"You." His eyes are black in the faint lighting as his gaze roams my face, skims over my hair, and coasts down my dress. "I have so many questions."

"Does one of them have to do with why I'm wearing a gown every time we run into each other? I swear I don't dress like this every day."

He laughs. "No, but now that you mention it, how are your feet?"

The first thing we did after we'd married was buy me a pair of sneakers. I had no intention of walking the Las Vegas Strip in my wedding heels.

"My arches are killing me." I've been standing in my slingbacks for over three hours. Murder for a gal who lives in work boots.

"Doubt we'll have any luck finding a shoe store at this hour. There's a pub up ahead. Let me buy you a drink instead."

Getting off my feet sounds heavenly. "I'd love to have a drink with you."

Aaron holds open the door, his hand lightly grazing my back when he follows me inside. The pub is dimly lit and loud. A live band plays Irish folk music in the back. I text Emi that I ran into Aaron and that we've gone out for drinks as we snag a booth near the entrance and away from the band. But we're forced to sit close on the green velvet bench to hear ourselves over the music. Aaron's elbow bumps my arm when we order beers and bacon cheeseburgers, his thigh pressing against mine.

"Confession," he says while we wait for our food, angling his body toward me. "It's the same for me. I haven't stopped thinking about you since the airport."

Since our goodbye kiss. There was something different in that kiss. Unspoken promises. Missed opportunities. Regrets about things that would never happen.

"You're engaged," I remind him. But how fun it would be to flirt with him.

"No, I'm not."

I frown. "Then why did Fallon introduce herself as your fiancée?"

He sighed. "We broke off our engagement a couple weeks ago. For our parents' sake, we agreed to wait until after the gala to announce it. Does it bother you I was engaged?"

"Only that it makes me wonder if anything you told me about yourself is true. You said marriage wasn't your thing."

"I didn't lie to you, Meli. I had no reason to."

"Then why get engaged only to break it off?"

"She wasn't my choice."

His remark sweeps at the dusty corners of my memories. We stopped at the Bellagio to watch the fountains, and I asked him why he'd accepted my dare. What had compelled a single man with an aversion to marriage to wed on a whim only hours after meeting his bride?

He stayed quiet for a long while, watching the fountains dance to "Fly Me to the Moon." The song finished and I thought he'd forgotten my question. But then he quietly spoke. "You were my choice." His parents had wanted him to marry for a variety of reasons—family

51

legacy, upholding the family's image, continuing their dynasty. And they'd pressured him to propose to his mom's friend's daughter. That was the second time he'd mentioned Fallon to me.

"Your parents finally talked you into marrying her?"

He taps a finger on the table. "It's more complicated than that."

Our server interrupts us with our drink orders, and before I can ask Aaron to elaborate, he lifts his beer. "A toast to second chances."

My mouth twists to the side. He knows I'm not interested in relationships. I was quite clear about my choice not to marry when I told him why I'd left Paul. Artisant Designs would always come first. "What happened to never seeing each other again?" I figured we'd go our separate ways once I convince him to retract Savant's interest in my uncle's shop.

"Fate. That's what happened. It's brought us together again."

I doubt fate is at play here. My frustration over my situation has been mounting since yesterday morning, and I unwittingly unleash it on him. "I think you're part of the reason I could lose Artisant, and that has nothing to do with fate. My uncle came to you with an offer you didn't refuse. I told you about his shop, how it's been in my family for decades. You knew how important my work is to me. It's the whole reason why I broke off my engagement to Paul. You should have said no when Uncle Bear approached you."

"Hey, hey, hey." Aaron leans back, palms in the air. "It wasn't like that at all."

"Explain, then. Tell me how the letter of intent I read yesterday isn't you ripping my future right out from under me." He might as well rip out my heart along with it.

He sets down his beer before drinking any of it. "When we met, I was the director of acquisitions. My job was to discover top-notch artisans and bring them aboard. Or strike up a deal that gave us exclusive rights to distribute their work. I was on my way to Vegas to meet with one such artisan, but she canceled on me."

"I remember, but what does that have to do with Artisant Designs?"

"Nothing directly but hear me out. After we got back, I might have obsessed over you." He ducks his head and starts picking at a spot of dried food on the table. "I searched you online, a lot. I saw your work, what you did. I stalked your Instagram feed. And yes, it crossed my mind more than once to approach you with an offer. But our company has a strict nonfraternization policy, and I selfishly didn't want you to come work for us. I remember how passionate you are about your uncle's shop. I remember you telling me you looked forward to inheriting it. You'd be the third generation to own Artisant, and I admired that about you, especially since our situations were similar and I wasn't enjoying the path my parents had put me on. I didn't want to be the one to convince you to come work for us and not pursue your dream. I didn't want to take that from you."

"Then why are you taking it from me now?"

"It isn't me. I left the acquisitions department three years ago. Yes, as acting COO, the department reports to me. But when Artisant came up during a strategy meeting, I asked about you. I was told Bernard approached us and that you were on board and eager to start with us if we moved forward."

"The only way your director would have thought that was if—"

"Your uncle told her you were," Aaron finished.

"He lied." I slump on the bench, feeling a renewed wave of betrayal and violation as the utter disappointment in my uncle weighs me down. He taught me everything I know about woodworking with the intent of giving me the shop upon his retirement. Why would he go back on his word? Why are my parents going along with him? And why have they been negotiating in secret?

Because they knew I wouldn't go along with it. They probably thought they could finalize the sale and package up my new role at the Savant House like a gift on Christmas morning. An offer I wouldn't refuse because they'd gaslight me into believing they had my best interests at heart. For once.

What would Grandpa Walt think of this?

He wouldn't because selling Artisant Designs would have never crossed his mind.

I must stop the sale.

"Your company needs to back off," I demand. "I can't convince my uncle to change his mind, so you need to order your team not to pursue. Tell them I'm not part of the deal. That should dissuade them." Without my talent, Artisant Designs is a less attractive acquisition.

"I don't think you removing yourself from the equation is enough to change the team's mind, no offense, not with your uncle so willing to sell."

Does the Savant House want our copyrighted designs that much? Are they that determined to see us out of business? We're just one shop of many. While we have a reputation with high-end clientele, we have minimal market share compared to the Savant House's reach.

I pull out the card I'd been saving, the promise he made me in Vegas.

"Do you remember what you said to me on the High Roller?"

The High Roller is a massive Ferris wheel that overlooks the Las Vegas Strip, carrying up to thirty people in each gondola. Aaron bought us tickets for a thirty-minute ride, and as our gondola slowly rotated and we took in the bright lights of Vegas, we talked about our careers. We were stunned to discover we not only worked in similar industries but also in family businesses. That's where the similarities ended. I was passionate about my craft. He was unenthusiastic about his job. He hadn't been given a choice about working there. He also envied that I worked with my hands and looked thoroughly entranced as I spoke enthusiastically about what I wanted to do with the shop once Uncle Bear transferred ownership to me. I had a multitude of ideas to expand our reach and broaden our offerings.

Aaron made me a promise, which I wholeheartedly reciprocated in kind.

"If you ever need my help achieving your dreams, come find me. I'll do whatever is within my power to help you succeed," Aaron says, repeating what we promised one another five years prior.

"I'm here, Aaron."

He stares at me for a long moment. Then a solemn nod. "I'll see what I can do."

I rest my hand on his. "Thank you."

He flips his hand and threads his fingers through mine. We sit like that, holding hands as we'd done many times during our short week together.

The band finishes a folk song and launches into a jig. Our burgers arrive, and as we eat, we catch up on the last five years. Aaron has mostly worked, regularly changing departments within the company, going wherever he's assigned. I tell him about the table I'm working on for Isadora and show him photos of my progress. He compliments my work, and when the check arrives, he insists on paying. We leave the pub and he reaches for my hand as if it's the most natural thing to do.

"My feet thank you for the rest, and my stomach thanks you for the food." I pat my full belly.

Aaron chuckles, retrieving his phone to order a ride. It's almost 1:00 a.m. The air is balmy, the sky clear, the night perfect. Almost. We're about to part ways again. Goodbyes have always been hard for me. Probably because when my parents left when I was ten, they never truly came back. Not as the same people they'd been before. They're friendly toward me now, but never loving. They're more reserved than open, more guarded than trusting.

I should order my own ride, but I'm amped from being with Aaron. I'm not quite ready for the night to be over.

I turn to Aaron. "I'm not tired."

"I want another twenty-four hours with you," he says at the same time.

My mouth quirks. "Another dare?"

"No dare. Just you."

His declaration sends a jolt of heat through me. Warmth sparkles in my fingers. I slide a hand up his arm and over his shoulder. I gently comb my fingers through his hair, desiring him in a way I resisted before because I hadn't been in the right headspace given the circumstances that led me to him. Just because I'm not interested in pursuing a relationship doesn't mean I don't still crave a connection. And if Aaron and I ever came together that way, I wanted it to be with a clear conscience.

Tonight my conscience is clear.

"Meli," he whispers roughly. A shiver moves up my arm.

I lift my face just as he lowers his and our lips meet, my eyes fluttering closed. The shock of his mouth on mine slams into me, and I shudder. He groans, and the next thing I know, we're pressed together like two pages in a book. Somehow, he pockets his phone and finds my hand, holding me against him in a one-arm hug. His other hand cups my jaw and angles my face to deepen our kiss. The kiss quickly turns heated, an open-mouthed clash of teeth and tongues as we cling to each other.

Kissing Aaron feels as good as I remember, better even. But this kiss isn't a discovery like that first kiss in the back of an Uber. It isn't playful like it was when we showed off to a plane full of passengers. It's not a tender goodbye. This kiss is for us. And it's electrifying, arousing, provocative.

I don't know who breaks it off first. Maybe we both lift our heads at once. But we're breathless when our eyes meet. His lips glisten and his gray eyes shimmer like polished silver. My fingers are in his hair.

"Aaron." His name is a breath across my swollen lips. I want, I want, I want. *You.*

His hand cradles my face and he draws his thumb along my cheek. "Come home with me."

CHAPTER 9

From the Heart

We barely make it through the front door of Aaron's Beacon Hill town house before we collide in a tangle of mouths and limbs, heartbeats and breaths. This is a first for me, that feeling where I want to climb into someone and bathe in their affection and adoration. And I want to do that with Aaron.

Our ride from the pub was quiet, the air between us thick with anticipation. We didn't talk or touch. We just sat in the back seat looking at each other, caught in our own orbit. Back in our bubble. A smile played on the edges of his mouth, the world muted outside. And every block we drove was a brushstroke of longing.

Aaron somehow manages to kick the door shut without breaking our kiss. I think I hear a bolt latch and the beep of a house alarm, but that's all I register. Anything beyond us is nonexistent as he backs me up against a wall. I push his tux jacket over his shoulders. He shakes the sleeves down his arms and the jacket lands on the floor in a tumble of richly textured fabric.

We spin around and Aaron's back slams into the wall, his hands coasting up my spine. There is the whisper of a zipper, the soft slide of expensive material, and my gown floats to the floor in a cloud of tulle and silk, where it joins Aaron's jacket.

I help him out of his shirt while he pushes down his pants. We step out of our shoes and all the while, we're kissing and exploring. His teeth nip my jaw, then his mouth travels down my neck, leaving a trail of damp heat. I'm on fire, my skin crackling, and I've never felt more alive.

I'm desperate to make Aaron feel as good as he's making me, so I suck his earlobe between my teeth, nip the skin, and run my fingers through his hair before skimming them across the contours of his abs. He groans when I reach the elastic waistband of his briefs. I want to kiss him there and everywhere. I need to feel his weight on me.

Who knew he could make me feel like this, like I wouldn't be able to spare a single breath if I were to walk away? Who knew he could make me ache for him so? Why didn't we do this on our wedding night? Why didn't we sleep together in Maui? Why have we waited so long?

"The fuck I know. Bedroom." Aaron grabs my wrist and we run up the stairs with my embarrassed laughter bouncing off the ceiling. I guess I asked those questions out loud.

Off come Aaron's briefs. Down go my panties. I'm not wearing a bra, and Aaron freely palms my breasts as he backs us down a long, dark hallway. Like a Hollywood movie, we leave a trail of clothes. And like a Hollywood movie, I remind myself this isn't real. It doesn't mean anything. I won't get emotionally attached. I won't let tonight deter me from my work.

I won't fall.

We're just scratching the itch we had in Maui.

We reach Aaron's room and he flips on a dim light. I briefly catch amber finishes with caramel tones, a king-size bed, textured drapes, and soft, rich layers that leave me with the impression of masculine coziness before a voice running over gravel draws my eyes up to Aaron's face. "I want to see you," he says as he turns on another lamp in the corner.

After years of him pervading my dreams and dominating my thoughts, I almost beg him to look all he wants. I want my fill too.

But a sudden shyness that belies my usual confidence in the bedroom settles over me. "It's been a while for me." His dark eyes find mine. I see a question in them. "I haven't dated in five years. You were my last kiss, *husband*," I say, keeping it honest between us. And there hasn't been anyone in my bed since Paul.

Heat flares in his gaze. "I have so many questions about that. *Wife*."

Why is it so goddamn hot when he calls me "wife"? I'm just about to ask when he nudges me back. My calves bump into the bed and I lose my balance, collapsing onto the mattress. Aaron crawls over me, stalking up the bed until he's right where I want him. He balances his weight on his forearms as my legs brace his. My toes skim his calves, the hair on his legs tickling the soles of my feet.

He lowers his head for a short kiss. "Is this what you want?"

I press the back of my head deeper into the pillow to look directly up at him. "Don't you want this?"

"Yes, but I want to be sure we're on the same page."

"We're reading the same book, Aaron." I fit my palm to his cheek. "I absolutely want this *with you*."

A groan rumbles in his throat before he kisses me hard. The nightstand drawer scrapes open and foil crinkles. He shifts on the bed and I reach for him, guiding him to my center. Our gazes lock and he pushes inside me.

Then everything but Aaron and the way he moves over me and in me falls away.

———

I stare at the ceiling, willing my heart rate to slow. Beside me, Aaron breathes heavily. His body glistens with sweat. I'm damp everywhere. Used and abused in the most delicious of ways, Emi would quip if I told her about tonight. She'd punctuate it with a high five.

I suck my bottom lip between my teeth. I can't tell Emi that I just had the best sex of my life, not if I want to keep the origins of my relationship with Aaron—if I dare call it a relationship—secret.

"What took us so long?" Aaron echoes my question from earlier, drawing me out of my musings.

"Right?" I grin at him.

The back of his hand grazes my pebbled nipple, and a pleasurable warmth blooms across my chest. My hand finds his. He studies my palm, his smooth fingers gliding over my hand, tracing patterns between the calluses like he did in Maui while we watched the sun set or lazily lounged poolside. The world shrinks to his touch, his teasing exploration a slow burn of desire. But my rough skin embarrasses me, and my fingers involuntarily curl over my palm. He presses them open. "I love your hands."

"They're in terrible shape." Dry, cracked, and scarred from years of labor. If anything, they're in worse condition than five years ago. I rarely remember to apply lotion.

"They show me that you love what you do. I'm jealous." He traces the outline of my hand.

"Of my hands?" I stare at my palm, amused we see it so differently. My hands are tools. They let me create furniture that enriches people's homes and lives. But like any tool, with so much use they've become worn and beaten up.

"If I have anything, it's an education." Aaron graduated from Yale with an English and Literature degree. "Other than strategies that keep Savant in the black, I have nothing to show for my work."

"As if this is nothing?" I circle an arm in the air at the extravagant primary suite. His room looks like a page from the Savant House catalog. I can only imagine the value of this property, given its location.

"Family money."

His tone insinuates trust fund, but he isn't bragging. I sense a quiet acquiescence. His life is what it is, and there isn't much he can do about it. His parents really did force him into the family business.

"I've taken a few trade classes—Intro to Woodturning, Elements of Design, Joinery."

"Really? You didn't mention that." I roll onto my side, fascinated.

"Because you're so skilled and my stuff is child's play." He turns to me, his hair flopping over his forehead. I gently sweep it back and his eyes close, giving me the sense he's savoring my touch.

"What have you built?" I ask, bemused at his embarrassment. Aaron is humble, but he's not someone who's easily mortified.

"A few pieces I will never show anyone."

"I want to see. I promise I won't laugh."

"Not happening, so get over it." He presses his forehead to mine.

I pretend-pout and he gently flicks my bottom lip. "Favorite thing about my job?" His arm loops my waist and he pulls me closer. No part of me is not touching him. "Not my current one, but when I was the acquisitions director? I loved meeting artisans in their workspaces. There's something sacred about woodshops. They're vibrant, teeming with activity and creativity, and full of possibilities. To have the skill to shape wood into something useful, something more than its original form and purpose? I wish I could do that."

I stare at him. I knew he didn't like working at the Savant House and wanted to do something more. But the way he described what it feels like to work in a shop like Artisant? It's like he understands why I do what I do.

From the moment I met Aaron, I felt like he understood me. That we understood each other on a level nobody else did. But I didn't give much weight to the feeling, because how could we relate to each other better than friends and family who'd known us much longer?

That feeling comes rushing back now. This time, I grasp hold of it.

"The first breath I take when I get to work in the morning is my favorite. The wood shavings and resin. Most people don't like the chemical odor. I relish it."

"I find everything about you and what you do interesting. I envy that."

"Then why are you still working for your parents?"

"It's where they need me."

"You should quit if you're not happy."

He sighs. "I owe it to them to stay."

I admire his dedication, but I hate that our families wield so much control over our futures.

I cup his jaw. His eyes flutter closed and he presses his cheek into my palm.

"Why did you break off your engagement?" I ask. Maybe he is taking control of his destiny.

"I didn't. Fallon did. She wasn't happy, and she could tell I wasn't either. We're better off with other people."

"Is there someone else for you?"

He meets my gaze. His eyes are piercing. "I hope to find out soon."

Same is the first thought that lands in my head, along with a flutter in my chest. To have his companionship and affection. What a life that could be. But a cold dread settles in my stomach. Any meaningful relationship will inevitably come down to me having to choose between loving him and loving my craft, a road I don't care to travel again.

I turn the conversation back to Fallon. "Why weren't you happy with her?"

"Truth?"

"Don't we always tell each other the truth?"

"We do, and that's what I like about us. We're honest about our feelings." He threads his fingers with mine. "Truth is, I kept thinking about that stupid list."

"What list?"

"The one we made on the plane."

"The marriage-material list? Wow. I wonder what happened to it." We rushed off the plane. I thought I put the napkin in my purse, but I couldn't find it when I arrived home. I assumed the list fell out at some point during our night in Vegas.

Aaron nudges me onto my back and leans over me, reaching for the nightstand.

"No," I say as he tugs open the drawer and shows me the napkin. "You kept it." Not only that, he kept it close by.

Aaron rolls onto his back. I take the napkin from him and he scoots closer, plastering against my side. I hold it up so we can both read. The ink has faded, and the paper is crinkled as if it's been handled often.

"'Marriage-Material List.'" I read my own handwriting. "'Someone you want to wake up with every morning. Someone who prioritizes you over friends and family. Someone who will dance with you.'"

"Fallon didn't like to dance."

"Oh." I glance at him. I remember that. He shrugs his shoulder. "I like to dance," I say.

"I know you do." His eyes meet mine for a beat, and I wonder if he's thinking about the club in Vegas or tonight. He easily led me in a waltz. We just clicked into place as if no time had passed.

He nods at the napkin, beckoning me to read more.

"'Someone who will sing your favorite songs with you,'" I continue. "'Someone who doesn't resent you because of your work. Someone who supports your passions. Someone who understands *me time* doesn't mean you don't want to be with them. Someone who means it when they say *I love you*.'"

"It has to be from the heart," Aaron murmurs by my ear, and my stomach tightens. Exactly what I said when he'd added how he wanted to hear "I love you." He didn't want those three beautiful words to become a salutation, like an automated response when you ended a call.

I scratch a spot behind my ear, uncomfortable with the effect our list is having on me. Is this what Aaron meant when he said he couldn't stop thinking about it? I would love to have this with someone. I want to have this with someone. But at the risk of not being able to devote my full attention to my work? I know my family. I know myself. I could never successfully manage both. I failed with Paul. I'd fail with anyone else.

I continue reading. "'Someone fun and playful. Someone willing to try new things with you. Someone compassionate, respectful, and kind. Someone who will stand behind you. Someone who will stand up for you. Someone not afraid to stand up *to* you.'"

I finish and we're both quiet.

"We set the bar high," I say, breaking the silence.

"It's a lot for someone to live up to."

Which is why it would never work. But I joke, "We ruined each other for anyone else. We should just marry again."

"We should."

I look at him. "You're not serious."

He doesn't say anything.

"I was kidding, you know that, right? You and I agreed marriage isn't our thing."

Aaron makes a noise in the back of his throat and moves over me. He kicks my legs apart. Then he kisses me, moving down my body, and my breaths deepen and my world narrows on the attention he starts lavishing.

"If this is your way of convincing me, it's not going to work."

With his mouth pressed to me, I feel his laughter vibrate my bones. He then adds a finger and I groan, my head falling back and arms folding over my face.

I am a goner.

CHAPTER 10

ANOTHER DARE

Aaron isn't in bed when I wake up to burnished sunlight pooling on his empty pillow. My first thought is he regretted last night and that's why he isn't here. The only thing I regret are the new memories of him that will haunt me for a long time. It won't be easy, walking away after only one night with him.

But as much as I want to fall back to sleep, I can't linger in bed. I have a table to sand, and I want to know what Aaron plans to tell his team come Monday. When does he expect an answer? When will Savant notify Artisant? That's my window to prepare my offer to Uncle Bear. I need numbers from the registers Mom manages and approval for a business loan before Uncle Bear seeks another buyer once Savant pulls out.

I roll from bed to go search for Aaron only to stop when I spot a pair of women's running shorts and a thin T-shirt, threadbare from many washings, folded on the nightstand. The clothes weren't there last night. Nor were the flip-flops on the floor beside the bed.

They must belong to Fallon.

That thought comes with a sting of envy.

Still, I put them on, feeling a little weirded out because they're his ex's. But what choice do I have? I don't want to wear a ball gown home, and my feet will disown me if I put them back in my heels.

Following the scent of bacon and eggs, I go downstairs. I spot my gown draped over the back of the couch in the living room, my heels tucked nearby on the floor, ready for when I leave.

Aaron's back is to me when I enter the kitchen, a large, bright room that runs the width of the house. Emi would salivate over this space. Tall windows open to a small, square yard. Morning sunlight drenches the marble countertops and white tile backsplash. Aaron stands at the stove, plating scrambled eggs and crispy bacon. He wears gym shorts and a workout shirt and looks as if he went for a run. His hair is messy and damp. Two mugs wait by an expensive-looking espresso machine. I smell the nutty aroma of freshly ground coffee, and my stomach rumbles.

"Morning," I say.

"Hey." He turns with a friendly smile. "I was just going to come wake you. Hungry?"

"Starving." I slide onto a stool at the island. "How are you even awake?" We stayed up well past 4:00 a.m., talking and doing other stuff, and it's only 8:30 a.m. now.

"Never fell asleep," he says. "Coffee?"

"Please. And please explain why you didn't sleep. I don't know how you're functioning. I'm exhausted," I say around a yawn, covering my mouth.

"I couldn't stop thinking." He gestures that his mind was buzzing and puts a mug in front of me. He then retrieves oat milk from the Sub-Zero fridge and sugar from a cabinet, then sets them both beside my coffee. I stare at them, a little stunned he remembers how I take my coffee—oat milk with two sugars. In the entire year we were together, Paul never could get it right.

Then I register what Aaron said and my stomach concaves. "Do you regret last night?" We shouldn't have mixed business with pleasure. It never works.

"Hell, no. Last night was . . . It was amazing, Meli." He looks straight at me and a flush moves up my chest.

I duck my head with a pleased smile.

"How are you feeling?" he gently probes.

"I hurt in all the right places."

Aaron's grin is instant and full of male satisfaction. My face flames. "I can't believe I said that." I slap a hand over my eyes.

He sets two heaping platefuls on the island and sits beside me. "Your secret is safe with me," he teases.

Steam from the eggs rises past my face. "This smells fantastic." I dig in. "Cook like this every morning, and I'll marry you again."

"About that . . ." He folds a strip of bacon into his mouth.

"I shouldn't have said anything." I wave my hand in a poor attempt to erase last night's joke. "I wasn't serious."

"I am."

Egg falls off my fork. "Come again?"

"We should get married."

I stare hard at him, then cackle. "You *are* sleep deprived."

"This is why I didn't sleep."

I wait as he shovels egg into his mouth, chews, swallows, and takes another bite. Whatever he plans to say, he's nervous about it.

"Remember that nonfraternization policy I mentioned?" he says, and I nod. "This is confidential, but a few years back, one of our furniture curators was having an affair with the sales director. They'd worked out a scheme where he was stealing pieces, pocketing cash on the side, and she covered for him, manipulating the numbers on her reports. Long story short, the company lost a lot of money, and the incident sparked company-wide conversations about boundaries between employees and the importance of maintaining a balance between work and personal life, especially if the couple works together."

"Which is impossible," I interject.

"Needless to say, HR put a nonfraternization policy into place, and it's actively enforced. We can't legally ban coworkers from dating, but it's strongly discouraged."

"Where are you going with this?"

"If we get married, there's a viable chance Savant will retract its interest in acquiring your uncle's shop."

"That's slightly extra in terms of strategy, but my interest is piqued. On what grounds would us being married deter Savant?"

"Off the top of my head: conflict of interest, lack of transparency, corporate governance." He ticks off his fingers. "I'm sure there's more."

But marriage? His strategy seems a tad drastic. I should be freaking out and racing for the nearest door. He's proposing to me! (Is this a proposal?) The only reason I'm not panicking is because this is familiar territory for us. Maybe "our thing" is to do the outrageous.

I tap a bacon slice against the plate rim. There has to be an alternative solution. "Why can't you just tell your company to not buy the shop? You are the COO."

"I don't have final say with acquisitions. Before we move forward with a letter of intent, we must have CEO or board approval, depending on how significant the financial investment is. Legal is another matter. While a letter of intent isn't binding, there could be legal consequences if it's retracted without proper justification. Something I'm already risking by proposing this. What's to stop your uncle from suing us for malicious intent? But"—he continues before I can ask why he's willing to put his job and company reputation on the line for my sake—"our marriage could dissuade the board's interest due to undisclosed conflicts, like employee favoritism, nepotism, and all that BS."

"You've put a lot of thought into this."

He dips his head until our eyes are level. "I was up all night."

"If I'd known that . . ." I give him a flirty wink.

He groans and finishes his coffee.

"Why would you do this for me?" He isn't proposing a twenty-four-hour dare. This could last longer, much longer. He's also risking a lot—lawsuits, company reputation, his credibility. "What's in it for you? And don't say more of what we did last night." I point my fork at him and his pained expression is comical. "Won't this piss off your parents?"

"Absolutely."

"You want to piss them off?"

"To say they'll be displeased when they learn Fallon and I broke off our engagement is an understatement. My mom will be on my case until we're back together. But if I'm already married . . ."

"Oh boy. They're going to love me," I drawl.

"They'd be stupid not to. Either way, when it comes to my family, I will stand beside you, behind you, and up for you. You have my word."

Our list.

I stare at Aaron before looking at my plate. I nudge the eggs with my fork as an odd, unusual feeling washes over me. Never has anyone advocated for me so profoundly. What if . . .

Stop right there, Meli.

I'm not really considering this, am I? Marrying Aaron? Again! Yes, he's sweet and nice and gorgeous. He smells incredible and is phenomenal in bed. But marriage? Haven't I confirmed it isn't something for people like me? I'd risk losing myself in a relationship again. I'd risk being forced to choose between him and my craft.

Wait. Wouldn't I be marrying *for* my work?

"I'd never let my family hurt you." Aaron's certainty interrupts my conflicting thoughts.

I look at him, and once again I feel that unsettling sensation that he understands me like no one else. That he sees inside me, the real me. The me who's frightened. Can he sense how deeply my parents once hurt me? How they continue to make me feel like I'm not enough to be truly loved and valued?

"I still can't believe your parents were forcing you to marry Fallon," I say, turning the attention back on him. He's studying me too intently.

"I wouldn't say *forcing*. More like *strongly encouraging*."

"Still. It's your life. You have the right to do what you want with it." We both do.

The lines in Aaron's forehead deepen. "Promise you'll consider my offer."

I slowly nod. It isn't the proposal I imagined receiving. Then again, I haven't imagined ever being proposed to again.

I catch the time on the kitchen clock. "Oh! I have to run. I have a table to finish." I slide off the stool, as much in a rush to leave and process our conversation as I am to get to the shop.

"I'd love to watch you work someday."

I smile. I would love that too.

I take our dishes to the sink and rinse them.

He retrieves his phone. "I'll order you a ride."

"You don't have to. I can take the T."

He follows me to the front door. "I want to." His thumb taps in an order after I give him my address.

He now knows where I live.

That fact leaves me feeling pleasantly elated.

"Thank you." I collect my gown and shoes. "Thanks for the walk-of-shame clothes too." I tug at the shirt.

"They're my sister's." A smile lifts the side of his mouth. He knew I assumed they belong to Fallon.

My ride arrives and Aaron gives me a long, lingering kiss goodbye. "Think about it," he says again.

How can I not? It isn't every day that a girl has the opportunity to marry a practical stranger, not once in her life, but twice.

CHAPTER 11

GOING DOWN?

I view my life in three separate acts: before, during, and after. Unoriginal, but whatever.

The before years are the ones leading up to when I was ten. Take away the scary times Mom forgot me in the grocery store or Dad left me for hours alone in the car while he visited a friend in an apartment building stained with graffiti, or the mornings I missed school because my parents had been up late partying. On those mornings, I often woke to the musty smell of pot, powder on the tables, and wine-stained glasses cluttering the sink. Sometimes there would be a stranger passed out on the couch. They'd stare bleary-eyed at me when I poked them awake, asking who they were.

Apart from that, I was my happiest self in those years because we were together. We laughed constantly, and they comforted me when I was sad. Mom and I visited the library almost every afternoon, reading books in the aisles, whispering passages to each other, giggling when someone would shush us. Dad and I acted out my favorite fairy tales at the park before we fed stale bread to the geese. On weekends, my parents and I hunted for shells on the Cape and ate lobster until the stars came out.

The during years were the ones where I lived with Uncle Bear. Eight years, to be exact. I spent my time with him holding my breath, waiting for the day my parents returned. I clung to the good memories, even though Uncle Bear would remind me of the bad times when he had to rescue me from my parents. I loved Mom and Dad to the moon and back, just as they had loved me. They weren't perfect. We all had our faults. And those times they hurt my feelings or inadvertently left me somewhere? I know they didn't mean to. I just knew when they came back, everything would go back to the way it was before.

But it hadn't.

Enter the after years.

I was sixteen when they returned, and like any teenager who felt abandoned, I was angry. And when they didn't invite me to come live with them, my animosity toward them only magnified. So they gave me space.

You're better off with your uncle, Mom told me when I asked why they didn't want me to move back home.

Wouldn't moving be a hassle? Dad answered.

Eventually, my anger cooled and we were at least civil toward one another. Dad would watch the Patriots game with me and Uncle Bear. Mom would drop off an extra casserole on the nights Uncle Bear or I didn't have time to cook because of work or school. But the chasm had been formed, and outside of working together at Artisant, they never tried to close the distance between us.

After I turned eighteen and moved into my own apartment on a floor sandwiched between my uncle and my parents, I started seeing a therapist. She advised I needed to let go of my childhood fantasy. My family would never be the same as we were before. Not only because I grew up but also because my parents were different people. They'd been through a lot.

It still doesn't change that I want to be with my family, even when it seems they don't want me around, or know how to act when I am. I just keep hoping things will change between us. It's why I live in the same building and want us all to keep working at the studio. Artisant Designs is the only place where we feel like a family. That shop holds us together.

After this morning with Aaron, though, I feel like I'm on the precipice of my fourth act. How can I not be? Between Uncle Bear selling and Aaron's proposal, my life will change again in a big way.

After I shower and change into my coveralls and boots, I give Blueberry breakfast and some much-needed attention because I don't usually work on Saturdays. I then head out for the shop. On the way down, the elevator stops on my parents' floor.

"Oh, hello, Meli," Mom says, surprised to see me there. This isn't the first time we've run into each other on the elevator. Yet she always seems shocked when we do.

"Going down?" I ask.

"Yes." Her gaze drops to my boots. "Off to the shop?" she asks, stepping into the elevator. She's wearing high-waisted jeans that hug her round hips, white sneakers, and a white shirt with orange and pink roses printed along the neckline and sleeve hems. Her overstuffed, worn leather purse hangs from her shoulder. She has several reusable shopping bags tucked under her arm.

"I have to finish Isadora's table since I left early on Thursday." I push the button to close the doors. Mom stands apart from me, facing the doors. She's quiet as the elevator descends. "How's Dad? Is he at the shop?"

"He might be. He and your uncle were heading to the Cape for a delivery."

Shoot. I glance at my phone. Hopefully I can make it before they leave.

Mom chances a look at me and smiles. I smile back. She looks forward again.

"So, um . . . what about you? Where are you headed?" I ask.

"I thought I'd go to the farmers market, then the library. There's a new Nora Roberts book they're holding for me."

I almost ask if I can join her. The question is right there on the tip of my tongue. A sunny morning with Mom sounds like my ideal way to spend a Saturday. An ideal morning that would only work if Mom and

I had a closer relationship. We could talk about books and pick out our favorite local vegetables. Maybe I would buy her a honey wax candle or she would invite me over for dinner. We'd make a salad with the fruit and lettuce we bought at the market. But I have too much work left on Isadora's table and a business plan I need to start drafting if I have any hope of qualifying for a loan. I also know Mom will politely decline. I spare myself the disappointment.

The elevator settles on the ground floor. "When you get to work on Monday, can you send me some numbers?" I ask. "I only need a few spreadsheets. I'll email you a list."

She frowns. "Whatever for?"

"I'm putting together a business plan. I'm going to apply for a loan and make Uncle Bear an offer for the shop."

"Don't be silly, Meli. The shop has run its course. Let your uncle handle it. He already has a buyer."

"What if the buyer falls through?" And they will, I want to tell her. "Shouldn't he keep his options open until the deal closes?"

"Everything has already been arranged with the Savant House," Mom says as the elevator doors open and she steps out.

"But I don't want to go work for them," I argue, still grappling with my shock and anger. Uncle Bear was the one man I thought I could count on who understood my craft is, and always will be, my first and only love, and that Artisant Designs will forever be the one place I feel is home.

Mom hums behind a forced close-lipped smile. "Have a wonderful day," she says, failing to acknowledge that I'm having a hard time with Uncle Bear's decision. "I'll see you at work on Monday." She quickly leaves the building with me gaping after her.

The elevator doors start to close. I throw my hand up to stop them and hurry after her. I look up and down the sidewalk, but she's gone. She must have snagged a cab. Also gone is my chance to talk her over to my side. Someone has to help me convince Uncle Bear to hear my proposal.

And that certainly isn't Dad. He never opposes anything his brother says. If anyone in our family is a pushover, it's my dad. But I'll never forgive myself if Savant, or any other company, acquires Artisant Designs and I didn't at least try to talk my parents into helping me.

When I arrive at the shop, Dad and Uncle Bear are in the alley, loading up the old U-Haul my uncle bought used at a deep discount years ago. The shop's roll-up door is open. Sawdust motes dance in the late morning sunlight. Uncle Bear heaves an oak side table onto the truck bed. Dad waits nearby with the matching coffee table.

"Nice to see you again," Dad says when I join them. "Wasn't sure you were coming back," he teases with a wink.

"Wasn't in the mood to work yesterday." Not after I stormed out on Thursday.

"Still angry?" Dad lifts the coffee table onto the truck bed when Uncle Bear motions he's ready for it.

"Do you think Uncle Bear should sell the shop to Savant?"

Dad shrugs, looking at the ground. I'm disappointed he won't say anything. Either he refuses to oppose Uncle Bear's decision or he's going along with it because Artisant has to be sold for some reason I'm not privy to.

"What are you and Mom going to do without the shop? Where are you going to work?"

"Not sure. We haven't figured that out yet."

"You don't have a plan?" My parents hardly have any retirement put aside. I know that because Mom's always complaining they don't have money. Dad likes to spend. "Is there any way I can convince you to help me talk him out of selling? I'll keep the business running. You and Mom can work with me. We'll continue as we have been." And we'll stay together.

"Meli . . ." Dad stalls, pursing his lips. His gaze slings to me only to dart away like a mouse scurrying across the floor.

"I can tell you don't want him to sell. Help me talk him—"

"I'm right here, Meli," Uncle Bear says above me. He looks down at us from the truck bed.

"I want to talk with you about selling."

"Not a good time. We have to get to the Cape and back before tonight's tournament." He and Dad compete on the same bowling team, the Woodchucks.

Uncle Bear grunts under the weight of the coffee table as he tries to move it farther into the truck. Dad pulls himself up and helps. They cover both tables with shipping blankets and strap them in so they don't shift during transport.

"I went to Savant's gala last night," I announce.

Dad's eyes widen before briefly meeting Uncle Bear's gaze. Uncle Bear covers his shock by staring at his gloved hands. He tears off the gloves. "Glad you did. They're nice people."

"I told them I wasn't going to work for them."

Unease crinkles the skin between my uncle's brows. "Now why would you do that?"

I just revealed my hand. I'm intentionally undermining his negotiations. But isn't he doing the same, undermining my plans to inherit the shop he promised me? Neither of us are playing fair.

"I never wanted to go work for a large corporation. I want Artisant. We've talked about this for years. You promised me the shop."

Dad jumps off the back of the truck. Uncle Bear follows him down. "You're passing up a good opportunity, Meli," my uncle says. "I'd hate to see that for you."

"Then give me the chance to make an offer. I probably can't match Savant, but we'd be able to keep the shop in the family. Grandpa Walt would have wanted it that way."

Dad's face tightens and he quickly looks away.

"Give me a few weeks to put some numbers together and get approved for a loan."

"I'm not considering other offers," Uncle Bear says.

"Artisant isn't just a shop to me," I push on. "It's our family's legacy. My legacy. Everything you, Dad, and Grandpa Walt built, everything we poured into this shop . . . You aren't just giving it away; you're taking it from me. For what? So you guys can leave me again?" I glare accusingly at Dad. "I honestly don't understand why you're selling, and why you're only considering selling to the Savant House. Are they holding something over you? Are they blackmailing you?" I couldn't see how or why, but it's worth asking.

Uncle Bear's face is a mask. "You don't want this life, Meli. Operating a shop like this is hard, unforgiving work." He talks to his hands, picking at his calluses. "Look at your dad and me. My back is messed up. Your dad needs another knee replacement. We're lucky we made it this far with all our fingers. You deserve better."

"Shouldn't that be for me to decide?" I'm twenty-nine. They're treating me like I'm twelve.

Dad turns around and walks to the front of the truck.

"What I deserve are answers," I argue. Ones that make sense.

We watch Dad step up into the cab. I wish more than I ever have before that he'd back me up. He shuts the door, his arm falling out the window. His fingers impatiently tap the metal.

Uncle Bear smacks his gloves against his thigh. "Don't you see I'm trying to protect you, Meli? Give you a fresh start? Artisant is a sunk ship. There's no salvaging her."

I lurch back. "How's that possible?" We're selling more product than ever. We can barely keep up with orders, even with the price increases I finally convinced Uncle Bear to implement. He always undervalued our work.

"Doesn't matter. I'm done discussing this." Uncle Bear pulls down the truck's roll door and slides the lock into place. "We'll be back after hours. Lock up when you leave." He climbs into the driver's seat with a grim expression. The engine coughs, chokes, and then revs. With a shudder like a bear shaking off dust, the truck drives away, the rear tire crushing an empty soda can, like my dreams.

CHAPTER 12

A WIN-WIN SITUATION

Less than an hour later I'm at Aaron's door. He answers after a few short knocks, his face splitting into a grin after his initial shock of finding me on his porch.

"Hi, Meli." He glances behind him into the town house. "Did you forget something? We were just heading out to the game." The *we* is a man and woman seated in the living room, dressed similarly to Aaron. He wears jeans, a navy tee, and a well-worn Red Sox baseball cap.

My heart pounds in my ears. "Were you serious about getting married?"

Aaron gestures for me to keep my voice down and joins me on the porch, closing the door behind him. I catch the warm notes of his Bottega Veneta cologne, the scent that has lingered in my memories. I saw the bottle on his bathroom counter this morning, the same brand he had with him in Maui.

"What's going on? Are you okay?" His gaze darts over my face anxiously. Concern darkens his expression.

I wipe my damp forehead. I feel flushed and my neck is sweaty, my hair tangled and windblown. I'm sure I look half wild. "Were you serious this morning? Because Bear won't budge. I can't change his mind. He won't even consider an offer from me as long as your company is in the picture."

Aaron stares at me, then opens the door. "Come inside."

I follow him into the living room. His guests watch me curiously, nursing beers.

"She your date, Aaron?" the woman boldly asks, assessing my frazzled state. I can tell the woman is tall. She has the same dark hair as Aaron's, trimmed in a blunt, chic cut that skims her shoulders. Her designer jeans and shirt are iron-crisp, her sneakers a pristine white.

"She's a friend," Aaron corrects her, and to me, says, "The rude one is my sister, Charlie."

I look at him. *That's riiiiight.* He has a sister. He adores her. I've wanted to meet her ever since he told me about all the fun scrapes he used to get into with her when they were kids. I wish I was here under different circumstances and had time to get to know her.

Aaron offers me a small smile. I'm sure he's remembering our conversations about her five years ago in Maui. "That's her husband, Murphy." He points at the guy unfolding from the couch.

"Hi. I'm Meli." I introduce myself to Charlie and shake Murphy's hand.

"You should come with us," Murphy says brightly. Red tinges his cheeks and I wonder how many beers he's already had. "We have an extra ticket since *someone* isn't joining us."

Charlie makes a shushing noise at her husband. Aaron clears his throat. He faces me fully with a lifted brow. Is that a question? Does he want me to go with them?

"Thanks, but I have to get back to work. And we . . ." I gesture at Aaron with a look. Does he have time to talk? "Maybe I should come back later." I don't know when the game starts. He said they were on their way out the door.

"Now's good. You guys go ahead," Aaron says to his sister and brother-in-law. "Meli and I have a . . ." He looks wide-eyed at me.

"A pressing business matter to deal with," I fill in for him. I crack my knuckle with a loud pop.

Charlie and Murphy exchange a look. "That's okay, we'll wait." Murphy settles back on the couch with a smug grin. Charlie smacks his chest with the back of her hand, but she's grinning too. I glance between them, wondering what I'm missing.

Aaron rolls his eyes. "Ignore them," he says and leads me into his den.

"And here I was going to thank Charlie for the clothes," I say, turning to him.

His ears redden and with a sharp laugh he shuts the door on his nosy family. Both Charlie and Murphy are leaning out of their seats to get a better look at us.

"Did you tell them about Fallon?" I wonder if the extra ticket belonged to her.

"Right before you arrived. They weren't surprised."

"Do your parents know?"

"Ah . . . No, not yet." He rubs his palms together, his expression clearly showing he isn't eager for that conversation.

I continue to pull at my fingers, taking in the room. Smooth leathers and earthy colors juxtaposed with polished woods and natural textures tie his home office together. There's a framed jersey on one wall and an electric guitar in the corner. A large oak desk squats in front of the window. Books fill the shelves on the opposite wall, and a sleek bar cart stocked with top-shelf liquors and vintage decanters occupies another corner. The room is warm, inviting, and full of personality, a space where I easily picture him relaxing and recharging. It's casual, breezy, and unflappable, just like the man I met on the way to Vegas.

Aaron leans back against the desk, his hands curled around the edge, facing the room. Facing me as I pace, really. Twitchy apprehension and all that.

"Tell me what's up," he says.

I take a breath and recap my morning, running through the conversations I had with Mom in the elevator and with Uncle Bear and Dad at the shop. I stop in front of him when I finish. "Do you really think Savant will retract the offer if we marry?"

"Are you sure you don't want me to try to talk to my people first?"

"Are you changing your mind?"

"No, but this morning you were wary. Now we can't get married fast enough." He grins wryly. "I want to be sure we're still reading the same book," he says, repeating back to me what I said to him in bed last night. "Don't forget, we each want something out of this."

"You pat my back; I pat yours. It's a business arrangement. I get it." I wave both hands. I'm a bundle of jumpy apprehension. I'm talking *marriage*. I'm actually considering marrying him.

"More like a marriage of convenience."

"Right. Sure." I can do this. We'll partner for practical reasons, not because of a genuine connection. Love isn't the driving force. I won't have to choose between him and my art. In fact, I'd be doing this for the love of my art, to preserve my family's legacy.

Which brings up another matter.

"How long do we stay married?" I hadn't put much thought into it on my way over. But offhand, I anticipate three to four months, six months tops.

Aaron sighs and crosses his arms. "Depends how soon my parents are convinced who I marry doesn't make a difference. Marrying Fallon won't bolster the family's public image any more than marrying you or the barista who makes my Americano every morning."

I blink. "Thanks? I think."

He waves off his remark. "It won't affect how I run the company when I'm promoted. Yes, they want grandkids." My eyes widen and Aaron gives me a weak smile. "Don't worry. Charlie and Murphy plan to have several. But more to the point . . ." He pauses and his gray eyes meet mine. "My parents can't influence me through you."

"Where they can through Fallon?"

His smile is close-lipped. "Fallon and I grew up together. Our moms are best friends. Fallon adores Kaye. She agrees with her on almost everything."

"Except for you two spending a lifetime together."

"Fallon's values are more aligned with my mom's than mine are. She'd likely give in to pressure to have kids before either of us are ready, and Mom is very good at making her feel guilty for not spending enough time with her or for not following their wishes."

I make a face at that. His mom sounds a lot like Paul's mom, Cheryl.

"But," Aaron says, "for all of Fallon's faults, she won't sacrifice her happiness."

"Nobody should sacrifice their happiness to please someone else." I look pointedly at Aaron.

"Yes, well." He glances at the floor. "My mom will do her best to get into Fallon's head and change her mind once she hears we broke off our engagement. Fallon is a people-pleaser, and Kaye is very good at getting people to do what she wants. That's why she makes an excellent president."

My protective instincts flare. "Well, she can't pressure anyone if you're already married." He nods. "So how long, then?"

"A year, maybe two. Three at the most. Does it matter if I can't give you a definitive answer just yet?"

I crack a knuckle, thinking. Can I commit to three years? It's a long time considering I promised myself I wouldn't marry. But this isn't for love. This is a business venture, one that supports the love of my art. I'm investing in a future I control. But like any agreement, our partnership needs an opt-out.

"I don't need a definitive answer as long as we agree that when one of us wants out, no matter when or why, we get divorced. No arguments, no trying to change the other person's mind."

Aaron's mouth flattens. "I can do that."

"We keep everything separate too. Our jobs, money, social life, everything. We leave the marriage with what we came in with. Except Artisant. That's all mine," I clarify since I don't technically own the shop yet.

"I'll agree to whatever you want, Meli, on one condition." He raises a finger.

"What's that?" I ask with a wary lift of my chin.

"You move in."

"No. No, no, no," I say, waving my hands in front of me. Marrying for business is one thing. But living together? I'm too attracted to Aaron. He's too appealing. I don't trust myself to keep business and pleasure separate. Not that I'm in love with Aaron, but I see myself doing what I had done with Paul, devoting all my spare time, and then some, to Aaron and his family. Or the exact opposite: me spending all my time at work, making myself unavailable to Aaron, which would only frustrate him. This has the potential of becoming a Paul 2.0 relationship.

"Nobody will believe our marriage is legit if we live separately, not my parents, the company, or your uncle," Aaron says, approaching me until I'm forced to tilt my head to meet his intense gaze. "For all intents and purposes, we need to act like a happily married couple, or my parents will cry bullshit. We have to convince the company and your uncle that any deal between the Savant House and Artisant Designs is a conflict of interest, that acquiring Artisant's talent—that being you— breaches Savant's nonfraternization policy and rings of nepotism."

"Just so we're clear, how do you expect us to act happily married?"

"Apart from moving in, you'll accompany me to some events. It could be dinner at my mom's or a corporate function. Lunch with a colleague and their partner. Whatever comes up. A little bit of public affection might be required when the occasion calls for it." His cheeks redden when he says this.

I give him a skeptical look. "What sort of affection?"

"Hand-holding, kiss on the cheek, maybe the lips. Remember, we'll be newlyweds. Think you can handle it?" He looks smug.

I glare at him. "One condition. No sex." I don't trust myself not to fall for him. "I mean it. Last night was really great—"

He leans in close. "It was unforgettable."

My mouth dries. "Yes, well, this is a business relationship, not pleasure. We can't mix the two."

His head falls forward in exaggerated disappointment. "If that's what you want."

Want isn't the issue. I'm protecting my interests and emotions. I know my boundaries.

"I'll sleep in a separate room."

Aaron sighs deeply. He stares at me, then offers a hand. "You have a deal, *wife*."

I shake his hand. *"Husband."*

A knock on the door has us jumping apart. I roughly exhale, shaking off my nerves.

"Ready for this?" Aaron asks, striding for the door.

"We're going to tell them now?"

"I don't see why not. Do you?"

"They won't try to talk you out of it?"

"My parents? Absolutely. Charlie and Murph? Nah. They'll understand why I'm doing this."

Before I can say anything further—before I can prepare—Aaron opens the door. On the other side are his sister and brother-in-law.

"All set to go, bro?" Murphy asks. He and Charlie glance between Aaron and me. I wonder how much they overheard. Given the glint in Murphy's light-blue eyes, I wouldn't be shocked if they'd had their ears pressed to the door.

Aaron reaches for my hand, then turns his grin on Charlie and Murphy. "We're getting married."

"You're joking." Charlie laughs.

"No joke," Aaron says, serious.

Charlie must have seen something in his expression because her smile disappears.

Then hers and Murphy's jaws fall open. Aaron beams like he's the luckiest man on the planet. A beer bottle slips from Charlie's fingers. Glass shatters on the floor.

I gape at Aaron. We are fucking doing this. Holy crap.

He just shrugs and mimes ripping off a bandage.

Murphy finds his voice first. "I guess that means we're family, Meli. Welcome!"

CHAPTER 13

DINNER FOR FOUR AND A HALF

Shortly before 6:00 p.m., after showering and changing into a mixed-print off-white midi dress with puff sleeves, I cross the hall and knock on Emi's door for her dinner party. I've brought lemon posset, a tart pudding I whipped up from three simple ingredients—cream, sugar, and lemon juice—topped with fresh raspberries and chilled before I left for the shop this morning. I also picked up a chianti from the wine store I pass every day on the way home from the T. I don't know much about food and wine pairings, but I searched online to find what complements an artichoke-stuffed beef tenderloin and these came up.

The door flies open to laughter and the aromatic scents of shallots, thyme, and smoked paprika. Emi stands there, holding a coupe glass full of a shimmery lavender cocktail, looking casually elegant in a paisley-patterned maxi dress. Her hair is in a high bun and wrapped in a scarf. Large gold hoop earrings swing from her lobes.

"Meli!" She air-kisses my cheek since my arms are full and leans back to peer at my face. "Are you all right?"

I wear my emotions, and my head has been buzzing since I left Aaron's town house. I'm still processing what we decided, and I'm not sure how I'll tell Emi. I don't think I can just announce out of the blue I'm getting married, like Aaron did to his sister and brother-in-law. Emi will try to talk me out of it. She'll be as disappointed and angry with me as Charlie was with Aaron. Though he somehow convinced Charlie and Murphy to support him, I doubt I can convince Emi.

So I paste on a smile and pretend it's just another normal Saturday night with my friends. "I'm good."

"And last night? How was it?" she asks over her shoulder as I follow her into the apartment. "As far as I know, you didn't come home last night, and you haven't answered any of my texts today except to say you were coming tonight. Thanks for replying, by the way. Shae and I were about to break down your door. We're all dying to hear about Aaron." She stops with an assessing look. Then her whole face opens. "Oh my God. You slept with him."

"Slept with who?" Tam asks. She gets up from the emerald-green velvet couch and hugs me. She towers over me and really should be gracing glossy magazine covers. She's a walking Ralph Lauren ad with her fresh complexion; fine bone structure; long, golden hair; and crisp fashion sense. But she prefers working behind the camera along with her wife, Shae.

"Her future boss," Emi supplies.

"Isn't her uncle her boss?" Shae's mouth purses in disgust. Or maybe to kiss me, which she does on the cheek. "Hello, Meli."

"Hi, Shae." It's good to see her. She's half the size of Tam, with jet-black hair, and just reaches my shoulder. She and Tam do video production at Stone & Bloom, photographing remodeled kitchens and filming training tutorials. I don't know how they do it, work and live together, doing what they love with the person they love while staying disgustingly in love. They argue a lot, bicker constantly, but also ceaselessly compliment one another. They never stay too hot or too cold for long.

"Eww, Shae, don't be gross," Tam says, referring to her wife's comment.

Shae opens the chianti for the wine to breathe. "I'm so lost."

"Catch them up on what's going on with Artisant," Emi says to me. "Then tell us what happened last night after I left." She mixes us lavender lemon-drop martinis while I tell them about the Savant House's letter of intent to acquire Artisant and how determined Uncle Bear is to sell. I explain how, even though he promised I'd inherit the shop, he won't consider an offer from me. Not yet anyway. I'm still determined to change his mind.

"That's not cool," Shae says of Uncle Bear.

"Talk to an attorney," Tam suggests. "Bear promised you the shop. Isn't that why you've kept working there? You should sue him."

"I'm not going to sue my uncle."

Emi passes around drinks. "She has other plans."

I startle, momentarily thinking she knows about my marriage plans. But she's only referring to my plan from last night about talking with Aaron at the gala. If I know Emi, she won't be pleased with this morning's development. Charlie and Murphy were shocked when Aaron announced our engagement. Then Charlie and Aaron started arguing.

"You can't be serious," Charlie shrieked after her bottle of beer shattered on the floor.

"Dead," Aaron said.

"Why?" She stared hard at him and Aaron remained silent. "Does this have to do with—"

"Charlie," Aaron snapped, and my posture tensed up at his passionate reaction.

"Quit Savant."

"You know I can't."

Charlie's face softened with pity. "When are you going to stop blaming yourself?"

"Don't—"

Charlie talked over him. "It wasn't your fault."

His face went blank. "I respect your opinion," he said in a slow, calm voice, which only further frustrated Charlie.

"Well, I can't respect your decision. I'm sure you're a great person," she said to me before turning back to Aaron. "But you're marrying for the wrong reason, and that just makes me sad."

"That's why it's a marriage of convenience."

"I feel sorry for you."

A flicker of hurt rippled across Aaron's face.

Charlie backed away from him, and I caught a sheen to her eyes before she ducked her head. "Excuse me. I need to take a walk." She left the house, both Aaron and Murphy watching her go.

Murphy shot me a look of apology and said to Aaron, "I'll clean up."

When he retreated to the basement to collect a broom and dustpan, Aaron moved closer to me. "Sorry you had to see that," he said quietly.

"You said she'd understand. We don't have to marry if this is going to cause problems with you two." I didn't want to come between them, not for my sake.

"She'll come around. She always does."

"Do you argue often?"

A hint of a smile appeared on him. "This was mild compared to others. It'll be okay." He rubbed my arm.

I'm not sure if Charlie ever made it to the game, but I chose to believe Aaron. After helping Murphy clean up and saying a quick goodbye to them both, I left for the shop to sand Isadora's table so I could start staining on Monday. It would need a couple of weeks to off-gas before delivery.

"I know Aaron Borland, Savant's COO. We met at a show a couple of years back," I explain to the gals, mildly surprised at how easily the lie comes. "I told him last night that my uncle's been negotiating a deal that involved me without my consent. He agreed he'll look into it."

"Because you slept with him," Tam deadpans.

I choke on my bittersweet cocktail. "When you put it like that . . ."

"You should have seen them dance the waltz. This guy has moves. And the way he was looking at Meli." Emi folds her hands over her heart. "Swoon."

I roll my eyes. "It wasn't like that. She's exaggerating."

"Am not. Not once did Paul ever look at you that way."

"Are you going to see him again?" Shae asks.

I open my mouth, on the brink of telling them we're getting married. But no, now isn't the time. I'll wait until Shae and Tam leave. They won't understand. Emi won't either, but she knows me better. She was there after I'd jilted Paul. In fact, she was thrilled I'd ditched my wedding.

"She saw *a lot* of him last night." Emi waggles her brows.

I blush.

"We want details." Shae presses her palms together and claps just her fingers.

The oven timer buzzes.

"Hold that thought," Emi says. "Dinner's ready."

We bring the food to the table—the tenderloin, a salad, and some sides—and load our plates. Emi opens a bottle of prosecco and Tam pours the chianti. Shae toasts to good friends and delicious food. Then to my relief, the conversation veers to Tam and Shae's latest project. When they were filming a fancy new faucet installation, Raj, their enthusiastic host, triggered the high-pressure setting and drenched the crew. I only half listen as I watch them finish each other's sentences and touch each other with affection and respect to emphasize a point or expound on another. The adoration on their faces when they compliment each other. I've never witnessed my parents treat one another in such a way. I doubt Uncle Bear has ever come close to treating anyone like that.

"How do you do it?" I interrupt.

Conversation stalls as they all turn to me.

"Do what?" Tam asks.

I circle my hands at them. "This. You. Together. All the fucking time. And you still love each other. Don't you get upset Tam spends more time editing videos than she does with you?" I ask Shae. She once confided that she spent a lot of weekends alone because Tam couldn't pull herself away from a project.

"Of course I do." Shae's expression darkens over my betrayal. That wasn't kind of me. Whatever. I'm trying to make a point. "But it goes both ways. Sometimes I'm the one hyperfocused on work. Remember that one project where for weeks I worked nights until one in the morning?" she asks her wife.

"That was the worst. She was so tired. The project wasn't going well."

"We argued all the time," Shae says. "I took my frustration out on her."

"She was a bitch."

"And you were okay with that?" I ask Tam.

"Of course I wasn't, not at the time."

"But you're still together."

"Because we love each other." Shae reaches for Tam's hand. "She more than made up for it when she booked us a room on the Cape."

Tam kisses Shae. "We both love our work and each other. It's about communication and balance."

"Balance is bullshit."

Emi blinks at my outburst. "Meli."

"Actually, she's right," Tam said. "It's impossible to give equal amounts of devotion all the time. There's a lot of give and take. A good partner will give you a nudge when you're hyperfocused on one thing too long."

"She isn't shy about nudging me away either. We don't want to smother each other," Shae adds.

"I can't balance. Multitasking for me is a joke. I can't even walk and talk on the phone at the same time." Emi tries to lighten the mood.

"Same," Shae agrees.

"Yeah, but what are the chances of finding a partner that perfect? We're talking lottery odds, am I right?" My parents aren't perfect. They bring their marital troubles to work. I'm sure they bring their work troubles home. There's no separation, the lines too blurred. Uncle Bear has never found the perfect partner, let alone tried to look for one as far as I know. Paul definitely wasn't perfect for me. We couldn't balance my work with his family. "That's why I'm never getting into another long-term relationship. I don't want anyone distracting me from my woodworking. That's what I really love."

"That's so sad." Shae pouts.

"Pitifully sad," Tam agrees.

"Why? I'm happy."

Emi frowns at me, a dubious crinkle between her brows.

"Aren't you lonely?" Shae asks. "I'd be lonely."

"I have you guys."

Emi's frown deepens.

"Well, I'm my happiest when I'm with you." Shae gazes moon-eyed at Tam and displays their linked fingers.

"And we're going to be even happier soon."

"Should we tell them?"

"Yes, let's," Tam says.

"Tell us what?" Emi asks.

"We've picked a baby daddy," Shae announces.

"We're going to be mommas," Tam says.

Shae squeals and claps.

"That's wonderful!" Emi exclaims, truly happy. She pours another round of prosecco and we raise our glasses. "To new family additions."

"And promotions," Tam adds.

Shae and I look at each other. "Who got a promotion?"

"I did. I found out yesterday." Emi smiles.

"That's awesome! Why didn't you tell me?" For over a year Emi has been vying for a senior designer position that comes with a raise and a team to manage.

"It didn't feel right talking about it after your news with your uncle."

"Not all my news is bad," I announce before I have the sense to stop myself.

They all look at me. I should make something up but I don't. Because somewhere between reading Savant's letter of intent and negotiating with Aaron, I've lost all sense of reason.

"Aaron and I are getting married."

They gape at me.

You could hear a pin drop.

———

Two hours later, after Shae and Tam leave, Emi roughly handles the dishes, scrubbing hard at the plates before putting them in the dishwasher. I spoon leftovers into plastic containers.

"You didn't have to stay," Emi says, keeping her back to me. Water sprays in the sink.

"You're angry." Once the gals got over their initial shock, I shared the plan Aaron and I had devised, clearly explaining to them that this is a business arrangement. We aren't committing to forever.

"I'm not angry. I'm disappointed." As I knew she would be. She slams off the water. "Okay. Maybe a little angry."

"People marry for convenience all the time."

She turns to me. "People do. Not you, not my friend."

"Does this have to do with Paul? You didn't want me to marry him either."

"Because he didn't love you, not the way you deserved." My parents' lack of interest in and affection toward me always bothered her. She thinks them living in the same building as me, barely talking to me, and rarely visiting is toxic. That it eats at my mental health like a cancer. Maybe so, but they are my family. "Besides"—she dries her hands with a dish towel—"your heart was never really into him. I could tell."

Emi is a romantic. I can't fault her for that.

"Love doesn't have anything to do with Aaron and me."

"Are you sure?"

I frown. Why would she even ask that?

"That's not what this arrangement is about."

"You keep saying that, and I think that's why I'm sad for you. I'd hoped . . ." She shakes her head.

"Hoped what?"

"I don't know. The way he was looking at you—the way you looked at him, and don't you dare deny it—you guys were into each other. There was a spark there."

I know that. I felt it. I refuse to pursue it.

"I guess after everything that happened with Paul and your parents, I kind of hoped you'd hold out for someone who really loves you. Who sees in you what I do. You deserve to be loved, Meli. After what I saw last night and hearing that you went home with him, I thought it could grow into something meaningful one day. You'd been celibate for five years."

"You make me sound like a nun."

"You practically are. Or were. Come on, Meli. I'm your best friend. I know you're lonely."

I lift my chin. "Am not. I have you, the shop. I'm not losing the shop."

"You don't know Aaron. You haven't even given yourself the chance for something to develop. But marriage? For business?"

"This won't be long term. Three years, tops."

"You're moving in with him. He's a stranger."

"Would it help if I told you that I know him better than you think I do, that we were already married once?"

I freeze, mouth agape, tongue turning to lead. Did I just say that?

Emi lurches back. "Come again?"

I wince. "I should go. It's late."

Emi blocks my exit from the kitchen. "You're not leaving until you explain."

I pull at my fingers, crack a knuckle. "I might have lied about how I know Aaron." Emi crosses her arms, not so patiently waiting for me to spit it out. "I might have met him on my flight to Vegas."

"The one you took after you left Paul?"

"We might have had too much to drink. And I might have dared him to marry me. Vegas, baby." I lift my hands. *Ta-da.*

Emi shrieks. "You what?"

"I dared him to marry me for twenty-four hours, and he said yes, and we had a lot of fun. And he might have gone to Maui with me."

Emi's mouth falls wide open.

"We divorced as soon as we got back. It was super quick and quiet. We didn't tell anyone."

Emi shakes her head, backing away like she doesn't know me. I'm a stranger in her house. On top of her anger and disappointment in me, she looks hurt.

"I'm sorry I didn't tell you," I say, following her from the kitchen. "I thought—"

She shows me her palm. "I can't be with you right now. I just . . ." She waves her arms around, then points at the door. "You need to leave."

"Emi."

"Not right now." She retreats to her room and shuts the door.

I stand alone in the middle of her apartment.

Now probably isn't a good time to ask her to be my maid of honor.

I swipe up my keys and cross the hallway. Blueberry is in the midst of a cleaning session, and my arrival startles him. He hisses at me, arching his back, and stomps off, giving me his one eye.

Great, snubbed by my friend and my cat.

CHAPTER 14

I Do 2.0

One week and one marriage license later, I stare at my reflection in the floor mirror. I'm alone in one of Aaron's spare bedrooms, a decent-size space pleasantly decorated in neutral tones that remind me of the coast. There's a queen bed sandwiched between two rustic oak sideboards I recognize from the Savant House catalog, and a matching dresser. A gallery wall of scenes from the Cape is on one side of the bed, and on the other, two tall, narrow windows that overlook the street. Sunlight pours into the room, puddling on the floor between the bed and wall. Dust motes float like specks of light.

The room suits me, which is a good thing. Starting tonight, it will be mine. Today I am marrying Aaron for the second time. And I am nervous. I still haven't decided whether to tell Uncle Bear and my parents I've temporarily moved from our apartment building and why, or if I'll wait until my uncle receives word from the Savant House. They'll demand an explanation then.

I also haven't spoken to Emi all week because she isn't speaking to me.

As I continue to gaze at my reflection, I'm reminded how different this wedding day is from my last one, where I also stood before a mirror in a wedding gown. Cheryl's gown, because it had meant so much to her to have her son's bride wear it. And my agreement to wear her dress pleased Paul because it pleased his mom. But I wasn't pleased, and looking back now, I see how unhappy I was. Despite having the gown tailored, the material was scratchy and the fit uncomfortable. The style just wasn't me. I didn't feel like me wearing it. And Emi noticed.

After Cheryl had left the church's antechamber to go sit with her family, Emi stood by my side. "I can tell something is bothering you. What is it?" she asked gently.

I pressed my lips into a tense line so she wouldn't notice them tremble.

"Is it the gown?"

"I shouldn't have let Cheryl talk me into wearing it." But I'd wanted to please my future mother-in-law and husband. I'd just wanted them to love me.

"Take it off."

"And wear what? It's too late." The ceremony started in fifteen minutes.

"It's not too late, Meli." Emi turned me to face her. Her eyes searched mine, which had begun to water. "I've always liked Paul. I've always thought he and you were a good match. But after what he said to you, I have to wonder if I was wrong."

I'd told her that Paul asked me to quit the shop, and she'd been angry on my behalf since. I'd also been complaining about Paul's mounting frustration over the amount of time I spent at Artisant, so his request had come as no surprise to her.

"I wonder too," I whispered.

"Whatever you decide, I'll support you. I just want you to be happy."

"Thank you."

We turned to face the mirror again, and my gaze lifted over my shoulder to meet my uncle's. Uncle Bear stood in the doorway, and by his expression, I knew he'd overheard us talking.

And just like that, I almost wish my uncle was here to see me now. He'd say something wise and encouraging to settle my nerves. "The strongest joints are those that have been taken apart and put back together. They know where they fit best," he'd tell me like he did when

I was younger and missing my parents. He encouraged me to be strong, just as I need to be now. Stay the course, see this marriage through, and I'll get what I want. Artisant Designs.

A knock sounds on the door to Aaron's spare room, and my chest clenches, my thoughts going straight to Emi since she was already on my mind. But I know it isn't her. She isn't coming.

"It's open," I say.

Charlie pokes her head in. "Got a second?"

"Yes." I'm happy to have someone with me—anyone, really. I'm overthinking, getting stuck in my head, and I need a distraction to pull me out.

Charlie closes the door behind her and smiles softly. "You look beautiful."

"Thank you." I smooth my clammy palms down the front of the dress I picked off the rack earlier this week. It's a short, off-white, chiffon wrap with long balloon sleeves and a deep *V* neckline that ties at the waist and reaches midthigh. The bohemian cut is more to my taste than any of the previous dresses I've worn around Aaron, and I'm quite impressed that I picked it without Emi's help. She's the stylist between us two, but I managed to pair the dress with single-strap nude heels and sweep my hair into a soft updo, leaving a few tendrils to frame my face.

"I'm glad you're here." For Aaron's sake. I wasn't sure Charlie would come, not after their argument last week.

Her eyes sparkle. "I couldn't let my big brother get married without me. I'm going to witness this thing between you two from its wacky start to fireball finish. Front row, center seat, girl."

In its own way, today's wedding, though intimate, will be a spectacle.

From what Aaron told me about his sister last week as I helped clean up the glass and spilled beer, Charlie is Savant's chief marketing officer and very much aware of the pressure their parents put on them about image, reputation, legacy, and dynasty. Charlie was on the receiving end of Kaye's machinations while dating Murphy. Aaron clarified for me that Charlie couldn't understand why he doesn't just quit the Savant

House instead of going to the extreme of marrying me. He obviously isn't happy working for the family. She thinks he's been pandering to Kaye's and Graham's whims for too long. Charlie wants him to stop. For reasons Aaron refused to express, at least in my presence, he can't quit.

Charlie comes farther into the room. "I was planning to check on you, but Aaron said you wanted to see me?"

"My best friend Emi can't make it."

Charlie levels her gaze on me. "Can't or won't?"

"Won't." I sigh.

"I'm sorry."

"I wanted to ask if you'd be my maid of honor. I know you're Aaron's best woman, and since Murphy's officiating, do you mind?"

Charlie crosses her arms. "Aaron told me a couple of days ago about your first marriage."

"He did?"

"I threatened to tell our parents he's marrying a stranger."

"We still kind of are strangers."

"Exactly why I don't agree with what he's doing for you, but I understand."

"This isn't just for me."

"I know." Charlie turns away with an expression that says she's struggling with what not to say.

"Are you about to give me a don't-break-his-heart speech?" I try for levity.

She turns back. "That goes without saying. Aaron's a good man, too much for his own good sometimes. Fallon wasn't right for him. She was right to end things; we all know that." Charlie tilts her head and scrutinizes me. "I've been worried all week about Aaron marrying someone he doesn't know, but there's something about you, Meli. Aaron hasn't been this genuinely happy since . . ." She pauses. "For a long time. He's been different since he's been around you. He's different when he talks about you."

"How so?" I ask, as curious as I am wary. Do I really want to hear what she's about to say?

"Stop frowning. It's a good different." Charlie pushes back her shoulders and grins. "Yes."

"Yes, what?"

"I'll stand in for your friend."

I let loose a long breath and smile, my first genuine one of the day. "Thank you."

"Now, unless there's anything else you need, we're ready for you downstairs."

"I'll be right behind you."

Charlie nods, understanding I need one last moment to myself.

"I'll let Aaron know. Welcome to the family, Meli." She touches my shoulder and leaves the room.

I turn back to the mirror and speak to my reflection. "You're not being reckless." Not like I was when I had dared Aaron to marry five years ago. While also temporary, this marriage has a mutually beneficial purpose. We'll be a team on this adventure in pursuit of our own goals.

The muffled sound of the doorbell breaks through my thoughts. Voices drift up the hallway, and I feel a momentary pinch of panic. Could it be Aaron's parents? Are they here to stop the wedding?

Worry along with a strong urge to go stand up for Aaron chases me from the bedroom to the top of the stairs. Aaron notices me first. His smoky gaze drinks me in and his jaw slackens. He quickly snaps it shut when his stare meets mine, and a smile spreads across his freshly shaven face that speaks volumes. *You're perfect. You're mine. I'm yours.* Everything at once. Thoughts and emotions I refuse to give weight to. Promises I won't acknowledge.

As if remembering we aren't alone, Aaron moves aside. "Emi!" I exclaim. She came. Elation bursts inside me. She's wearing a short navy-blue one-shoulder A-line dress I recognize she wore to a coworker's wedding last fall. She looks up at me with a mix of hope and hesitation.

"Sorry I'm late." She clutches a simple bouquet of three white peonies wrapped in olive branches. Only Emi would add such a symbolic touch.

"You're here and that's what matters." I join them downstairs.

"Can we talk?" she asks.

"You can use the den," Aaron offers.

I lead Emi into the room and shut the door. We turn to each other. "I'm sorry," we say at once and both giggle.

"You go first," Emi says.

"I'm sorry we fought. I'm sorry I didn't tell you about Aaron and that I'd lied about him."

"I'm sorry for avoiding you all week. I don't like fighting with you. I'm just worried about you."

"I love you." I hug her so she can't see I'm about to cry. All these years, I've been starved for my parents' affection, and I've had Emi all along.

"Are you sure you know what you're doing?" she asks.

"Absolutely not," I say with a watery laugh, blotting the corners of my eyes. "If it doesn't work out, we'll divorce and I'll move back to my apartment." Of course, that would mean I don't have Artisant Designs either.

"As much as I want us to be neighbors again, I don't want you to get hurt in the process. You have a big heart. You're too forgiving."

"Let's point out all my flaws, why don't we."

"They aren't flaws. For you." She thrusts the flowers at me. "I know it's just a marriage of convenience, but you still need a bridal bouquet."

I take the flowers. The bouquet is beautiful in its simplicity.

"I never got the chance to be your maid of honor," she says.

"What happened? Bride ditch the wedding?"

"She bailed big time. But if you'll still have me . . ."

"I'll always have you." I hug her again.

A soft rap sounds on the door. "Come in," I say, dabbing my damp eyes again.

Aaron enters the den. Dressed in slim slate trousers and a blue dress shirt, his dark hair is casually disheveled. Emi drinks him in and I glance at her funnily. I know that look. She had it the other night when I first pointed out Aaron to her. He's striking, with a smile that melts hearts. But what appeals to me most about him is his quiet confidence and genuine sincerity.

The man is just plain nice. A good nice, not the nice used to describe someone when you can't think of anything original to say about them.

Emi leans in close and whispers from the corner of her mouth. "Someone woke up in a lucky clover patch."

"Shush." I lightly smack her arm. "Sex is off the table."

"What about under?"

"Stop."

Aaron glances between us, rubbing his palms, his tell that he isn't quite sure what he's walking into. He did the same thing both times we applied for a marriage license.

See? I'm getting to know him.

"Emi is staying," I say, putting him at ease. He probably thinks she's here to talk me out of the marriage. All is good between us.

Aaron clasps his hands. "Wonderful."

"We haven't been properly introduced. I'm Emi, Meli's best friend, maid of honor, and the bane of your existence if you so much as harm an eyelash on her."

His eyes pop but he shakes Emi's hand like the gentleman he is. "Noted."

"You're both crazy. Too bad you're not crazy for each other." She looks between us. "I need a drink. Got any liquor?"

"Go see Charlie," Aaron says. "She opened champagne."

"I like Charlie already. See you kids outside." Emi pistol-shoots us with her index fingers and leaves the room.

Aaron meets my gaze. "You look beautiful."

Warmth spirals down my arms. "You clean up nicely yourself, Mr. Borland."

A frown replaces his smile. "Sorry. Forgot we aren't saying those kinds of things to each other."

"It's fine. A compliment here or there isn't going to kill us." They'll just make me fall for him faster.

No, no they won't. I give my wrist a mental slap.

"Look, ah . . . I want to ask you something."

"Uh-oh. Sounds serious."

He smiles weakly. "Have I in any way manipulated you into doing this?"

"The marriage?"

"I'm not forcing you to marry me, am I? I didn't guilt you into agreeing?"

"Did Charlie say something?"

"No, this is me asking."

"Emi might disagree with me, but I'm of sound mind and body. Nobody is forcing anybody today. At least I don't feel that way."

He pushes out a weighted breath. "Good. Then let's—"

From out of nowhere, Billy Idol's "White Wedding" blasts through the Sonos speaker system. Aaron groans.

"What in the world?" I cover my ears.

"I gave Charlie control of the music," he yells over Billy.

"She's going to be fun."

Aaron shoots me a pained look. "She's something all right," he says dryly, and presents his elbow. "Ready, *wife*?"

"Ready as I'll ever be, *husband*. Let's get hitched. Again."

———

Our wedding ceremony is brief, more of a formality than anything. After we say "I do" and seal our commitment with a short kiss, after pizza, cake, and a cutthroat game of pool in Aaron's basement, after we send off a tipsy Charlie and Murphy and pour a drunk Emi into a waiting Lyft, Aaron closes the front door and turns to me, hands in his side pockets. We were go-go-go all week, and suddenly, life stalls. The house is still, the quiet descending on us like a plane coming in for a hard landing. We're alone for the first time since Murphy married us hours ago.

What now? Do we retreat to our respective bedrooms? Does he watch a game on TV while I go read a book? Should we give each other space? I did insist we keep everything separate. Does that include downtime at home? Does it include certain parts of the house? Maybe we should set a defining line and run tape along the floor. His side and mine. Or maybe I'm overthinking again. I crack my thumb knuckle.

Aaron's hand twitches as his thumb spins the onyx wedding band I put on his finger hours ago. I twist the narrow titanium band with a single embedded diamond on my finger. They're dressier than the wood ring and dented silver band from our first marriage. We bought the rings after we'd ordered our wedding license. For appearances' sake. Whatever helps us make this marriage look legit from the outside. The band feels as foreign as our new status. Husband and wife. Official, once again.

Aaron looks around the house, and my gaze follows. Glasses with melting ice and plates painted with dried frosting clutter the dining table. Charlie and Emi must have played half Aaron's vinyl collection. Albums are scattered about. The state we left the living room and dining room in reminds me of my teenage bedroom. A glorified mess.

Aaron rocks up on his toes. "Ah . . . I should clean up."

"I'll help," I offer, eager to do something with my hands. Keep myself busy.

I stack dishes on a tray and Aaron collects cups as we effortlessly move around each other like a couple who've been together longer than we have. With a team effort, we've cleared the dining room and living room of dishware within moments, and while I stack glasses in the dishwasher, I leave Aaron to organize his albums. He's flipping through the albums in his media cabinet when I join him in the living room.

He glances at me over his shoulder. "Have you heard of the Easybeats?"

"Sounds like an eighties alternative rock band." I approach him.

"Nope. Try again."

"Seventies?" He shakes his head. "Sixties?"

He points a finger at me. "Winner." He tips out the record and sets the vinyl on the turntable's platter, turns on the system. "Their first hit was in sixty-five. Here, listen." He lowers the toner arm on the album and music fills the town house.

"Sounds punkish." I swing my hips to the broken, bluesy rhythm that reminds me of the Kinks. "I like it. What's the name of the song?"

"'For My Woman.'" He turns to me and erratically sways side-to-side, swinging his arms with his thumbs out.

I burst out laughing. "What are you doing?" He looks like a goof.

"The Hitchhiker."

I laugh harder. And because this is Aaron and I can't help myself, I swirl my hips with bent arms. "The Twist!"

"Brilliant." Aaron switches up his moves. "The Funky Chicken." He flaps his elbows, knocks his knees together, and thrusts his chin back and forth. I'm dying, doubled over with laughter, when I feel a subtle shift inside me. I no longer feel ambivalent about my place here; rather, I feel that I'm in the right place, right alongside Aaron.

The track rolls into the next, and then the next. We dance without rhythm or care through the entire album, and when it ends, we collapse on the couch, grinning and out of breath.

I tilt my head to look up at the ceiling. "I forgot how much fun we have together." In Maui, we played Marco Polo in the pool and made faces underwater while we snorkeled. Several times I got water up my nose because he made me laugh. I was always laughing hard with him.

"You're fun."

I turn my head to see Aaron watching me. My smile comes easily. "We do know how to have a good time together."

"We do."

A moment passes before my smile fades and a calm comes over me, a comfortable warmth stirring inside. "Do you think it'll always be like this with us?" I ask tremulously.

Aside from Emi, Aaron is the only other person I've effortlessly clicked with. We get along as well as get each other. Our conversations flow, and whenever I'm around him, I feel a sense of comfort and belonging, almost as if I've known him forever. I felt that way when we wrote our Marriage-Material List.

And now? I feel at peace when I'm with him. But I'm also anxious, as if I'm waiting for something to come. As if I already expect this won't work. Though I can't pinpoint exactly what I think won't work: Savant retracting their offer or Aaron and me. I'm too jaded to see beyond this day.

Aaron reaches for my hand. His expression turns hopeful. "Wouldn't that be something?"

I look at our linked fingers. "Thanks for getting us to dance. It was the perfect icebreaker."

He makes a face. "Icebreaker?"

My other hand flops around. "After everyone left it felt weird between us. Like I don't know what we're supposed to do here when it's just us two, when we're not having to prove to our families we're happily married. Is it just me, or is this going to be weird?"

"It doesn't have to be."

I release his hand and run my palms over my thighs. "So do we say good night now or . . ." My voice drifts off. I'm terrible at balancing relationships and work. But how am I supposed to do a relationship that isn't really a relationship?

"We could." He holds my stare as I debate holding on to the night. It's late and I'm tired. Tomorrow I have a long day in front of my laptop. I need to start drafting my offer to Uncle Bear and shop for business loans. I also have to get Blueberry from my apartment and pack more clothes. But am I ready to say good night? Am I ready to start treating Aaron as a roommate rather than a husband or friend? I kind of want to sink into this moment and just hang out on the sofa with him, talking. And if I'm being honest, I have time later this week to work on the plan. It doesn't have to be tomorrow. Isadora's table is stained and off-gassing. A few new orders came in last week. I'll start those on Monday. I'm waiting to hear back from one client. I have a question about the bedside table's dimensions for another. The console table—

"Where did you go?"

I stop mid-thought and grimace. "Nowhere. Just overthinking."

"About?"

"Work. Life."

Aaron leans back and studies me. "We have a good rapport, Meli. We get along and we talk easily. It doesn't have to change because we're married and agreed to keep everything separate. We're friends."

"We are?"

"We are. We can do stuff together."

Yes, I want that. As long as I don't let it distract me from my goals.

Aaron untucks his shirt and rolls up his sleeves, getting more comfortable. "Got a question? Ask me anything. I don't know what it is, but there's something about you. I want you to know me. And I want to know you."

I stare at him for a long moment before my eyes drop to the tattoo on his forearm. It's his only tattoo, and I've been curious about it since I saw it on the plane to Vegas. Once in Maui while lounging by the pool, I asked him what the design meant. But a waiter interrupted us to take our drink order, then a couple of newlyweds drew us into a volleyball game, and well, our conversations never tracked back to his forearm. Plus, I figured since I already asked and he knew I was curious, he'd tell me if he wanted to. He hadn't, so I didn't bring it up again.

But since he's inviting me to ask anything . . .

I gently clasp his forearm and trace an ink line. "Tell me about this. What does it mean?"

His face goes blank, and I can tell he immediately feels uneasy. But he doesn't pull away from me or cover the tattoo. He stares at the bird with the missing wing, falling from the intertwined branches, one of them broken. He clears his throat. "I got it after my brother died."

He had a brother? All our time together in Maui and he didn't mention this once.

Oh, Aaron.

"What was his name?"

"Liam. He was ten months older than me. We were thick, really close. People thought we were twins."

"How old were you when he died?"

"Seventeen." He swallows roughly.

My hand finds his. "What happened?"

A pause. "It was stupid. We were hiking, messing around. He fell and broke his neck."

"I'm so sorry."

"It was a long time ago. A few more years, he'll be gone as long as he'd been alive."

Rising onto my knees, I hug him, pressing my face into his neck. He stiffens, then his arms come around my back. He lets me hold him. After a moment, he lifts his head and I sit back.

"What was that for?" he asks, pinching his nose bridge, not meeting my eyes.

"I wanted to." He seemed like he needed it.

We sit quietly for a beat. "Well," he finally says with a shaky laugh. "That was heavy."

"Go big or go home, I always say. Thank you for telling me."

"I don't like talking about him."

I have the impression he doesn't talk about his brother at all. This is something he doesn't share with anyone. I'm honored he told me.

He rubs his palms along his slacks. "What's up for tomorrow? I don't have any plans. Want to do something?"

I have so much to do. Loan applications, number crunching, planning for the upcoming week. But couldn't that wait until Monday? I could afford one day off.

"I'd love to."

CHAPTER 15

LIFE IS NOT A ROM-COM

Aaron is waiting for me downstairs the next morning. He proposes we handle the day like we had our night in Las Vegas. No plans. See where our wanderings take us.

"You're pulling a Ferris Bueller on me," I tease, wondering what sort of trouble we'll get into. After Calvin had dropped us off at the Venetian after our first marriage, Aaron indulged me with a visit to KAMU, an ultrahip karaoke bar Emi once told me about. We tossed back a few drinks to settle our nerves and befriended a couple who'd just eloped. We told them our wild story, that we'd met on the flight here and married on a dare, and they invited us to join their wedding party in a private karaoke suite. We took turns with the mic. Aaron had been honest on the plane when we wrote our list. He couldn't sing. But that didn't stop him from hogging the spotlight and crooning "Sweet Caroline."

Perhaps today will hold a similar adventure. "What do you have in mind?" I ask.

"Up for playing tourist?"

His question triggers a flood of memories of spending time with my parents as a kid. There's much to see and do in Boston, from the Freedom Trail to public art displays, and we spent many weekends exploring, making up stories about the people we saw along the way. I miss those days, and I especially miss us being a family. But I guess Aaron's my family now, at least temporarily. Better than not having one at all, I suppose.

"I'm up for it. Let's do it. Where do we start?" Dad used to poke a city map, like playing pin the tail on the donkey, and that's where our day began.

Aaron grins and swipes his ball cap from the table by the front door. "We start with coffee," he announces, and outside we go.

It's a gorgeous late-spring day, and he takes me to Perkatory, a coffee shop a few blocks from his town house, for coffee and egg sandwiches. We sit at a window table and people-watch, guessing where they're going. When I tell him about the game I used to play with my parents, we start making up stories about their lives. I point at a man walking his golden retriever and tell Aaron that he's quitting his hedge-fund-manager career tomorrow to start a dog-walking business.

Aaron nods at the elderly woman shopping for flowers at the florist stand across the street. She's confessing to her granddaughter that she had a clandestine affair with King Charles and he is her biological grandfather. I laugh around a bite of sandwich and start coughing. Then I'm wheezing and chugging down water and laugh even harder. Aaron delivered his story with a horrendous British accent. I appreciate what he's doing, creating new memories to fill the void between my childhood and now, even if he's not aware of it.

When we finish, we walk to Boston Common to pick up the Freedom Trail. Aaron hasn't walked it since a fourth-grade field trip. We follow the painted red line to the State House and Park Street Church, and on to the Granary Burying Ground, where we leave Boston Common to take in the King's Chapel and Benjamin Franklin's statue. Each site reminds me of my youth, and I realize I've long avoided swaths of the city because I ventured there with my parents.

"Did you know oysters are an aphrodisiac?" Aaron asks at lunch. He tosses an empty shell in the bowl between us and picks up his beer.

"Are you telling me you're horny, Aaron?"

He slaps a hand over his mouth before he accidentally sprays the beer he just gulped. "No."

"I'm teasing you, and that's a myth. There's no scientific proof."

"It worked for Casanova. Boosted his libido," he says. I roll my eyes, but I'm grinning and Aaron smiles. "There she is."

"What do you mean?"

"You seem to be having fun. I'm having a great time. But there have been a couple moments when, I don't know . . . Are you okay, Meli? If you don't want to do this today, we can go back to the house."

"No, I'm having a great time." I attempt a smile that falls flat. Aaron gives me a look clearly stating he doesn't believe me.

I rest my spoon in my chowder bowl and fold my hands in my lap. The posture brings down my shoulders. "I used to play tourist with my parents when I was a kid. It's bringing back a lot of memories." Like when Dad and I made up stories about the people buried in the old cemeteries along the trail.

"Good memories?" he asks.

"Yes and no." After my parents had to go away, Uncle Bear tried to fill the void they left by taking me on art walks through the city, but it wasn't the same. Either he stopped trying to fill in for my parents or I lost interest. I'm sure it was a little of both. But the outings eventually stopped and we spent Saturdays working at the shop.

"Meli, I'm sure much hasn't changed since Maui. I'm going to assume you still don't like talking about your parents. But if you ever feel the need to, you can tell me. I'm here for you."

"Thank you. That means a lot."

He gives me a slight smile as he nods and goes back to dressing up another oyster with lemon and vinegar, and my heart opens a small back door I didn't know existed. If I do end up talking to anyone about my parents, other than Emi, for what little I've shared of them with her, I think it would be Aaron.

"I'm having a great time with you," I repeat with genuine cheer. I always have fun with him.

His smile broadens. "Just wait until you see where we're going next."

After lunch, we take the T to Cambridge and spend a few hours browsing shops until we find ourselves in a bookstore at Aaron's suggestion, perusing new releases and wandering the aisles. It's the perfect end to what has been one of the best days I've had in a long while. Aaron can't find a book that interests him, and I offer to select one for him.

"What if I don't like it?"

"You'll like it," I say confidently. "I'm a book whisperer. I've never recommended one that someone doesn't like. Emi's always asking me for titles."

"How do you know she reads them? Maybe she's just being nice and doesn't want to hurt your feelings."

"Thanks for the vote of confidence," I scoff in mock offense, and he playfully nudges my arm with his elbow. "I know because she posts reviews. They're all positive."

He returns a bestseller with an old merchant ship on the cover to the shelf. "All right. Pick one."

I tap my lips. "If you were stuck on a deserted island with a magically powered TV—"

His mouth pulls to the side with his raised brows. "A magically powered TV?"

"There's no electricity. Just go with it. There's a magically powered TV with one series that plays over and over, but you get to choose the series. What is it?"

"Sherlock."

I make a note of that. "Would you rather spend a weekend in a haunted house, be chased by dragons, or explore a forgotten temple?"

"These are the strangest questions."

"Book whisperer, remember?"

"Forgotten temple."

"Cliff-hangers or no loose threads?"

"No cliffs."

I smile. "Got it."

"Just from that?"

"I might even have two. Follow me." I lead him to the historical fiction section, find the book, and give it to him.

"*The Alienist*? Isn't this a show on cable?"

"The book is better. I have one more." I take him to the science fiction aisle and show him *Project Hail Mary.*

"I've heard of him," Aaron says of the author Andy Weir. He reads the back cover copy and asks, "Have you read it?"

"No."

"How do you know I'll like it?"

"I'm a book whisperer." I puff out my chest. "But I also have on good authority that it's good. Uncle Bear read it last year. He wouldn't shut up about it. I already know how it ends. It's a page-turner, trust me."

"I'll give these a try. Thank you."

"You're welcome."

"Now it's my turn."

"You're going to pick a book for me?" This should be interesting.

"Oh, ye of little faith. Choose a number between one and five."

"How is that supposed to help?"

"Immensely. Now choose."

"Three?"

"You don't sound so sure of yourself."

"Fine. Three." I cross my arms.

"Pick a number between one and"—he glances down the aisle—"six."

"Five."

"Pick another between one and five."

"Again? Two."

"Between one and . . ." He looks at the shelf beside us. "Let's go with fifty."

"Odd, but whatever. Thirty-six."

He grins and starts walking.

"Where are we going?" I tag along. He turns down an aisle, and almost at the end, he stops, counts the books on the shelf, and grabs one. He presents the book like a prize. "Don't freak out, Meli, but you're a romantic."

"Susanna Kearsley's *The Winter Sea*?"

"You're going to love it."

"How do you know?"

"You picked it."

"I did not pick this."

"Yes, you did. Third aisle, fifth bookcase, second shelf, thirty-sixth book."

My numbers. "Very ingenious of you, *husband*."

"Works every time, *wife*."

"And how many times have you used this process?" How many women has he selected books for? I hate that I'm even asking myself that.

"Once."

I give him a lingering sideways look, admiring his technique. I tap the paperback against my palm. "Let's see if it works."

All the chairs in the store are taken, so we settle on the floor in the same aisle he found my book with our legs pressed together and noses in our novels. Two pages in and I'm hooked. Before I know it, an hour passes. When I look up, Aaron is already a quarter through Weir's book.

I nudge his leg. "What do you think?"

His head jerks up and he blinks. "It's good. Yours?"

"It's not something I would have chosen for myself, but I'm enjoying it."

He glances at his watch. "We've been here awhile."

"We should go. I have to feed Blueberry." And bookstores aren't libraries.

I insist on purchasing Aaron's books when I buy mine, and when we make it to my apartment, it's a little after 5:00 p.m. Blueberry is vocal, clearly displeased over my being gone. Aaron, who hasn't had a cat since he was a kid, takes to him immediately. The feeling is mutual. Blueberry rubs against his legs, his motor kicking into overdrive when

Aaron picks him up. They watch while I prepare Blueberry's dinner, Blueberry nuzzling Aaron's chin.

"You two get along well," I remark. Blueberry is friendly with visitors but rarely lets anyone pick him up.

"He's a good judge of character."

I have to agree.

Aaron puts Blueberry down when I set out his bowl. Blueberry runs to his food, and Aaron follows me into my room while I pack more clothes, tossing shirts and shorts into a laundry basket since I already took my suitcase to Aaron's. I know he's as curious about my personal space as I was about his when I first visited his house, so I let him poke around. He picks up a photo of me and Uncle Bear from my dresser. The picture was taken aboard the USS *Constitution* during a class field trip. Uncle Bear had to fill in as chaperone since my parents were too hungover to attend.

"You were cute," Aaron says.

"Were?"

He grins. "When was this? Your uncle looks young."

"Twenty years ago. He chaperoned a class field trip." Aaron looks at me. "My parents were unavailable, which wasn't new," I explain before he can ask.

"I'm sorry."

"Don't be. I was used to it."

"You shouldn't have had to be." The corners of his mouth turn up slightly in a subtle show of support. He returns the photo to its spot on the dresser. He picks up a photo of me and Emi from last summer. We're sitting on a blanket at a concert in the park, toasting our wine tumblers to the camera. Aaron smiles. "Whatever happened to the photo of us on the roller coaster?" The one I couldn't resist buying after we rode the coaster at the New York–New York resort. We spotted the camera at the same time and threw up our arms. We both looked truly frightened. "I'm shocked you don't have a photo of your husband."

"All right, smart-ass." I retrieve the glossy picture with the paper frame from my nightstand. Our eyes make contact when he takes the photo. I'm sure he's thinking the same thing I thought when he showed me our Marriage-Material List. I kept it close because I looked at it a lot.

"I have the video." He returns the photo. "Calvin sent it to me."

"Our wedding video?" I can barely contain my surprise as we sit on the edge of the bed. I never expected to see it. Aaron brings up the video on his phone, and there we are, sitting in Calvin's back seat, looking utterly petrified but determined to go through with our dare.

"Look how young and scared we were," Aaron says.

He's right. But I also see something else. With our knees pressed together, our bodies leaning toward each other, our gazes don't waver from the other, not once. I don't recall Paul ever looking at me the way Aaron is in the video, as if I'm the one he was searching for. I never believed something like that could happen any more than I believed in love at first sight. Until now. Except for when he tenderly touches my cheek, his hands don't stray from mine. Anyone else watching would believe we were in love.

Then we kiss . . . and what a kiss. I remember how it felt. Hesitant, but exciting. A glittering heat that sparked like a jolt of electricity. A collision fueled by adrenaline and the salty tang of the unknown. But to watch it? Emotions rush through me. Nostalgia, regret, the sheer intensity of the situation. It makes me lightheaded. The attraction I feel for this man resurfaces as a physical warmth spreading through my body. My heart beats faster. Aaron inhales deeply beside me, and I wonder what's going through his head. Is he feeling any of what I do? Then Calvin shouts, "Congratulations!" And the video ends.

Outside my window a horn blares. Blueberry joins us on the bed and cleans his face. Aaron and I don't speak. I can't bring myself to look at him, afraid I'll be unable to stop myself from touching him should I see the same intensity in his expression that I feel inside me.

I watch him put his phone away. We don't get up and we don't move apart. He smells so nice and it feels so right just being here with him. I could easily lean into him, lift my chin and close my eyes and . . .

I shoot to my feet. "I'm packed. We can leave."

"Yes, right . . ." Aaron rubs his hands over his thighs.

I scoop up Blueberry and put him in his carrier, then run around the apartment, gathering his supplies.

Aaron orders us a ride and picks up the laundry basket. "Ready?"

I look around my apartment one last time. I'm sure I'll return soon for more clothes, but I can't help feeling like my home for the past ten years is no longer home. It's wherever Aaron is.

"Ready."

We take the elevator down with Blueberry complaining the entire ride. He doesn't leave the apartment except for trips to the vet, so he isn't happy. I'm talking to him, trying to calm him while we wait at the curb for our driver, when I see my parents walking toward us.

Aaron notices my panic. "What is it?"

"My parents." To tell him I have a weird relationship with them is not the same as him witnessing how awkward we are with each other. I tense as they draw near.

"What do you want to tell them about us?" he asks, as if my parents were actually curious about my social life.

"Nothing. They aren't going to stop and ask."

And they don't, because outside of the shop, they don't seem to care about me or what I do. They're both wearing jeans and sneakers. Dad has on a nice shirt and Mom wears a blouse. I wonder if they went out to dinner. Dad notices me first and waves. Mom says, "Hello." And that is it. They don't ask how I'm doing or who I'm with, where I'm going. They just head into the building, making me feel like I'm a nobody. Just another friendly face they might pass on an evening walk.

I should be grateful. I don't have to lie to them about who Aaron is and where I'm going. But I'm already lying to myself when I say their indifference doesn't sting. Feeling invisible to them is one thing, but in front of Aaron?

Deflated, I turn back to the road with a dull ache in my chest. It takes everything in me not to cry, especially when Aaron gently cradles my neck and kisses my head, showing without saying how much he understands what I'm feeling. Insignificant.

CHAPTER 16

BOTTOM LINE BLINDSIDE

I spend Monday morning at the shop, and for once, I'm grateful my parents don't have any interest getting into my business. Mom and Dad didn't bring up last night when they saw me outside our apartment building with Aaron, their new son-in-law. It saves me from lying about who he is and what we did over the weekend. Or telling the truth. *Guess what, Mom and Dad, I got married!* Besides, I don't want them to have a head start. If they know I married Aaron Borland, they'll tell Uncle Bear, who will contact the Savant House for damage control. Aaron and I agreed he'll announce our marriage to his team and let the news move up their internal channels. Then we'll deal with the fallout. Fingers crossed it's in our favor. Aaron is confident it will be.

Uncle Bear keeps to himself most of the morning, working quietly at his station staining a headboard. The brief conversation we had earlier updating each other on our current projects was strained. The Savant House's acquisition offer is a squatter in the building. I'm still angry and Uncle Bear refuses to budge on his decision. Our words were clipped and rude, so we have an unspoken agreement to leave each other alone. We aren't talking.

Around lunchtime, I'm reviewing my designs for a pair of bedside tables I'm about to start for a new client, and I wonder if this will be the last thing I build for Artisant Designs. If Uncle Bear sells the shop, the buyer will own the copyright. But if I tweak the leg just so—

"We're off to lunch," Uncle Bear announces, bursting into my thoughts.

"We might be a few hours. Lock up if you leave." Mom collects her purse and a short stack of manila folders.

"You aren't going with them?" I ask Dad after they leave. Kidder is already on his lunch break.

"They're meeting somebody."

"Who?"

"Don't know."

It's probably someone from the Savant House. Aaron's telling his parents and staff today that we married over the weekend. He'll let them take that information and do with it what they want. The acquisitions team will present this new development to the Board of Directors, who will reevaluate the viability of acquiring Artisant Designs. At least we hope that's what will happen. It could take weeks, maybe even a few months before they make a decision. The board needs to reconvene.

I keep checking my phone. Aaron said he'd text after he meets with his mom, Kaye Borland.

Dad is cleaning his workstation and putting away tools, so I return to working on my laptop, modeling a new bedside table that I can copyright under my name.

"Want to go to lunch?"

I shriek, my finger sending the cursor across the screen. "Dad, you scared me."

Dad stands at my workstation, his hands in his front pockets. "Didn't mean to."

I press a hand to my racing heart. "What did you just ask me?"

"Lunch. You hungry?"

"I heard you. I just . . . really?" We'll eat lunch together at the shop, but we never go out to eat together. We haven't since I was ten. I invited him multiple times after I got over my anger that he and Mom had left me, but after a while, I got tired of him declining so I stopped asking.

"I'm buying," he says.

I'm speechless. I also can't pack up my laptop fast enough. Feeling like a kid whose dad just offered to take her to the amusement park, I don't want to miss this chance with him. Just the two of us, like it used to be.

I'm supposed to meet Emi for lunch so I text her to meet up for coffee this afternoon instead as I follow Dad out of the shop. He takes me to an old-style deli four blocks away. He orders a Reuben with a watery coleslaw and I get the BLT on Dutch Crunch. We take our sandwiches and fountain sodas to a table outside.

"Weather is nice," Dad says, unwrapping his sandwich, looking up at the sky.

"It is," I agree. There's a smattering of clouds and it isn't too humid.

"Saw you yesterday."

Nerves flicker in the center of my chest. "You did."

"New boyfriend?"

My mouth works. "You could say that."

"Nice-looking guy. He treat you right?"

"He does."

"Better than that Paul fellow?"

"My ex? Um . . . yeah. I didn't realize you noticed." Or have an opinion.

"I noticed." He stares at his sandwich on the table while he chews.

I look at my sandwich as the silence between us goes on a few beats longer than is comfortable. Our conversation is sputtering. At this rate, whatever Dad is trying to strike up between us will fizzle out like a deflated balloon.

I put down my sandwich. "Why did you ask me to lunch?"

"I was hungry."

"Dad."

He wipes his hands and leans to the side, pulling a roll of papers held together by a rubber band from his back pocket. He removes the band and gives me the papers.

"What's this?"

"Look at them."

I skim them with a catch to my breath. Artisant's financial records. Balance sheets, profit and loss statements, account ledgers.

"Did Mom tell you I asked for these?"

He nods.

"What changed her mind?" She told me it was a waste of time to pursue an offer with Uncle Bear.

"Nothing. She doesn't know I gave them to you."

"You printed them?" I ask, shocked he even has access to the shop's QuickBooks. Even I don't.

"You said you needed them. Want the rest of my sandwich?"

"What? No. You eat it."

"Maybe later." Dad rewraps the remaining half of his Reuben. "I'm going to head back." He's building a desk. So far, it's some of the most exquisite work I've seen him do. It's also the last project he'll build at Artisant Designs. I can't express how sad that makes me feel.

"Are you working this afternoon?" he asks.

"I think I'm done for the day. Thanks for these," I say of the papers. And for lunch. And for spending time with me.

He stands to leave and stops at my chair. "My brother isn't always right, Meli. You deserve a shot." He claps a hand on my shoulder and walks away.

———

Two hours later, Emi and I stand in line to order coffee. I'm deep in my head, revisiting what happened at lunch, when Emi nudges me with her elbow. "You're quiet," she says, sensing my mellow mood.

Even though I don't like talking about my parents, this afternoon was bizarre. I have to tell someone.

"Dad took me to lunch."

"As in invited you and paid for it?" I nod and Emi's mouth parts in shock. "Did you ask him why the fuck he and your mom ignore you?"

"They don't ignore me. Whatever," I say when Emi challenges me with a look. I don't know why I'm arguing. "Dad waved and Mom said hello. They saw me with Aaron outside the apartment building. They didn't even ask who he was."

"Isn't that good? You didn't want them to know yet."

I nod.

"Sorry I missed you when you were there. That Charlie girl can drink."

I laugh. I'm not surprised Emi was hungover yesterday. "I'm glad you had fun. Anyway, Dad wanted to give me the shop's financials I'd asked for. I need them for the loan application, and he, shockingly, believes I deserve a shot."

"Damn straight," Emi says. "I'm glad someone in your family has some sense, present company excluded." Her shoulder bumps mine. "So what were you and Aaron doing yesterday? I didn't think you guys were going to do the hang-out-together thing."

"It was for only one day." I tell her about us playing tourist and spending hours at a bookstore before we swung by the apartment to pick up Blueberry.

"That sounds like a date to me . . . Hmm."

"We were just having fun." Then again, Aaron and I always seem to have fun together.

Emi's grin is evil, and I'm pretty sure she's about to say something smart-ass, like how everyone but me can see I'm falling for him, when it's our turn to order. Since Emi has to return to her office and I want to start reviewing the spreadsheets Dad printed, we order our coffees to go.

"Wouldn't it be something," Emi says on our way out the door, "if you and Aaron fall in love?"

She ended up saying something smart-ass anyway. But it doesn't come across as sarcastic as I expected.

"We aren't going to fall in love."

"If you say so." Emi hugs me goodbye. "Text me later." She wants an update after I hear from Aaron. He hasn't called me yet, and by the time I return to his town house, I still haven't heard from him. I try not to worry, trusting he'll make the announcement to set everything in motion, but I'm nervous the news will fall flat and Savant won't lose interest in acquiring Artisant. I mean, that is a possibility.

Meanwhile, there isn't anything I can do except work toward my own goals. But after a few hours, I'm still sitting on the floor in the living room, my back against the sofa with Blueberry purring in my lap, going over Artisant's numbers. June London plays on the turntable, and spread on the floor before me are the sheets Dad printed. I'm stumped. I've come across six large, uncategorized withdrawals with an empty payee field over the past six months. They can't be distributions because Mom would have labeled them as such. She keeps meticulous records, making the uncategorized entries stick out.

I hear Aaron's key in the door. Still unused to the house and sounds, Blueberry flies off my lap and up the stairs just as the door opens. Aaron startles at the ball of fluff that blurs past him.

"Whoa!" he shouts before seeing me there on the floor. "Hey." He looks drained.

"Long day?" I ask, anxious for news.

"Long day," he echoes. He tosses his jacket over the sofa and drops his backpack on the floor. Rolling up his sleeves, he joins me in the living room, settling on the sofa across from me with a heavy sigh. "I told them."

"Your parents?" He nods. "How did they take it?"

"As expected." He predicted his dad would be upset, but his mom would have a much more passionate reaction. Both would demand he get an annulment. Bottom line, he told me, they couldn't legally do anything about our marriage. But his mom would make his life miserable.

"Are you in the doghouse?" I ask of his mom.

"If it's located in Hell and doesn't have an HVAC system, then yes, I am."

I wince and open my mouth on the cusp of telling him how sorry I am.

He stops me. "Do not apologize."

"How did you know I was going to?"

"Because I'm getting to know you, Meli. This isn't your fault. I put myself in this position. I wanted them to react this way."

I got so caught up in my own goals that I forgot he has an endgame too. I do wonder if there's more to it than him not wanting his parents to control him through his spouse as he'd shared with me when we first negotiated this marriage of convenience.

"Now we wait?" I ask.

"Now we wait."

We watch each other for a drawn beat. I have the urge to crawl across the floor and into his lap, to kiss him.

A flush moves up my chest and I glance away, look out the living room window. The sky is the pinkish gray of twilight.

"Have you eaten?" he asks.

"Um . . . dinner? No. I lost track of time."

"Up for some Thai?"

"Would love some. Want a beer?"

"God, yes. I'll get them," he says when I start to get up, eager to splash my face with water.

He orders our dinner and returns with two Blue Moon ales. Handing me one, he sits on the floor beside me. "What are you working on?"

"I'm going through Artisant's accounts so I can apply for a business loan. Something isn't adding up, though. I came across some large, uncategorized withdrawals, and I don't know what they're for," I say, taking a risk sharing this with him. I have to trust he won't pass the information along to the acquisitions team. But it's likely they already know if Uncle Bear has shared the shop's books. They would have done a valuation. "The withdrawals put the shop deeper in the red each month. It's been going on for six months. My mom's accounting is clean, but this seems careless even if it's intentional."

"I'm sure there's an explanation. Have you asked her?"

"She doesn't know I have these. She didn't want to give them to me. My dad printed them."

"I guess you can't ask your uncle either."

I shake my head.

"Let me know where I can help. Happy to lend you the money if it doesn't work out with the bank."

"You've done enough for me already but thank you."

"I don't mind." He picks at the beer label.

I knock my foot against his. "Sexually frustrated?" I ask, referring to the urban myth about peeling labels off beer bottles.

He laughs, his cheeks darkening. The doorbell rings.

"Saved by the bell." He can't answer the door fast enough, making me giggle.

We eat on the floor, our legs and shoulders brushing like they did yesterday at the bookstore. "How did your sister and Murphy meet?" I ask, making conversation.

"Murphy and Fallon grew up with us, but Charlie always liked Murphy, whereas Fallon and I never felt anything romantic between us."

"Wait. Are Murphy and Fallon siblings?"

Aaron nods.

"Wow. Your parents really do want to keep it all in the family."

"Their grandfather owned a construction company that did historical renovations. He used to be my parents' top junk supplier."

"Junk?"

"Old knobs and cabinet handles. Cast-iron tubs. Copper pipes. Things they could upcycle after a demo. That's how my dad got started. He used to own a restoration store near your uncle's shop."

That, I knew.

We finish our meal and I start to help Aaron clean up when he says, "I'll get it. I know you want to work."

"Thank you." I sit back down.

He takes the food containers and trash to the kitchen and brings me another beer, opening one for himself before retreating to his den.

We work apart for a couple of hours. When I'm not any closer to figuring out the uncategorized entries, but I'm at least able to plug some hypothetical numbers into my business plan, I pack up my things. Exhausted, I go to the kitchen to make myself a chamomile tea. On a whim, I make one for Aaron and take our mugs to the den. Blueberry is sprawled on Aaron's desk, his belly exposed, Aaron absently stroking the cat's fur, zoned out, gazing out the window. It's now dark outside. The only thing I can see is us and the room reflecting back.

"There you are. I was wondering where you went off to. Traitor." I put Aaron's mug on the desk.

Aaron snaps upright. "Who, me?"

"The cat. I brought you tea."

He blinks at the mug and picks it up. "Thank you."

"You can nudge him off if you don't want him up there."

"He's fine." He scratches Blueberry's chin. "We're becoming buds."

"I'm not surprised. You're very likable, Aaron."

He looks over at me with a tender smile.

"Well," I say as that seed of attraction blooms larger in my chest. "I'm headed up for bed. I just came in to thank you again for all that you're doing." It has evidently taken a toll on him today. "And to say good night."

"Good night, Meli."

I turn to leave.

"Why don't you like talking about your parents?"

I stop.

"Never mind; I shouldn't have asked. Forgive me for prying." His finger taps the desk. He absently stares inside the mug of tea.

My instinct is to put off his question. I fear things will change between us if I tell him. He won't look at me the same. He might not want to be around me. Paul never understood my relationship with my parents, since he was close to his mom and dad. He acted uneasy whenever I brought my parents up in conversation, so I just didn't. But Aaron confided in me about his brother, letting me witness how the loss has affected him. He chose to trust me with that knowledge, his emotions. If that wasn't him being vulnerable, I don't know what is. I want to reciprocate.

I slowly turn back to him. "It's embarrassing. I mean, who willingly works with their parents, lives in the same building as them, and constantly subjects themselves to their indifference? You saw them yesterday. It's like that almost every time we run into each other. Imagine being stuck in an elevator with them."

"That happened?"

"Longest five minutes of my life." The power temporarily went out in the building. It could have provided a great opportunity for us to reconcile. But Mom chose to use the time to shop online for a plastic juice pitcher. I stood there like a fool, afraid if I forced her into conversation she wouldn't talk to me again, not even at work.

"What happened with them?"

"At the risk of you wishing you didn't marry me?"

"I'd never wish that."

My mouth flattens. Doubtful. But I sit in one of the two armchairs facing his desk. Blueberry notices and leaps into my lap. I like to think he senses my unease and came to comfort me. I put my mug on the desk and pet my cat.

"My parents were functioning addicts. They missed a lot of me growing up because they were too drunk or strung out. I was too young

126

at the time to realize what was going on. I just remember the fun times, the times they weren't using. It would go in phases, I guess. That's what Uncle Bear told me. According to him, he was always running interference, saving me when things got really bad with them, especially with my dad. He was caught up in a rough crowd. He'd been like that since high school, the typical messed-up kid with the tragic past. His mom died when he was young, and my grandpa Walt raised him and my uncle. From what Uncle Bear tells me, Grandpa Walt only spent time with them when they worked with him at the shop. Otherwise, he wasn't around.

"I remember some mornings waking up and there'd be some stranger passed out on the couch, sleeping off their high. Randoms would open my bedroom door at night, looking for the bathroom. We lived in a small apartment. You'd have to be pretty out of it to miss where the bathroom was."

"Unless they weren't looking for the bathroom." Aaron says what I won't. I can't think about everything that could have happened to me.

"I know."

"Jesus." He's appalled.

"Nothing happened." I was lucky.

"One day, my dad got caught dealing to an undercover cop. It wasn't his first offense, so he was sentenced to six years in prison. Mom went into rehab and Uncle Bear became my legal guardian. I was ten when I went to live with him. Mom eventually got out. I don't know where she went afterward. I think she was living somewhere near the prison so she could visit Dad. But she didn't come back for me, and when I asked, Uncle Bear wouldn't take me to see her. He said she wasn't herself.

"I was sixteen when Dad was released. He and my mom moved into our apartment building two floors down from my uncle. They'd visit him when I was there, but they never invited us—or, more specifically, me—over to their apartment. It was partially my fault. I was angry when they got back, which only pushed them away. But once I cooled off, the damage had been done: They didn't want me to move back in with them. They said my uncle was my legal guardian now; I should stay with him. Which I did until I could afford my own place.

"I know addiction is a disease and they've been treated. I forgave them a long time ago. But I don't know what I did to make them not want me back or, at least, get to know me again. I wasn't the same kid they'd left behind. But I got over my anger a long time ago. I keep hoping one day they'll say they still love me. I know, sounds pathetic. And wow." I blink, stunned at myself. "That was a lot more than I planned to say." I look down at my lap and keep petting Blueberry. He purrs deeply, a gentle vibration I feel in my legs.

Aaron doesn't speak. He pushes away from the desk and comes to stand in front of me. He moves a sleeping Blueberry from my lap to the other chair. Then he takes my hands and pulls me to my feet. He hugs me. I stiffen in his embrace, and when he doesn't let go, I slowly relax as a thought occurs to me: I'm exactly where I want to be.

His arms lower and I look up at him. "Where'd that come from?"

"I wanted to."

He probably thought I looked like I needed it.

I did.

CHAPTER 17

SCORE ONE FOR BLUEBERRY

The following morning, Aaron leaves on a four-day business trip to Los Angeles. Isadora's table isn't scheduled for delivery until next week, and I'm still in the design phase of my next project, so I could work from the town house. But it's too quiet with Aaron gone, and if these are the last weeks I can work alongside my family, I don't want to waste any hours. I also don't want to miss anything if they talk about the acquisition. I'm still determined—and convinced—I can swoop in with an attractive offer and sway Uncle Bear to my side. I should be the third party he sells to. So I spend mornings at the shop, working on my new client's bedside tables, and afternoons with Blueberry at the town house, drafting not just my business plan for the loan application but also my proposal for Uncle Bear.

And all the while, I pretend to ignore the obvious: I miss Aaron.

We text, brief check-ins with status updates. He hasn't heard anything further about the Savant House's stance on the acquisition, but that doesn't mean the company isn't reevaluating their decision. Aaron has planted the seeds that the deal won't reflect well internally.

Then there are his other texts: a picture of the ocean while he dines at Nobu in Malibu Beach, him asking for a photo of Blueberry. He misses my cat. I send him a picture of Blueberry snuggled in the crook of my neck while I work from bed. I just happen to be in the photo too. He follows up that text with a selfie, him toasting me good night. He's at a business dinner in LA.

And the text on his last night away: I don't think I've ever looked so forward to going home as I have on this trip.

Rough week? I reply, trying not to read into his text that he couldn't wait to come home because he misses me as much as my cat.

Yes, but that's not why.

I leave our conversation there and remind myself why I'm living here, why I need to stay focused. Any sort of relationship we have is because I'm trying to save Artisant Designs from being sold off. I've also learned from experience and observation that, like my parents and uncle, I'm incapable of dividing my attention, passion, and affection. And I already feel like I'm being split between the two: Aaron and my art.

But there's a little voice inside me that's convinced I can love both equally. She's getting louder. And the thing that scares me? I'm starting to believe her. Because I don't think he'd ever ask me to give up my craft, even if our marriage was real.

Friday night, I'm working at the kitchen table, adding final notes to my proposal, when Aaron returns. Once again, Blueberry, who is lounging on the table, batting at my pen, shoots through the house and up the stairs to his hiding spot under my bed when Aaron opens the door.

I hear him park his luggage and backpack in the foyer and walk toward the kitchen. He appears with his shirt askew and sleeves rolled to his elbows. His face looks drawn and he has dark circles under his eyes, shadows covering his jaw. He sees me and a slow smile replaces the exhaustion. He visibly relaxes.

"Hello." I give him a little wave.

"Hi."

He comes into the room, sees the empty place at the table, and asks, "What did you have for dinner?"

"Fettuccine in a wine sauce. Hungry? There's extra."

"Starving."

"I'll fix you a plate." I pick up my dirty dish and put it in the sink.

"I got it," Aaron offers. He turns to the stove.

"Let me," I say, already getting a bowl from the cabinet. I want to do this for him.

He grabs a beer from the fridge while I scoop pasta. We turn at the same time and almost bump into each other. His bloodshot eyes startle me. He looks tired enough to make me think he'll collapse from exhaustion before he finishes eating. He doesn't move away, and my gaze drops to his mouth, then to his neck where his clavicles meet. His breathing deepens. I thrust the plate at him. "Here."

He grabs it before the pasta spills onto his shirt. "This smells amazing."

I mixed in fresh basil leaves, halved cherry tomatoes, garlic chunks, sliced olives, and marinated artichoke hearts. The tip of his tongue swipes across his bottom lip.

"So, uh . . . how was the expo?" I return to my chair and he sits in the one across from me. "Any new trends?"

He shakes his head, shoveling in a bite of pasta. "Nothing worth mentioning. I was there mostly to negotiate bulk deals and renew relationships with some of our suppliers. Lots of bullshitting and handshaking."

"I haven't been to that show. I hope to go some year."

"You should. Your work would blow away most of what I saw. What are you working on?" He nods at my laptop.

"My proposal to my uncle to buy him out."

"How's it going?"

"Mmm . . . okay." I wiggle my hand in an iffy gesture.

"Want to talk it out?"

"Promise not to steal my ideas?"

He mimes zipping his mouth. "This house is a vault. Nothing you say here leaves."

I stare at him and decide I believe him. "Sure, why not." Typically, I would ask Emi for feedback on anything work related, but she's not here. Other than a few training videos Tam and Shae helped me record a while back, I haven't done this big of a presentation since my trade-school days. I angle my laptop for him to see, and he scoots closer. I'm instantly aware of his nearness. The appealing scent of him, the space he takes up.

I direct my attention to the screen. "I'm confident about my ideas and number projections. Profitability should increase dramatically when I align our pricing with our reputation. We should be charging more than we do, by fifteen percent, at least."

"I agree. What other ways do you see increasing revenue?"

"To start, I'll diversify our offerings beyond one-off custom orders." Aaron nods at the rhythm of my words, and it's all the encouragement I need. I share my ideas about partnering with homebuilders and architects, hosting woodworking workshops, and creating DIY furniture kits with precut and predrilled pieces. I then tell him about my magnum opus, the offering I'm most excited to launch: digital packages that include furniture plans and woodworking templates, matching each with a series of educational videos designed to inspire and spread my love of the craft.

Aaron's expression is alight with interest through the entire presentation, and he asks a lot of tough questions that challenge me. But when I finish, he falls silent.

I wiggle the pen with unease. "Say something."

I worry my ideas are terrible. My parents have never shown interest in hearing them, and Uncle Bear rarely gives me permission to implement anything I've suggested in the past. He thinks my ideas are over the top. "Just make the table, Meli, and forget the rest. Our clients don't want all those extras," he told me. How do I get them to listen to me now when they haven't before? I worry my efforts will be fruitless.

Aaron clears his throat after a stretch of silence that just reaches the point of feeling strained. "This is brilliant, Meli."

"Really?" My doubts aren't easily chased away by a fancy compliment.

"I almost want to convince you to come work for us. You'd be an asset. Have you recorded any videos yet to test your idea?"

"A few. The gals helped me. Tam, Shae, and Emi," I say. I open my file explorer. "Here's one. We recorded it about six months ago. It's for a small dining table."

"May I watch?"

"It's almost an hour long."

He shrugs. "I'm not going anywhere."

"All right," I say with a little reticence. I haven't shown the video to anyone apart from my friends. I play the video, cracking my knuckles at a few points while Aaron quietly watches the tutorial. The video finishes and he immediately compliments my work.

"Thank you."

"My only suggestion is to break it into shorter clips."

"Emi said the same thing."

"You're a natural teacher. Send me the link? I want to watch it again when I'm not so tired."

"You just want to see me in a hard hat," I joke, disguising the guilt I feel for keeping him up so late. I send him a link to access the video.

"Your ideas are solid, Meli. So are your projections. I think you're on the right track. Why are you worried?"

"Uncle Bear. He hasn't been open to my ideas in the past, and so far, he won't consider an offer from me. Who's to say he'll listen to me now?"

"You can always open your own shop."

"True, but it wouldn't be the same." Apart from my family not working with me, I'd truly have to start from scratch. But with Artisant Designs, even if my parents and uncle don't work there, the shop would be where it's always been. I'd be able to work around the memory of them. I'd still feel connected to my family's legacy so long as I'm within those walls.

Aaron yawns and I notice it's after midnight. "You should get some sleep. I've kept you up long enough."

"I don't mind." He yawns again. "Yeah, I should head up." He takes his bowl to the sink. "Are you coming?"

"I want to run through my numbers again. You go ahead. I'll lock up."

He stares at me. I think he wants to say something, but he turns around and starts to leave, only to stop at the kitchen doorway and glance over his shoulder with a soft smile. "Good night, wife."

I easily smile back. "Good night, husband."

I hear him go upstairs and long to follow him. Clients compliment my work. Friends, followers, they all admire my designs. But my parents never praise me, or each other, not like Aaron just did. I'm feeling good about myself, confident for the first time in a while.

I want Aaron to feel the same, and I start to think of ways to make him happy. He's seemed mellow and somewhat distracted since Monday when he told his parents and staff about marrying me. Maybe I can take him to coffee tomorrow. I should find another book for him. He might have finished reading the ones I bought him. I could make him dinner on Sunday.

There are so many things I want to do for him and with him that I'm struck with a sudden realization: I feel good, not just about myself, but about everything.

Is this what it feels like to be in a positive and rewarding relationship? Is a marriage like Tam and Shae's possible? One where the partners support one another's passions as much as their love and respect? A relationship where we aren't constantly vying for our partner's attention and don't guilt one another into spending more time with them because we're jealous of the time they spend nurturing their art?

I start to dream it can be possible for me, and the next thing I know, I really am dreaming, and floating. My eyes flutter open. Above me, the ceiling is cast in muted gray. My cheek rests against soft cotton. My nose is pressing into cool skin. I inhale a long breath that smells faintly of fresh water, mint, and man.

I jerk, coming awake, and flounder when I can't feel the ground underneath me.

"Shh. I got you." The words are softly spoken.

Aaron is carrying me upstairs.

I study his profile, the straight line of his jaw and his day-old beard. "What happened?"

"I came down after my shower to check on you. You were passed out at the table."

The last thing I remember is Aaron going up to bed. Then Blueberry came running down and popped onto my lap. I was petting him, then . . . nothing. I wonder where my cat is now.

"You're carrying me," I mumble, feeling myself falling back to sleep.

"I tried to wake you."

I mumble something about how tired I am and burrow into his chest. Then he's putting me into bed and pulling the sheets over me. The mattress feels cool and soft.

"Good night, Meli," he whispers by my ear. His fingers brush my hair back, lingering for a moment, and then he's gone.

———

I jolt awake, looking around, barely remembering how I got here.

Aaron.

It's dark out, the dim glow of the streetlamps outlining the shades in my bedroom. I glance at the time on my phone screen—3:47 a.m.—and look for Blueberry. He isn't on my bed where he usually sleeps.

I toss aside the sheets and step into the hallway to go downstairs and look for him, but I notice Aaron's light is on and his door cracked open. I go to his room, thinking he's fallen asleep with his light on. But he's reading in bed. And snoozing beside him is my cat.

Noticing me in the doorway, Aaron rests his opened book on his bare chest. "I was going to bring him to you, but he looked too comfortable. I didn't want to disturb him."

I walk into his room, stopping beside the bed. If Blueberry was asleep, he isn't now. He looks up at me with his permawink and chirps, but he makes no move to get off the bed.

"Traitor." I gently rub his exposed belly, and his purr becomes a deep rumble. "Fair warning: he does have a way of wheedling into your heart." He found his way into mine within seconds of me meeting him at the shelter.

Aaron doesn't bother to hide his guilty look. I suspect Blueberry has already burrowed into his heart.

"What are you reading?" I sit on the edge of the bed, not even thinking about what I'm doing or the line I'm crossing.

He shows me the cover of *The Alienist*. "I finished *Project Hail Mary* on the plane. Have you read yours?"

"Halfway through." I take the book from him, mark his place, and set it on the nightstand.

I should tell him to go to sleep, it's late, but I don't.

I should take my cat back to my room. But I don't.

Aaron watches me closely as my gaze drifts over him, from his eyes to his mouth, down to his chest and the smattering of hair there. I rest a hand on the cut lines of his abdomen where the sheet meets his skin, and he sucks in a sharp breath. The heat of him sears my palm.

"Meli," he whispers, and my eyes fly to his. He stares at me, waiting, unmoving.

I don't think. In fact, I think I stopped thinking the day we met. I lean forward and kiss him. I want to kiss away the unkind things I suspect his parents said to him this week. I want to kiss away the troubling thoughts occupying his mind, whatever it is that's keeping him awake.

My name is a sigh on his lips as his hands cup my face. Then they're in my hair, holding me against his mouth. He deepens our kiss, groaning into my mouth as I move over him, straddling his hips. I skim my lips over his chin and along his jawline, kissing the soft area below his ear. I kiss down his neck and across his chest, lavishing my attention on every contour of his torso. Every rise and fall of his chest as his breathing becomes erratic and our hands frenzied. He undresses me with impatience, pulling my shirt over my head and nudging down the lounge pants I fell asleep in. He shoves off his own sleep pants and guides me over him as I grip him and sink down onto him.

We groan, and then we move, our eyes never leaving the other. Our lovemaking is slow, every touch and every breath a tumble as I recognize the falling sensation I experienced when we wrote our list on the plane, and felt again when he slipped a dented silver ring on my finger, and yet again when he twirled me across the dance floor several weeks ago, and once again when we rocked out on our wedding night in his living room, and once more last week when we'd lost track of time and ourselves in the bookstore . . . And finally tonight, when he'd praised my ideas. All these times had been me falling for him, again and again and again.

Afterward, we lie on our sides, his front to my back, his arm protectively over my waist, his hand between my breasts, and his mouth by my ear.

"Stay," he whispers.

And I do.

CHAPTER 18

UP THE ANTE

Another two weeks go by without word from the Savant House. If Uncle Bear wasn't grumbling about them dragging their feet or that his contact there wasn't returning his calls, I'd be worried Aaron's and my plan isn't working. Aaron isn't surprised by the delay, and when I bring up my concerns, he reminds me that some decisions in the corporate world take time. Aside from marrying Aaron and living together without my family knowing, it's been life and business as usual. I'm not complaining.

I get up each morning and join Aaron for breakfast downstairs, like we did our first morning together since we had met up again, or we go for coffee at Perkatory, which has become a highlight of my day. He walks me to the T station, and I go to work at the shop. While Uncle Bear and Dad are winding down and closing out orders, I'm still taking on work. I had Isadora's table ready for delivery last week when she had called and asked for a delay until she returns from Italy. Her brother had passed away. So I started on a new walnut coffee table. Between that and the two bedside tables I'm finishing up, I've kept busy. All three pieces are new designs, both functional and transitional in style, that I plan to copyright under my name. Just in case I don't get ownership of Artisant Designs.

A bank approved my loan for a disappointing amount. Aaron offered again to loan me money when I shared the news and my frustration, but I can't accept. I don't want to owe him anything more than I already do. But also, wouldn't a loan from him extend our relationship beyond three years? Wouldn't it symbolize a deeper connection between us? Could it loosely mean we're in business together? He's beyond generous to even offer, but I can't get past thinking that accepting a loan from him is almost the same as working with him. And should we work together, I don't think I could handle the feelings I'm developing for him. What happens when we disagree or bicker, or he starts to resent me when I lavish more attention on my work than him? Or when I start to resent him when he spends more time on our business than with me? I'll leave him like I left Paul. Or we'll be miserable like my parents.

As much as I want to look on the bright side of this potential situation, I can't. History and family and personal habits have proved what's inevitable. I'll never successfully balance working with Aaron at Artisant Designs and a relationship with him. I'm destined to never have it all. So why get my hopes up? I was kidding myself to think it was possible. And that little voice inside my head? I tuned her out.

All this introspection could explain why I've avoided facing something else: where I've been sleeping every night, in his bed.

I keep telling myself tonight will be the last night, but then I think about my bedroom and how my clothes have slowly made their way into his closet and drawers, much like how my affection for him has sneaked through the back door of my heart. Or how Blueberry automatically goes to Aaron's room each night, which Aaron now refers to as *our* room, as if that's where we're supposed to be. And really, is it so bad that I want to be there? It won't be forever.

Goodness, I'm such a jumble of contradictory thoughts and emotions.

I'm thinking about all of this on my way to the shop this morning, so deep in my head that I walk straight into the man standing in front of Artisant Design's entrance.

"Sorry, didn't see you," I apologize, reaching around him for the door. He's a short man with a barrel chest and large shoes. Dressed in a dark suit and tie with a starched white shirt, he looks like a bald Agent Smith from *The Matrix*.

He doesn't move out of the way, watching me through his nearly opaque sunglasses. "Mrs. Borland?"

My stomach lurches at the name. "Who's asking?" I didn't legally change my name, but I nervously glance through the glass door at Mom seated at her desk, wondering if he went inside looking for me. Does my family now know I'm married?

"Kaye Borland. She'd like a word with you." He extends an arm at the idling black Escalade I just now notice. Aaron's mom wants to speak with me? I figured Aaron and I would eventually get around to visiting her at the Savant House or at a restaurant over lunch. It can't mean anything good that she's come to me. Not only that, she came specifically when she knew Aaron wouldn't be with me.

"And you are?" I hope he doesn't expect me to willingly get into the car. I have a morbid vision of him dumping me in the Charles River.

The corner of his mouth twitches. "She's waiting in the car and only needs a few minutes of your time." He opens the rear passenger door. "If you don't mind." He tilts his head, gesturing for me to get in.

"All right," I say, noticing Kaye in the back seat. As curious as I'm wary, I settle onto the black leather seat beside Aaron's mom, whose floral-and-citrus perfume greets me before she does. Dressed in a monochromatic dove-gray pantsuit and silk blouse, her arrow-straight silver hair is styled in a blunt shoulder bob that mimics her daughter's. Kaye is an older, well-aged version of Charlie, her long legs folded in the foot space on her side of the car. Her hands, the only part of her that hints she's older than her cultivated appearance, rest on the tablet on her lap. Thick-framed Chanel sunglasses hide half her face, which looks like it has benefited from extensive and expensive work. She's as put together as a military general who's red-carpet ready, exactly the way I suspect she runs her multimillion-dollar corporation. Highly polished, disciplined, precise, and in control. There's an air about her that speaks of her business acumen and savviness. She presents as someone accustomed to being respected before it's earned, obeyed when ordered, and listened to when she speaks. I notice her mouth. Her lips are painted a subtle pink, and they aren't smiling. I also realize I've been staring.

"Hello, Mrs. Borland," I say with a jolt when Kaye's driver shuts the door on us.

"I don't know you," she starts, "and I don't care to know you."

"Okay . . . Then why did you ask to see me?"

"I read the prenup you signed. It's inadequate."

Aaron and I signed a prenuptial agreement his attorney had drafted, the same attorney we used for our first divorce. Our agreement is fairly standard, stating our assets remain our own and anything acquired while in the marriage would remain ours alone. He would keep his town house and any other property he invested in. Artisant Designs would go to me in its entirety, assuming I get the shop.

The agreement is solid, and I trust Aaron. I don't trust Kaye, and I guess the feeling is mutual. I also don't owe her an explanation. But I find her lack of confidence in her son off-putting. There's an edge to her that makes me uncomfortable . . . and very protective of my *husband*.

"I believe your son capable of adequately protecting his and his family's interests."

"Then you don't know my son."

I didn't stand up for myself when I'd been with Paul because I'd been so enamored with him and awed that somebody wanted me and I didn't want to jeopardize the relationship. I've rarely stood up for myself or confronted my parents and their disinterest in me out of fear I'd push them further away. But something about Kaye diminishing Aaron's credibility makes me want to speak up.

"I have no interest in Aaron's wealth, and I don't want any part of your family's business."

"Do you love him?"

"What?"

"I don't think you do. How could you possibly? You don't know him. You don't know anything of our family. You say you aren't interested in what we have, but you can't guarantee that won't change. I'm not concerned about how you feel or what you think today. I'm preparing for tomorrow." She taps the tablet and the screen lights up. "Sign this, please. I insist," she orders.

I have no intention of signing anything. But I take the device from her, curious what she's giving me, which turns out to be a *post*nuptial agreement. I skim the document's legalese. I pause on the noncompete clause. According to that, I can't start or pursue any business venture that would compete with the Savant House or any of its holdings. They've absorbed multiple shops like Artisant Designs, so would this preclude me from buying the shop if the Savant House retracts its offer?

I read through more of the agreement. The Borland family would control my public image. My presence would be required at all family and corporate functions. There's even a timeline for producing an heir.

An heir?

Unexpected laughter bubbles up my throat. I clap a hand over my mouth.

"Something funny?"

"It's just . . . You don't really expect me to sign this?"

"I didn't come all this way for you not to."

"I . . . I can't sign this."

"I suggest you reconsider."

Her condescending tone and sense of entitlement push me to do the exact opposite. "No, thanks. Sorry you wasted your time." I open the door, anxious to leave.

"You know," Kaye says before I exit the car, "you aren't the first horrible mistake Aaron's made."

I look at her from across the seat. "I may not be your choice of a spouse for Aaron," I tell her, my voice frosting over, "but I trust your son's judgment. I . . . ." I stall. I don't want to say that I feel like I do love him. I can't admit that to her before Aaron. Before I've thoroughly processed and evaluated and picked apart exactly what I'm feeling for her son. A trimmed, silver brow peeks above her Chanel glasses. "I admire him," I concede. "He's charismatic, ambitious, honest, reliable. He believes in me. Your postnup?" I nod at the tablet I left on the seat. "It's an insult to his intelligence. I wish I could say it's been a pleasure meeting you, but we both know it hasn't been. Excuse me, I have to get to work."

"You'll find the agreement has been emailed to you. Think on what could happen if you don't sign it."

Her threat chases me from the car. Sheesh, she's something else. I wouldn't dare sign it without having an attorney read over the document, let alone discuss it with Aaron first. But I also have no idea how my signing, or not signing, would impact Aaron. Goodness, I'd be committing us to having a baby within a year.

"Have a good day, Mrs. Borland," Kaye's driver says to me. He shuts the door and rounds the Escalade to the driver's side. He pulls into traffic as my phone buzzes.

"I just met your mother," I say to Aaron when I answer.

"That's why I'm calling. I'm on my way. Don't let her bully you into anything."

"Too late. She already left." I hear an uneasy warble in my voice from the adrenaline rush. "You don't need to come."

"I'm already here."

I look up and a blue Mercedes rounds the corner and stops in front of me. Aaron is behind the wheel.

"I didn't know you had a car," I say when he meets up with me on the sidewalk. He pulls me into a hug. His arms feel so good around me.

"I came as soon as I heard. Charlie told me our mom was coming here to meet with you. Are you okay?"

"She wanted me to sign a postnup." I give him the highlights of what I read in the agreement.

"Did you sign it?" he asks, horrified.

"Hell, no."

Hands on his waist, he drops his head with a groan and peers at me through his lashes. "I'm sorry you had to deal with that. It was out of line, even for her."

"It's all right."

"It's not." Aaron is visibly upset.

I touch his arm. "I'm fine. Okay, I'm a little flustered," I amend when he looks at me like he isn't sure he believes me. "Did you really leave work to check on me?"

"Of course. You're my wife. We look out for each other. I . . ." He stops.

"You what?"

He shakes his head.

His phone rattles and he reads the screen. He hesitates answering and glances between me and the device. "I ran out on a meeting."

"Then you should get that. Or go, really. I'm okay." I put on a smile, but he hedges. "We can talk tonight," I reassure him.

Relief pours across his face. He even smiles a little. "Okay, we'll talk. Again, I'm sorry about her."

"Please don't be. Go," I push when his phone keeps rattling. He shouldn't feel guilty. His mom is at fault, and she's clearly a piece of work.

"Geoff, hey," he answers, returning to his car. He glances back at me. "Hold one second." He rushes over. Cupping my neck, he gives me a quick, hard kiss. Then another, this one soft as his lips linger on mine. "Thank you," he whispers against my mouth.

"See you at home," I whisper back.

Then he's gone, leaving me standing on the sidewalk, my fingertips touching my lips. It isn't until he pulls away from the curb that I realize he was wearing jeans and a T-shirt, not the suit he'd left the house in. Where had he come from, and where is he going? I stare after him until his car is swallowed in traffic. A passing bus honks at a jaywalker. I jump.

"Focus, Meli," I order myself and head into the shop only to find it unusually quiet. Rather than whining saws and buzzing drills, I hear the humming fridge in the kitchenette and the whirring of the overhead ceiling fans.

Kidder stands at the bin wall, organizing screws and nails.

"Where is everyone?" I ask him, making my way to the lockers.

"They're having a meeting out back." Kidder swings an arm at the metal door to the alley.

I don't recall a meeting on the schedule. "Do you know what it's about?"

"No, but whatever it is, Bear blew a gasket. Dean and Gemma took him out back to cool off."

I glance warily at the door. If he just received notice from the Savant House that they're retracting their offer, Kaye couldn't have timed her appearance more brilliantly. Her warning about what could happen if I don't sign the agreement has me wondering if the postnup is related to whatever is going on with my uncle.

"How long ago did they go out there?"

Kidder shrugs. "Five, ten minutes?" he guesses.

I toss my backpack into my locker and crack my knuckles. I'm nervous about how my family is reacting to the news. But I head for the alley anyway, determined to convince my uncle the Savant House retracting their acquisition offer is for the best and that I'm the best for Artisant Design's continuation.

"I wouldn't go out there if I were you." Kidder looks genuinely concerned.

"I can handle them," I say with a confidence that belies my nervousness and push open the door.

Uncle Bear, Dad, and Mom stand huddled over a sheet of paper. They're speaking fervently in hushed tones, but their conversation abruptly stops when the door bangs shut behind me. Three heads turn in my direction, their faces drawn in a mix of disbelief, shock, and anger.

I've been anticipating this day and this conversation, but a prickling of unease unfurls inside my chest. "Kidder told me I'd find you guys out here. What's going on?"

Dad takes a long draw on his cigarette and breaks from the huddle as if he wants no part of what's about to go down. He stares at the stained asphalt under his boots. Mom cuts me a withering glare, not even trying to hide her displeasure. My shoulders curl as if I'm ten years old.

Uncle Bear thrusts the paper at me. "What the devil have you done?"

I know he's asking about Aaron and me, but I hear myself saying, "What do you mean?"

"Read it," he demands, his rage deepening the grooves in his face.

I read the printout of an email he received not less than fifteen minutes ago.

Dear Bernard,

Please accept my apologies for not getting back to you sooner, but I'd been waiting on an internal audit before we spoke. Unfortunately, I have bad news. The Savant House has made the difficult decision to withdraw our offer for Artisant Designs LLC. This decision was not taken lightly, and the Savant House sincerely regrets any inconvenience or disruption this may cause. After careful consideration and further due diligence, we have determined that acquiring Artisant Designs LLC is no longer an attractive venture.

Sweet satisfaction ripples through me. I can barely contain my glee. "Savant retracted their offer?" I ask, too giddy to finish reading the letter. I look at my family for confirmation despite holding the proof in my hands.

Mom immediately calls me out. "Don't play dumb, Melissa."

I wince. She hasn't used my proper name in years.

"Did you ask why they don't want the shop?"

"I did." Uncle Bear plants his fists on his waist. "They gave me some bullshit about corporate governance issues, possible manipulation from both parties, and the loss of our key employee."

That would be me since I was no longer part of the deal.

"You know what else they told me?" Uncle Bear's complexion turns the same ruddy shade of the building's brick siding. He throws out his arms. "'Congratulations!' Like an idiot, I asked what for."

"Is it true?" Mom rubs her arms as if she's chilled. "Are you married to Aaron Borland, the CEO's son?" Her gaze drops to my naked ring finger, seeking proof that isn't there. I don't wear jewelry at the shop. It's too dangerous around the equipment.

"What have you done?" Uncle Bear yells, and regret fills me even though this is exactly what I wanted to happen. Marrying Aaron was the right thing to do. I couldn't wait to call him and share the news. Our plan worked. But never in the nineteen years since Uncle Bear became my legal guardian has he yelled at me the way he just did.

I lift my chin. "The only thing I could to save the shop."

"What do you think I was trying to do?" He smacks the paper I'm holding.

"We did this for you."

I look at Mom, not understanding what she meant. "I don't get it. You're selling off the shop when I want it. Why aren't you selling it to me?"

"Did you read the entire letter?" Uncle Bear growls.

I didn't, and I'm starting to clue in that something has gone over my head. With a shaking hand, I finish the email.

Please note this in no way affects the purchase of the property located at 10 South Street. That deal will proceed as planned and negotiated. Our site selection team is eager to see this matter through. Escrow will close on schedule in a matter of weeks.

It's been a pleasure working with you, and I appreciate the time and cooperation you've shown during our correspondence.

Regards,
Shelbie Wright
Director of Acquisitions

"You're selling the building?" I shriek.

"Why did you think I was selling the shop?"

"I have no fucking idea because you didn't tell me anything." I point at my family. "Not a single one of you."

But he's right. I've been so focused on stopping the sale of the business that it never occurred to me Uncle Bear was selling Artisant because he'd sold the building along with the land underneath it. Like the shop, the building has held our family together for three generations. I just assumed I'd pay Uncle Bear rent when he transferred the shop ownership to me when he retired, just as he'd done when Grandpa Walt retired.

"Your uncle knew this isn't what you and he had planned," Mom explains to me. "He had no option but to sell, but he didn't want to leave you without or in the position of finding a new location for the shop. Rental rates are abhorrent. That's why he negotiated a position for you at the Savant House. The money from Artisant's sale would have gone into a trust for you."

"But you let that ship sail," Uncle Bear scoffs.

Because of the size and location, the property was last valued close to $4.5 million. Uncle Bear has repeatedly received offers from real estate investors over the years. He always remained steadfast on his position of retaining ownership of the building.

"Why was selling your only option? What happened? What aren't you telling me?"

Uncle Bear's lips pucker. He doesn't answer me, and I catch Mom's subtle glance at Dad.

"What did you do?" I ask Dad.

"Not your concern, kiddo." Dad drops his cigarette butt and grinds it on the asphalt with his boot toe.

"I think it is. I'm part of this family, as screwed up as we are, whether you treat me like I am or not. I've dedicated my life to this shop, just as each of you have. I had plans, really, really good plans to expand and grow. What gives you the right or entitlement to make decisions about my future without involving me? I deserve an explanation," I demand, for once standing up for myself.

My parents glance away. I've never felt this hurt, this *less than*, or this insignificant. Am I truly not enough for them to love and value me?

Keys rattle and I notice Uncle Bear removing the key to his apartment from the metal ring that holds all the master keys for the shop. He pockets the key and grabs my wrist. He drops the key ring in my palm. "Shop's yours."

Mom gapes. "You can't be serious, Bear. You can't just give her the shop. There's paperwork and taxes."

"I just did. Do what you want with it, Meli. Shut her down or build her up. Either way, they want you out within the month. The Savant House is tearing down the building."

"They're what?"

"They're razing the entire block," Mom says. "Building a new flagship store."

"Bear, you need to give her something," Dad says.

"I've had enough from you," Uncle Bear snaps at his brother. "Both of you, let's go."

My parents look at each other, then humbly follow my uncle inside. I got the shop, but the shop won't have a home. And all I can think is that my husband knew. He's known all along about the building.

CHAPTER 19

SAWDUST AND APOLOGIES

It takes a moment to shake off the shock of what just happened before I follow my family inside. When I do, Uncle Bear and my parents aren't around. Kidder stands at his locker, packing up his stuff.

"Where'd everybody go?" I ask.

"They walked out."

Like they're on strike? I can't believe they took off. Uncle Bear I understand. But my parents? They didn't want me to live with them. They barely take the time to talk when we bump into each other at our apartments. Now they refuse to work for me? Uncle Bear might have left me the shop, but without him and Dad here to finish their orders, and Mom to handle customer service and the books, I'll quickly have a shop full of problems on my hands.

My fingers rub the worn master key to the entrance. A lot of good it will do once escrow closes. I don't have access to the shop's bank accounts or the office computer. In less than a month, I won't have access to the building.

Kidder slams the locker door and slings his backpack onto his shoulder.

"Are you leaving too?"

"Bear told me my internship is over."

"Oh." I don't move. Neither does he. I don't have it in me to argue what my uncle decided and ask Kidder to stay. "Well, thanks for your help."

Kidder looks at the floor, disappointed. "Yeah, it's been great. See you around, Meli." He heads for the exit.

"Kidder," I call when he reaches the door. He turns back to me. "Text if you need a letter of recommendation."

"Sure," he says without his usual spark. He leaves and the glass door swings shut behind him.

I call Aaron. I can't think about what to do next until I hear the truth. He answers on the first ring. "Hi, Meli."

"Did you know?"

"Know what?"

"About the building? Did you know your company bought my uncle's building?"

There is an extended pause. "Didn't you?"

He knew. I feel sick. I sever the call.

He immediately calls back. I send him to voicemail. He rings right back. Again, I terminate the call. This time, he texts. Please call me. I silence and pocket my phone and take in the abnormally quiet shop. I see dusty equipment and smell fresh-cut wood. But when I peer closer, I see the memories of working alongside Uncle Bear and hanging out with my parents. The ghostly echo of my grandfather. In less than a month, everything here will be gone. The equipment, the wood, the shop, my uncle, my parents, and the building that holds us together.

I'm too distraught and heartbroken to work today. I'm too ashamed that I trusted Aaron to go along with his idea of marriage.

I close up the shop and leave the building.

———

A half hour later, I enter Stone & Bloom's showroom. The employee offices are upstairs and not open to the public, so I go straight to reception and ask for Emi. She comes down five minutes later, looking summery fresh in a vibrant-orange, modern-print midi dress with Mary Jane heels and button earrings. I briefly consider giving up on Artisant Designs and coming to work for her so I can wear something other than shirts, coveralls, and boots to work. Then I imagine myself building the same kitchen cabinet boxes over and over and chase the thought away.

Emi rushes over to me with the biggest smile, super happy to see me. Her cheer doesn't nudge me out of my funk, and my composure falters as we hug. "Oh, Em." I cry on her shoulder.

She holds me at arm's length and searches my face. "What happened?"

"It's hopeless. Everything's falling apart." I wipe my eyes, mortified I'm crying in public.

"Let's go for a walk," she readily suggests. Emi knows me, and she knows I need to talk things out when I'm perplexed, disappointed, or upset. In this case, it's all three.

"It's too muggy outside."

"How about tea, then?"

I nod. Tea sounds good.

We walk over to the showroom's café, and Emi buys us each an herb tea. We sit at a high table with plush stools.

"I've been meaning to text you to meet up for coffee. I miss having you across the hall." She rips open her tea bag and lets it steep in the hot water.

"I miss you too," I say. We've texted and chatted here and there since Aaron and I married, but it isn't the same as when we were neighbors. We haven't talked these past few weeks as frequently as we used to. When I haven't been at the shop or working on my business plan, I've been with Aaron, and Emi has been adjusting to her new position at Stone & Bloom.

And all this time, not once did Aaron mention the building.

"Since I haven't heard from you much, I assume you're adjusting to married life and things are going well with your new husband?"

"They were."

"Uh-oh."

"Uncle Bear sold the building to the Savant House."

Emi's mouth falls open. "He what?"

"That's why he wanted them to buy the shop and create a position for me. He didn't think I could lease a space affordable enough to stay in business, or that I'd want the shop without the building we've always had. He figured if he could get enough money for the shop and put it in trust for me, with that and a job with benefits at Savant, he'd feel less guilty about selling everything. I mean, he didn't actually say all that, but that's definitely the way I see it."

"You should relocate the shop. You can always negotiate a lease. Businesses do it all the time." Emi sets her tea bag aside and blows across the hot surface before taking a tentative sip.

"I know, and I should, but it wouldn't be the same," I say, glum.

"You're right. It could be better."

I stare into my tea, shaking my head. She couldn't possibly understand. Her parents raised her. She grew up in a loving home, and she sees her family at least twice a month. They celebrate her career wins. And here I am, missing a family I never see outside of work, one that doesn't care about me or my worth. Artisant Designs could never be the same at a different location. I already know they wouldn't come with me if I moved the shop.

"Tell me what's going on with Aaron, then."

"He's known about the building sale this whole time and never said anything."

Emi's eyes widen. "That seems a tad passive-aggressive."

"If anything, it proves I don't know my husband." Not as well as I thought.

And he wants a wife who *gets* him. I almost roll my eyes, recalling our list, because that surely isn't me.

"Have you asked why?" Emi asks. I shake my head. "Did it ever come up in conversation?"

"No. It never crossed my mind Uncle Bear would sell the property." And that's on me.

No wonder Uncle Bear never gave my ideas to expand Artisant's offerings merit. I'd been oblivious to what was going on beyond my workbench. I should have insisted Mom keep me updated on the shop's income and expenses. I should have considered the property was part of the deal, or rather, *the* deal. The Savant House has been purchasing surrounding parcels for years. I, sadly, pretended it wouldn't affect me, falsely believing Uncle Bear would never sell. So instead, I chose to live in ignorant bliss. What sort of business owner does that? Not a successful one.

I etch my initial on my paper cup with my fingernail. "I wish Aaron had mentioned it."

"You need to ask him why he didn't."

"What's the point? We don't need to stay married." I don't. And after today, I'm not sure I want to see him again. He tricked me.

"Are you sure about that? I get the sense you both feel more for each other than you're letting on. You seemed really happy with him."

"Our marriage is fake. The idea of us? We're a lie." Everything about our relationship from the day we met has been pretend.

No longer in the mood for tea, I get up from the table and pour what's left in the trash.

"Where are you going?" Emi asks in a worried tone.

"Aaron's town house to get my cat and a divorce." The only good decision I've made these past weeks was to keep my apartment lease.

Emi slides off her stool. "Promise me something. Don't make any decisions until you talk with him first. Aaron seems like a really good guy, and I like him for you. You're good together. I'm sure he has an explanation."

"I don't see how he could possibly explain this." I hug Emi. "Thanks for talking."

"Anytime."

I turn to leave and stop when I remember. "I forgot to ask. How's the new job going?"

"Really well. I'm loving it. We'll talk more later. Go see Aaron. Text me."

"I will."

———

I'm upstairs packing when the front door slams and Aaron yells my name. I hear him calling for me from the kitchen. Then he's running up the stairs. He stops in the doorway to his bedroom.

"You're here." He's breathless and he looks relieved to find me. His hair is askew, face ruddy and sweaty, and he's still wearing the jeans and shirt I saw him in earlier. His clothes are dusty, and he's wearing work boots, something I didn't notice this morning when he rushed over to Artisant after his mom's unexpected visit.

"I've been looking for you. I went back to the shop, and when I found it closed, I drove to your apartment."

"I've been here."

"I know. Emi told me."

"You called her?"

He shakes his head. "I came home first, and when you weren't here, I drove to your old apartment, then to Stone & Bloom on the off chance you were there. I've been trying to reach you. You aren't answering my calls."

"I silenced my phone." It's probably why I missed Emi's text. She would have warned me Aaron stopped by the showroom and was on his way here.

"I figured." His arms drop to his sides when he notices the pile of my clothes on his bed. I'm trying to fit everything into my sole piece of luggage and the laundry basket I brought over. Blueberry's carrier is also out. I want to bring everything back to my apartment in one trip.

"What are you doing?" he asks.

"Packing. I'm leaving as soon as I finish here."

"Why?"

"My uncle gave me Artisant. There's no longer a reason for me to stay." Aaron might have been enough of a reason, but he deceived me by not telling me about the building. Who knows what else he hasn't told me. I hate that I started to care for him, maybe even fall in love with him. To think

I almost lost Artisant Designs—that I still could lose the shop—because of him. (Yes, I'm putting him in the same bucket as his family. They all work for the Savant House.) Thank goodness I insisted on an opt-out clause.

Aaron's face crumples. But his expression quickly flattens until it's unreadable.

"I want a divorce," I announce.

He goes very still. "Why?"

"We promised no questions asked if one of us wants out."

"I know. Just"—he takes a breath—"tell me why. Please."

"You lied to me."

"I've never lied to you, Meli. I have no reason to."

"Then you deceived me. Savant bought Uncle Bear's building. That's why he was selling the shop. It's the building your company has wanted all along. The shop and I were just the side deals."

"It wasn't like that at all," he argues, coming into the room. He stops opposite the bed from me. "Don't sell yourself short, Meli."

"You knew about the building, and you deliberately kept that information from me."

"I honestly thought you knew."

"You never brought it up."

"Neither did you."

We glare at each other. I hold the shirt I'm folding to my chest like a plate of armor.

Aaron sighs. "I'm sorry. I just assumed it was common knowledge. My mistake. A building is just a building. You can take Artisant Designs anywhere."

"It's not just a building, not to me. It's the only place where I feel like I have a family. We lose that building, I lose what little time my parents are willing to give me of themselves. You saw them when we went to my apartment. They hardly speak to me. Now they can ignore me completely as if they never had a daughter."

Aaron falls quiet for a long stretch. We stare at each other. I look away first to resume packing, but he says, "I'll be your family. If you'll have me."

His words puncture my heart. "Aaron." The shirt slips from my fingers to bunch on the bed. I take a long look at him. He doesn't hide what he's feeling. The slight pleading in his eyes for my forgiveness. His determination to regain my trust in the subtle clench of his jaw. The small nod that he understands me. I also see his regret and despair in the vulnerable way his hands flex at his sides. He's nervous I'll reject him. He doesn't want me to leave.

"Is there any way you can stop the sale?" I ask, not entirely without hope, even knowing there's no way in hell I can afford a $4.5 million piece of property.

Aaron shakes his head. "It's a done deal. For whatever reason, your uncle needs money fast. He insisted on a short escrow. Listen, Meli." Aaron cautiously approaches me. "I could kick myself for never bringing up the building. I didn't want to see that it was as important to you as Artisant Designs, and I'm sorry for that. I didn't intentionally not tell you. I was scared because I didn't want to lose you. I knew you'd leave. Can you forgive me? Please say you'll forgive me." He lifts his hand as if to brush back my hair but falters, and his hand falls away.

"I hate the way I'm feeling right now, like I've lost everything I've worked so hard to hold on to. It was right there and now it's gone. It makes me feel unworthy and useless and lost, and I hate this feeling." It's the most vulnerable thing I've shared with anyone. I'm sure I'll look back on this conversation someday and realize if I was in a different frame of mind, I'd question why it's so easy for me to open up to Aaron, to be more honest with him than I am with myself. I'd question why he selflessly offered to be my family, as if he's searching for one too. But I don't have much experience with relationships or love or being in love.

"Can I show you something?" he asks.

"Show me what?"

"Where's Blueberry?" He glances around the room for the cat.

"He took off as soon as I pulled out his carrier. He doesn't like it. I only use it when I take him to the vet. He's either under your bed or hiding in the closet."

"Put some food out for him. It's near his dinnertime, and this might take a while. We have to drive through traffic," he says, and his concern for my pet thaws some of my disappointment and anger.

"Are we taking your car?"

"Yes, why?"

"I can't get over that you have a car and I didn't know about it."

"I didn't not tell you on purpose, if that's what you're thinking. I hardly drive it. I keep it parked on the company lot since I don't have a garage."

"Oh."

"Will you come with me?" He holds out his hand for mine. Our eyes meet, and I see that same plea for my trust as a silver lining around his gray irises.

I take his hand.

Aaron's car is parked on the street a few doors down, and he drives us to an old four-story brick building on A Street. There's no signage, the building fairly nondescript aside from a small parking lot with three stalls and a docking bay for deliveries and pickups. Aaron parks his car and takes us to the main entrance.

"Whose building is this?" I ask as he unlocks the door.

"Mine."

"The entire building?"

He nods and I'm floored. I'm realizing how little we know about each other. We talk about . . . well, stuff. But we've never discussed money or our financial portfolios—rather, my lack of one—since I insisted we keep our finances separate.

"This is a big building."

The corner of his mouth lifts into a quirky half smile as he pushes open the door, moving aside for me to enter first. "I rent out the other three floors as office space. But I've kept the first floor for my use."

"It's empty," I say, looking around the space that's open-concept except for a couple of partitioned sections that could become an office and conference room in the future.

"Hopefully, not for long. I have some stuff in the back."

He leads me to a set of double glass doors and pushes through them. I follow him into an even larger room, stopping just inside the doorway when he does. It looks like a warehouse. An assortment of tools, drills, blades, hammers, and chisels hang on one wall. A bay of lumber sorted by type and cut runs along another wall. Workbenches and planers and table saws are spaced out across the floor. Everything looks new and shiny. The room is twice the size of Artisant Designs and has one docking bay door.

"What is this place?" I ask, wary he's brought me to a competitor's shop.

He fiddles with the key he used to unlock the entrance. "You aren't the only one with dreams."

"This is *your* woodshop?" I notice an unfinished table in the center of the room that looks vaguely familiar. "That's my table." I rush over to it.

"Or a sorry attempt at it." Aaron joins me. "It's not you, it's me. Your video is perfect. I'm just not that skilled."

"Wait . . . You built this from my video?"

"Your idea works, Meli." Aaron looks at me in earnest. "You taught me how to do this. I've always admired woodworking, but you've given me a new appreciation for the craft. I never would have had the courage to pursue this if you hadn't been so passionate. Think of all the other people you can inspire."

I'm stunned and speechless and confused until, slowly, I make sense of what he's saying and what this place is and what he's wearing and where he's been all day and what he's been doing.

"Are you opening your own woodshop?" Here I'm struggling to keep mine together, and he's been building his own all along?

"Not mine. *Ours.* Or yours, if you want it. I could be a silent partner."

"Excuse me?"

"Let's be honest. Compared to you, I suck." He knocks his fist on the table.

I study his craftsmanship. It's not a piece I'd sell but one Aaron should be proud to display at home. "Your joinery is borderline amateurish, but you made a solid effort. I'd grade it a C." I wink, pointing a pistol finger at him, surprised I have it in me to tease when I'm a jumbled mess.

He laughs. "I've accepted I'll never build a table as good as you, or any craftsman you hire."

"That I hire?"

"Yes, you. What I'm good at is implementing great ideas, and you have a lot of those. I've got this building with all this space begging to be used, and you have a business that needs a home."

I rapidly wave my hands in front of me. "Wait, wait, wait . . . You're giving me this?"

"Not exactly. I'm proposing . . . that maybe . . . you'd consider having me as your partner. We can put the showroom up front with my office. You and your team would have this entire area to design and build out our catalog."

"You want to go into business with me?"

"If you'll have me."

"It's a terrible idea," I blurt. I can't work with someone I'm married to. Not that it's a real marriage, but I like Aaron. Like, *really* like him. And working together on a permanent basis would ruin any sort of rapport we have.

Aaron's face shutters. His mouth flattens.

"I didn't mean that."

"Yes, you did."

I deflate. He's being nice and sincere and overly generous, and I've been nothing but rude, mean, and ungrateful. "I'm sorry. I'm just . . ." I look around, overwhelmed. Everything is changing. It's all happening so fast.

And what about his career at the Savant House? He's due for his promotion to president. How does he expect to manage that job and run a business with me that potentially will compete with his?

I'm about to ask him when he confesses, "I don't want a divorce. I want to stay married, Meli."

I gape at him. His offer completely goes against everything I believe in. How can we work together and be together?

Aaron moves closer until I have to tilt my head to meet his eyes. "You're scared," he says, his voice low and not at all condescending. "You're afraid we can't be together if we work together. It's okay. I'm scared too. But I'm not so scared that it'll stop me from trying to make it work with you. I care about you too much."

A rush of blood warms my face and time slows. Is he telling me that he loves me? That he wants to be with me? For real? No more fake marriage and relationships.

"This was just supposed to be a marriage of convenience."

"Nobody says it can't be more."

"What you're proposing." I slowly shake my head. "It won't work. We can't manage both. *I* can't do both. We'll either hate working together or hate being married. Maybe not right away, but what about a year from now? Two years? Five? We already know about me. I'll start resenting you for making me feel guilty about spending too much time at the shop. You'll start resenting me for not spending enough time on us. I know this because it happened before. Paul—"

"Wasn't right for you. It never would have worked out. You need an appreciation for art to respect the artist."

"And you're the right person for me?" I challenge.

"I appreciate art, and I respect you," he says with a hint of a smile. "As for me being the right person for you? Only you know that. What I do know is you're right for me."

My heart races. "How are you so sure this will work?" Even the temptation of having access to this location isn't enough to scatter my doubts.

"I'm not sure. What I am willing to do is try." He moves in even closer. I can feel his breath on my forehead. I can smell the scent of his cologne. Both make my heart pound faster. He tilts up my chin with the crook of his finger. "I think we're pretty good together, Meli. And I think you think so too. All it takes is for one of us to believe in us to get the ball rolling. But imagine how incredible we can be together if we both believe in us. Imagine what we can accomplish together. You aren't your parents any more than I am mine. Just because working together strained their marriages doesn't mean the same will happen with us. It might even bring us closer. This is *our* journey."

He cradles my face with both hands. His thumb tenderly brushes my lips as his steel-gray eyes search my face. "What do you say, Meli? We're committed on paper. Do we make it official here?"

He presses a hand to my heart, and my breath catches. I'm overcome with emotion. He's fighting for us. He's fighting for me, which is new. I've never had anyone stand up for me or stand by me, especially lately. But to have a partner? To feel that connection? To be a true team?

Despite my fears, I can easily visualize what Aaron described: us working alongside each other by day, building a life together here and at home. We'd film tutorials, design furniture, meet with new clients, attend expos to market our work and gain inspiration for new pieces. We'd try new restaurants and explore new hobbies, attend concerts, and go to the theater. Meet up with friends. We'd dance and sing and read books and talk to just talk, about anything and everything. Together. And for the first time since my parents left me with Uncle Bear, the weight of the loneliness and despair I've carried most of my life doesn't feel so heavy. Aaron offered to be my family. If I'd have him.

I think I will have him. I want him to be my family.

I nod, giving him a watery smile.

Air rushes from him in relief. He lowers his forehead to mine and thumbs the tears off my lashes. "Thanks for giving me a chance."

"I'm giving us a chance."

He lifts his head and he's about to kiss me when his phone trills loudly. He mumbles an apology. "Let me silence this," he says, staring at the screen. His brow furrows and he apologizes again. "I have to take this."

I nod and he turns away to answer. "What is it now?" he asks in a clipped tone, walking away.

I tune out his conversation, giving him the privacy he seeks, and study my surroundings. This isn't Uncle Bear's building. But for all that I'd miss should I move Artisant Designs here, even I can see the potential. Didn't Emi say just hours ago that relocating could make Artisant even better? What if that's true? And what if I gain a new family through Aaron and the team we build? Kidder would be the first person I'd hire. I'd offer him a real job, not an internship.

Aaron finishes his call and returns. "I hate to ask this of you after what happened this morning. Not to mention the timing's really shitty."

"What's wrong?"

"Dinner with my mom tomorrow night. You up for it?"

"She's upset I didn't sign the postnup."

"Yes, but I don't think that's why she's asking us over."

I get the impression she isn't asking.

"Will you come?" His eyes implore mine.

"Do you think it's a good idea for me to go?"

"She asked me to bring you. I think she felt like you two got off on the wrong foot. It would mean a lot to me if you came."

I sense he wants moral support given we're both in this marriage of convenience.

And I did agree to "show" how into each other we supposedly are. Kaye needs to believe this marriage is real.

"If it's important to you, I'll go." He's done so much for me in the short time we've been together. I'll stand beside him, behind him, and up for him.

Aaron watches me, his gaze questioning, patient. He brushes hair off my forehead, and I feel his touch all the way to my fingertips. "You really are incredible, Meli."

I think the same about him.

I take his hand and twine our fingers. "Let's go home."

CHAPTER 20

BRACE FOR IMPACT

Kaye Borland lives in an exquisitely renovated five-bedroom home on two acres in Wellesley. Aaron parks his car in the circular drive of the home he and his sister grew up in and shuts off the engine. He doesn't make a move to get out of the car.

"Are you okay?" I ask, releasing my seat belt.

He nods, but I sense a reluctance to go inside, unless that's me projecting.

"Anything I should know or expect about tonight?" Waterboarding? Lie-detector test? Torture chamber? My thoughts are dryly sardonic, but I wouldn't put anything past Kaye after yesterday morning's impromptu visit.

"We're just having dinner."

"Are Charlie and Murphy coming?"

"Not that I know of."

Graham, Aaron's dad, won't be here. He lives in Newton with his second, much younger wife, Oriana. Her name means "a fresh start," Aaron explained, and candidly, Graham had wanted exactly that: a fresh start after divorcing Kaye. Graham and Oriana leave for Florida tomorrow morning to embark on a four-week cruise to South America.

"I haven't spoken with Charlie since yesterday morning," Aaron discloses in a tone that tells me everything might not be right between them.

"When she told you your mom was coming to see me?" I ask and he nods. "Is she upset with you?"

He sighs. "Yes, at the moment. I'll explain after dinner." He takes my hand and rubs the back of it, looking quite dashing in his dark-wash jeans, casual-print button-down shirt, and blue sport coat. He polished off the look with brown derby shoes. His hair is a shaggy tousle I'm tempted to run my fingers through. I'm also tempted to whisk him away for a night of cocktails and jazz music at a club downtown, if only to lighten his mood and avoid another run-in with Mommie Dearest.

"All right." I give him a small smile so he knows I'm okay with that.

We didn't have much time to talk today about anything other than Artisant Design's relocation; otherwise, he might have explained the situation with Charlie already. When we weren't talking about the shop, I was trying to reach Uncle Bear and Mom. If my uncle is serious about transferring ownership, I want that on paper. I left them both messages, asking for the buy-sell agreement, if one exists, drawn up when Grandpa Walt formed the LLC or when Uncle Bear assumed ownership. The agreement would outline the transfer process. He, with Mom's assistance, will need to update the business license and supplier contracts to reflect the ownership change. Otherwise, I have to negotiate new contracts, which could give our suppliers an opportunity to increase their rates.

"Don't worry. Mom will be on her best behavior. She won't single you out, not in front of me," Aaron says.

"It's not that. I'm thinking about you and Charlie." I hold his hand in both of mine. He and his sister are close. I'm worried for him. I just hope my not signing the postnup isn't the cause.

"I'm fine, really. It's temporary. She'll get over it." He kisses the back of my hand. "Let's do this so we can go home," he says, opening the door.

How ironic. With a dry smile, I open my door. I'd kill to have Mom invite me over for dinner, and Aaron can't get through this evening fast enough.

After my first impression of his mom, I expected Kaye to have a house filled with staff. But she answers the door wearing a stained apron, of all things, over a black silk blouse and pressed white pants. Apparently, she cooked our dinner. Not a hired chef.

"I'm so glad you made it, dear." Kaye hugs Aaron first, then me, catching me completely by surprise. I almost drop the bouquet I bought on our way here. She also dives right into the heart of the matter. "We didn't meet under the best of circumstances, so I appreciate you coming, Melissa." She speaks with an exuberance at complete odds with the cold, calculating business executive I met yesterday. The one who insisted she doesn't want to get to know me. It's also not lost on me she's invited us onto her turf.

"We wouldn't miss this," Aaron placates. "What's for dinner?" He sniffs the air as we enter the house. "Smells . . ." He frowns. "Smells good. I can't place it. What did you cook?"

Kaye gives me a flat look. "It never changes, does it? Thirty-two years old and he still asks the same question every time he visits. 'What's for dinner?'"

"It does smell good," I agree.

"Excellent, because we're having buttermilk fried chicken legs, corn on the cob, and potato rolls. You remember whose favorite that was, don't you, Aaron?"

Aaron stands in the shadows of the foyer, hanging my light sweater on the coatrack, but I swear the color drains from his face.

"What's the occasion, Mom?" he asks in a tight voice.

"No occasion. I had a craving for comfort food. Are those for me?" Kaye asks of the flowers.

"Oh, yes." I give her the bouquet of alstroemeria flowers in a rainbow of colors.

"Cute." She hands the flowers off to Aaron. "Be a dear and put these in water for me."

"Of course." He juggles the wine we brought with the bouquet, apologizing for his mom with a look.

Kaye takes us into the kitchen, and if it weren't for a pot of cooling cooking oil and grease spots on the stove, I would have gambled she ordered KFC takeout. Her kitchen smells exactly the same.

"Dinner's ready, so let's sit right down." She removes the crispy fried chicken legs warming in the oven and sets the tray on the stove. Using tongs, she transfers the legs to a ceramic bowl.

"What can I help with?" I offer as Aaron puts the flowers in a vase of water and opens the bottle of wine.

"Grab the corn and rolls." She points to them on the large island. "We're eating on the screened-in porch out back. Aaron, darling, bring the plates and utensils. They're stacked behind you."

He recorks the wine, tucks the bottle under his arm, and picks up the plates and utensils. I get the bread basket and platter of corn. Kaye leads the way, and when we reach the porch, Aaron's step falters. He stares at the picnic table decked out with a red-checkered tablecloth.

Then he pulls himself together. "Where'd the table come from, Mom?" He sets down the plates and wine. "I thought you got rid of it."

The table seems like an oddity among the wrought iron patio furniture with plush cushions. Definitely out of place in Kaye's house of pristine white walls, polished walnut floors, and Savant House–catalog furniture.

"Your father had it." Kaye puts down the bowl of chicken and inspects the tabletop. She snaps her fingers. "I forgot the salad. Start serving yourselves. I'll be right back."

"What's wrong?" I ask Aaron after she leaves.

"Nothing." A tic pops in his cheek from gritting his teeth. We sit beside each other on a bench. He glances at me with a forced smile and rubs my back. Something about this table bothers him.

Kaye returns with a tossed green salad and sits across from us. Aaron pours the wine and we fill our plates. After a quick toast, I bite into a chicken leg. The meat is succulent and the skin crispy with just the right mix of spice.

"This is really good," I tell Kaye.

She's pleased and actually smiles. It completely changes her face. Now I see Aaron in there. Kaye is a beautiful woman when she isn't trying to appear so frightening.

"It's an old family recipe. It's been way too long since I've made it, but tonight felt like the right occasion. Don't you agree, Aaron? You're here; you brought your lovely wife."

Aaron smiles stiffly at his mother. He doesn't touch the chicken.

"Thank you for cooking this for me," I say. Though in reality, I'm shocked. I can't quite figure her out. Does she like me or not? Is she upset I didn't sign the postnup, or is all forgiven? Maybe she does want us to start over.

Then she goes and says, "I didn't do this for you."

I flinch and glance at Aaron. Did I hear her right?

"Mom." His tone is a warning as they stare at each other across the table. Kaye glances away first.

"Well." She leans back and rubs her hands on the napkin over her lap. "I'm just pleased you both could make it out here on such short notice."

"Of course," I say after a beat, feeling like I need to acknowledge her when Aaron doesn't. He still hasn't taken a bite. Rather he's using his fork to nudge salad around his plate.

For the rest of the meal, our conversation remains relatively pleasant. Kaye talks about meeting a friend of hers for lunch, giving Aaron updates about the people who run in their social circle, adding footnotes for me as to who they are and how they know them, why they're important to her. At one point it becomes clear to me she's talking about Fallon's mom. Kaye asks Aaron if he's seen Fallon lately.

"I haven't." He splits a bread roll in half.

"Well, if you do talk to her, tell her to call me. She's been rude, not returning any of my messages."

"How's Dad?" Aaron changes the subject. "Did he tell you what time is his and Oriana's flight to Florida tomorrow?"

Kaye sets down her fork. "Why did you have to go and bring them up? You know I don't like talking about that twat."

I gape at Kaye, then I look at Aaron to see his reaction. He has a staunch smile plastered on his face, but his foot is tapping under the table as her words hang in the air and an incongruous silence falls over us. I find her name-calling of her ex-husband's wife as off-putting as I found her lack of faith in Aaron yesterday morning. Do I even want to know what she says about me when I'm not around?

Absolutely not.

I no longer feel hungry, and I really don't want to be sitting here. In fact, I'd be happy to leave anytime. Now would be great, I think, looking at Aaron.

"Oriana has a name and she is his wife." Aaron coming to his stepmother's defense fills me with admiration and respect.

"She's as old as your brother would have been."

Aaron sits, unmoving. He then slowly, purposefully, puts down the two halves of his roll. Rage simmers under a surface of forced calm.

"Your father is more than twice her age," Kaye goes on. "Best thing he did was to have her sign the prenup. Can you imagine her on the board of directors when he goes belly-up?"

I have a hard time swallowing my corn as I stare wide-eyed at Kaye. Nope. She's still fuming over my lack of cooperation.

"If you must know, he canceled his cruise. With his retirement and Charlie stepping in as president now that the board has voted me in as CEO, I need his help with the transition. She wasn't trained as thoroughly as you. You're fortunate you still have a sister, Aaron."

I turn to Aaron. "I thought you were going to be president."

"I should have known there was a reason you invited us tonight," he says to his mom, his gaze fixed on her. "You always favored the dramatic,"

Kaye looks from him to me, then back to her son, and she slowly smiles. This one isn't a warm smile. "He hasn't told you?" she asks me.

"She doesn't know yet," Aaron answers.

"Told me what?"

"Mother," he says, terse. "Let me tell her on my own time."

Kaye turns to me. "He was fired."

Shock ripples through me.

"Is that true?" I ask Aaron. It would explain why he offered to go into business with me. He lost his job. "Why did she fire you?"

"You didn't sign the postnup," Kaye answers for Aaron. "I told you to be wary of the consequences if you refused."

———

Dinner spirals from there with Aaron announcing he's done for the night. He thanks his mom and tells her that we're leaving. As if she timed it, like I suspected she'd timed her arrival at Artisant with the email Uncle Bear received about the Savant House's retracted offer, Kaye receives a call that pulls her away from the table. I look at Aaron and my head spins. His own mother fired him.

He's practically shaking with pent-up rage. He stands abruptly. "Will you give me a moment? I need to take a walk."

"All right." Worried for him, I don't request that we just go home, and I watch him leave the screened-in porch and cross the yard. I would be outraged too. This whole dinner was a setup for her to humiliate him in front of me.

At a loss for what to do while I wait, I clear the table, which is more than Kaye deserves. I rinse the plates and put away the food, then return to the porch. Aaron has returned. With his hands in his pockets, he stands at the patio edge where the bricks meet the lawn. He stares up at the sky. I join him and look up. The stars are more vivid here than in the city.

"Beautiful night," I say.

"It is," he says, and after a moment, "I'm sorry about her."

"It's not your fault." No more than it's my fault for how my parents treat me.

"She hasn't cooked fried chicken since Liam died. It was his favorite."

"Aaron." I touch his back.

"That picnic table?" He thrusts his chin over his shoulder. "It's from when we were kids. He loved eating at that table with the family."

My mouth moves around silent words. I don't know what to say to make him feel better other than, "I'm sorry."

"Pretty pathetic, if you ask me."

"For her to do that to you? It was obscene." Not to mention disgusting, repulsive, shocking, and abusive. I could go on but I don't need to share what we both already know.

He stares at the sky. "It's nothing compared to what I did." He glances down at me with a wan smile. "She was different before Liam died. She used to be a good mom. Fun. Hard to believe, but we were close once."

"Why didn't you tell me she fired you?"

His throat works. "It happened at Mount Holyoke," he says as if he didn't hear me as he stares into the woods bordering the yard.

It takes me a second to realize what he's talking about. "Where Liam died?"

He nods. "It was my fault."

"No . . ." He can't take the blame for that. But as I think it, I wonder if this is what Charlie was talking about when Aaron told her we were getting married. If so, he's been holding on to this blame for so long.

"We grew up hiking there. Sometimes we went free-climbing. We never made it that far up any route. They weren't well marked and we weren't very good. But that one time . . ." He speaks slowly, looking beyond the trees. "I talked him into a route he wasn't keen on. Told him I'd do his chores for the month if he went up with me. He'd do anything to get out of cleaning the fish tank." A dry, hollow laugh. "We made it above the tree line when a loose rock under my foot gave way. I panicked and threw an arm out, knocked Liam in the shoulder." Aaron roughly swallows. "He lost his grip and fell into a tree. *Snap-snap-snap.* That's all I heard, the branches breaking as he went down. He didn't even yell. Not a sound from him."

The snapped branch on his tattoo.

"Aaron." I am crying. I reach for his hand.

He flinches and tightly folds his arms. "God, I miss him."

My heart cracks for him and the brother he lost. As much as I want to pull him into my arms and hold him, I refrain since he doesn't want to be touched. Whatever this is, whatever he needs to express, it has to run its course without my interference.

"My parents blame me. Hell, I blame me. I was the reckless one, always doing stupid shit, getting into trouble. But with Liam gone, they shifted their expectations of him to me. They ordered me to straighten out and get my shit together because one day, the Savant House would be mine. I didn't want to work there. I wanted to build furniture and travel and raise a family far from anything that had to do with Savant. I was that typical rebellious second child." He gives me a sad smile. "I didn't appreciate what I had. But I didn't argue with them. I didn't have a right to. I did exactly what I was told. I felt too guilty not to.

"So I applied to college, went to Yale like Liam would have, then went to work at Savant, working wherever they put me, loving and hating it at the same time. I thought about quitting, and a few times, I worked up the courage to do it. But I could never go through with it. The whole reason why I was there is because Liam wasn't.

"Then I met you. Beautiful you. There's so much life in you." He turns to fully face me. His fingertips briefly touch my cheek. "You know exactly who you are and what you want, and you aren't afraid to go for it. You fucking ran out on your own wedding. I mean, who does that? From the moment I met you, Meli, I've admired you for your bravery. I've looked up to you for your ambition. You inspired me. You're so passionate about your work and life, taking the good and the bad in stride. Lucky me; some of that rubbed off. I need to live for myself. I need to go after what I want, which isn't working at the family business for the rest of my life."

It occurs to me this is why he's compelled to always please his parents, especially his mom. Why he finally agreed to marry Fallon. He's been living up to their expectation of being the dutiful son because he believes he's to blame for Liam's death.

His first horrible mistake. I recall Kaye's words from yesterday and feel sick to my stomach on Aaron's behalf.

"Anyway." He runs a hand through his hair, agitated. "I've known since I was eighteen my parents would force my spouse to sign their prenup and that they'd disown me if she didn't. I knew what was in that agreement."

"Fallon would have signed it."

"She would have." Aaron's eyes shimmer and he cradles my face with shaking hands. "Your drive to be independent, to do everything on your own, to control your destiny . . . It isn't a flaw, Meli. It's one of the most stunning, enchanting things about you. It's what I love about you."

My breath shudders. "You gambled I wouldn't sign it." And in doing so, he forced his parents to follow through on their threat: to disown him, and in turn, to fire him. Based on my own brief interactions with Kaye, I know she would have made his life miserable had he quit on his own.

But a knot forms in my stomach, tightening as an unsettling thought comes to mind.

"Is this what you wanted to get from marrying me, for your parents to disown you?" I recall what he said to me when we'd agreed to our marriage of convenience. *Don't forget. We each want something out of this.* "Why didn't you tell me?"

He hesitates and I step back, his arms falling to his sides. I'm not sure I want to hear what he's about to say.

"You have a generous heart, Meli, but sometimes even the most generous shouldn't always be so."

"What is that supposed to mean?"

"I worried you'd sign it if you knew what would happen to me if you refused. I worried that you'd sign it even after I said that I didn't care if they disowned me because you wouldn't want to feel responsible for them doing just that. Your greatest desire is to feel close to your family. The last thing you'd want is to see mine push me away."

"I can't say in good conscience I would have ever signed that agreement, but I wish you would have trusted me to make the right choice, just like you'd asked me to trust you that our marriage would convince the Savant House to reconsider their acquisition offer."

"You're right. I should have. But I'm man enough to admit I was scared. I didn't want to talk you into something you otherwise wouldn't do."

I peer up at him in a new light. It makes sense Aaron has an innate fear of talking people into doing things they wouldn't normally agree to. It most likely stems from when he'd pressured his brother into free-climbing. It would explain why he was so adamant about knowing he hadn't manipulated me into marrying him. That the decision had been 100 percent mine. Now that I know about Liam, I see why Aaron behaves as he does.

Still, I feel uneasy about all of this.

I turn from him and look into the woods. "I guess we both got what we wanted from our marriage."

I feel Aaron's panic before I hear it. "What are you saying?"

"I don't know." On the one hand I'm reeling from what he told me about his brother and the ensuing fallout that's slowly torn his family apart. That couldn't have been easy for him to admit, let alone share. But on the other hand, I can't help thinking that through his fear of not manipulating me into marriage, he'd done exactly that.

CHAPTER 21

No Plan B

We don't talk much on the ride home, which is weird for us. We're always talking. Aaron keeps his attention on the road, but I feel him look over at me from time to time. I stare out my window at the city skyline sparkling against the backdrop of night, thinking about us.

I don't want to say Aaron used me. We used each other. That's why we entered into a marriage of convenience. But I was transparent about my reasons for getting married. From the beginning, he's known owning Artisant Designs has been my end goal. Aaron, though, was more translucent than transparent about his goal, keeping certain things to himself, and I can't help comparing how much that reminds me of Uncle Bear and my parents. Nobody tells me anything because I'm not important enough to them.

I know I tend to act rashly. I've done so on more than one occasion. And yes, maybe they worried I'd overreact and do something to spoil their plans. But by keeping everything from me, they, in essence, stole my agency.

"Are you okay?" Aaron asks when he parks in front of the town house and we get out of the car.

"I'm fine," I answer with a tight smile. We both know I'm not.

We climb into bed and we don't sleep. I toss throughout the night. I can't turn off my brain. I don't think Aaron could either. Come morning, he looks as exhausted as I feel.

"Do you want to get coffee at Perkatory?" he asks while we stand at the dual sinks in the en suite bathroom, brushing our teeth.

"I can't. I have to work." The chair Uncle Bear started won't finish itself. My own orders need work. I have to reach Dad today to ask him about the desk he's building. I couldn't find a job order, so I don't know when the client expects it.

Somewhere between these projects, I need to pack up the shop before escrow closes on the building. Everything must go to storage until I figure out what I'm going to do with my life. Because I don't think going into business with Aaron is the right thing to do, not if his lack of transparency is how he handles issues in our relationship, business or otherwise.

Aaron's expression flattens. He rinses his toothbrush and drops it in the holder. "What's wrong, Meli? What did I say to upset you?" His gaze seeks mine in the mirror, but I dodge eye contact.

"I need time to think. There've been a lot of changes lately, and I'm trying to process everything." I rinse my mouth and wipe my chin with a towel. "I'll be at Artisant all day. Someone has to finish Dad's and Uncle Bear's orders if they aren't going to."

"I can help."

"Thanks, but . . . I think I need some space."

His eyes dim. "I understand. I'll be around if you need me."

I nod and he leaves the bathroom. I hear him in the closet getting dressed, and I slip out the door.

I arrive at Artisant Designs half expecting my family to be there. They aren't, and I'm disappointed all over again. But as I crank the music and go to work on my set of bedside tables, then cut the lumber for the armchair seat on Uncle Bear's project, as I wait for someone—Mom, Dad, Bear—to return my calls, I steadily grow angrier. By the end of the day, I'm fuming over their silent treatment and how they've treated me in general through this entire situation. I need to speak up for myself.

I close up the shop and board the T to see if I can find my parents or Uncle Bear at our apartment building. On the ride over I mentally talk through my argument. Yes, I'd intentionally married so the acquisition deal would backfire. But what I did to them was no worse than what they'd done to me. Had I known Uncle Bear sold the building and why—which I still don't completely understand because he hasn't given me a full explanation—I believe we could have come to an agreement about what to do with the business and my part in it.

But they never gave me a chance.

Maybe that's why I don't get off on my parents' floor when I take the elevator up or press the button for my uncle's floor. They don't value me. Instead, I get off on my floor and knock on Emi's door.

"Meli! What are you doing here? Where's Aaron?" She pokes her head into the hallway.

"He's at his place."

Her brows dip at my annoyed tone. "Uh-oh. Did you ask him about the building?"

I nod. "Can I come in?"

"Of course. I was just heating up leftover lasagna. Want some?"

"Sure." But I doubt I'll eat. I'm too worked up.

"Talk to me," she says, serving me a plate, and I do.

We settle on the couch to eat. Or she eats. I get up to pace as I explain everything that's happened since we spoke the other day. I tell her about Aaron finding me at the town house packing after he came looking for me at Stone & Bloom, and about the building that he showed me that I never knew he owns, and that he wants us to go into business together. I complain about my parents, sharing my frustrations and hurt over them ghosting me, which is only stressing me out further. Then I tell her about dinner at Kaye's and Aaron's confession afterward and how I learned about the real reason he'd married me, that he deliberately hadn't told me about the nuptial agreement he knew his parents would insist I sign.

I even share with her that I ache for him about the loss of his brother, even though I don't tell her that Aaron blames himself for Liam's death. That's not my story to tell. But I do tell her what he asked yesterday—to consider our marriage more than a convenience—and that for a short time, perhaps for just a few moments, Aaron had made me feel wanted and loved. A person of value, a very important person in his life. I tell her that I think he's in love with me. Or he was before I told him I needed space.

It all comes pouring out of me. I'm a burst dam of thoughts and feelings, and I can't stop the flood of anger and frustration and disappointment and regret.

"After all that," I say animatedly when I finish, "I still can't separate what he did to me from what my parents and uncle have done. They just push me off to the side and make plans around me. Plans, you can bet, that affect me and my future."

"Wait, wait, wait." Emi swipes her arms in front of her face. "I get what you're saying, Meli, and you're absolutely right. They should have included you. They should have gotten your support, and you have every right to be upset with them. You definitely need to talk with your parents and uncle about that. Don't brush this off and let them continue to treat you as if you're not important. You've put up with that for way too long. You also need to talk to Aaron, *your husband*. But do you hear yourself?" she asks, standing up.

"Uh . . . yeess?" I drag out the word so that it ends up sounding like a question.

She stares at me with big, round eyes and a slight shake to her head, as if she's saying, *Hello! There is something right in front of you. Don't you see it?*

I stare back. "What am I missing?" There must be something I'm not getting.

Then I do see it.

"Oh my God." I press my hands to my cheeks. Aaron tells me about his brother, about how his family blames him for Liam's death. He reveals this after we sat through the most painfully awkward family dinner I've ever experienced with a woman who, in front of her son's wife, humiliates him by doing everything short of vocalizing out loud that he is, in fact, responsible for his brother's death. All of this happened after yesterday's conversation when he proposed for us to go into business together, admitted that he wants our marriage of convenience to be a real marriage, then, quite possibly, confessed he's in love with me. Of course, he wouldn't say it straight out because of what we put about saying *I love you* on our list. We never intended to fall for each other.

Unless he did intend exactly that.

Has he been in love with me all this time? Could getting me to fall in love with him have been his real endgame all along?

Then here I am, after he bared his soul, upset he was only 90 percent transparent about his motivations for marrying me, of which he's already apologized for, something else my parents and uncle have yet to do: apologize. Not only that, but Aaron also tried to talk to me about it this morning, tried to get to the heart of what's bothering me in an effort to fix this—yet another thing my parents haven't tried to do: repair our relationship. And what do I do? I lump his behavior with theirs. I brush him off. I push him away. I tell him I need space. When I should have stood up for him to his mother. And behind him. And beside him. And . . .

My arms fall to my sides. "I'm a terrible person." I've been caught so off guard. Kaye's dinner was all shock and awe. I mean, who behaves like that? I shouldn't have let her get away with how she treated my husband.

"No, you're not." Emi's mouth purses to the side, her way of saying "I told you so" without actually saying it. "But am I right to guess you figured out this was a simple case of crossed wires with a man who obviously adores you because you do mean something to him?"

"What have I done?" He's going to leave me. He's going to give me the divorce I asked for.

"You had a misunderstanding. Nothing any other married couple hasn't experienced before. Big question is, do you want to stay married?"

My head nods all on its own. *Wow.* I did not see this coming. But I can't imagine not having Aaron in my life.

"Do you want to go into business with him? Because, damn girl, with his industry experience and connections and your wood skills and that building he owns. And, fuck," she says, laughing. "Everything is awesome! Watch out, Savant House. You two have it going on. You're like the next Chip and Joanna Gaines. I'm seeing a reality show on HGTV. A podcast about couples going into business together and succeeding."

"Okay, okay, don't get carried away. But yes. Yes, I want it all. I'm so fucking scared, but I want it. I want him. Oh my gosh, I've been so selfish, Emi. I need to go talk to him. I'm sorry, I have to go." I hurriedly pick up my untouched plate.

"Leave it." Emi snags the plate before I drop the lasagna in my flustered state, and I rush for the door. "Don't forget to tell him you love him too," she hollers after me.

I stop, turning back to her with huge eyes and splayed fingers, my mouth gaping open.

She's grinning.

Do I love him?

Yes, yes, I do. I am in love with Aaron Borland. *My husband.*

What I feel for him is vastly different from what I've previously felt with anyone. It's more vibrant and richer and unyielding and never-ending. I just know without a doubt that with this kind of love, I can have it all—Aaron, my craft, our business. It's the kind of love I wouldn't risk losing any more than I'd risk giving up one for the other.

I squeal and, after running back to Emi, throw my arms around her. "Thank you for everything."

"I want all the details later," Emi shouts before I shut her door, and I laugh.

I order a ride so I can get to Aaron faster. Then I text him I'm on my way home, and that yes, I'm ready to talk. I'm so elated to see him, to tell him everything I'm feeling, that when I arrive, I throw open the door and shout, "I'm home!"

But Aaron isn't alone. I catch him and Fallon in a tight embrace. They jump apart at my sudden appearance.

I look between them. "What's going on?"

Fallon glances away and dabs her face, but not before I notice her red and swollen eyes. She's been crying. Aaron turns to me in a daze, his mouth slack and turned down at the corners. He says my name, then two words that destroy everything I've just convinced myself I could have.

"Fallon's pregnant."

All the epiphanies I rushed over here to tell Aaron wither and die on my tongue. I look to Fallon for confirmation. She nods tightly, hugging her arms. And I see it, their future. Them as parents cooing over a perfectly swaddled baby with a full life ahead. Dance lessons, soccer games, piano practices, birthday parties, family vacations, movie nights.

Then I see something else: my part in this family as Aaron's wife and the stepmother of his child. Parenthood will be an all-consuming role because I won't be like my parents. I will love and value Aaron's baby as much as I love and value him. But with the significant demand on my time and attention that raising a child requires, where does that leave room for my pursuits? How am I supposed to balance the passion for my craft, a marriage, and launching a business with Aaron, *and* parenthood?

No. I shake my head, hardly aware I'm backing away. I was fooling myself earlier. As much as I want it all, I can't manage it all, not according to my track record. Aaron will come to resent me, and the thought of disappointing him is too much.

"I'm sorry," Aaron says, so impassioned that I barely keep a lid on the emotions threatening to boil over inside me.

"Don't apologize. Not for this." Fallon didn't get pregnant to trap Aaron, not when she's the one who broke up with him. And she didn't get pregnant to break us up. I've been married to Aaron for only a few weeks. I wasn't even in the picture when she conceived. "I guess congratulations are in order."

Fallon's bottom lip trembles when she attempts to smile. "Thank you," she whispers.

"Meli . . ." Aaron shakes his head. He reaches for my arm.

I step back. "No."

"Can we talk?"

"About what? You're going to be a dad. You have a family to raise," I say. He told me last night about the dreams he had to give up.

"We haven't decided—"

I don't let him finish. I run upstairs, taking the steps two at a time. In his room, I shove what clothes I can into my luggage and have Blueberry tucked inside his carrier within minutes. Leaving now is best for us both. He won't have to worry about dividing his focus between me and his new family, and I won't be made to feel guilty for devoting too much attention to my craft.

Aaron is coming up the stairs when I head down. We both stop. "Where's Fallon?" I ask, looking around.

"She left. Meli, I didn't know. She wasn't going to tell me. I called to make sure my mom wasn't harassing her, and she told me she's been purposefully avoiding her but that we needed to talk. She asked if she could come over," he explains as I lumber downstairs with the carrier and suitcase. He reaches for Blueberry, trying to help.

"Please don't." I move past him, determined to leave before I become a blubbering mess.

"Where are you going?"

"Home, my apartment. That home."

His face contorts like he can't believe I'm actually leaving him. Then panic fills his eyes and he scours my face with a hungry intensity. He's desperate for a way to change my mind. Blueberry yowls his annoyance. Through the front window, I see the car I ordered upstairs pulling up to the house. I set down my luggage and open the front door.

"Meli, would you please listen?"

"You can't marry her if you're still married to me."

"Who said anything about marriage?" Aaron picks up my bag, and after a brief tug-of-war, I give up and take off down the porch steps. He follows me out with my suitcase. He drops it beside me on the sidewalk. "Fallon and I haven't agreed to anything yet. We aren't planning to marry," he says when I open the passenger door and put Blueberry inside.

"Can you pop the trunk, please?" I ask the driver. She does, and when I try to pick up my luggage, Aaron grabs the case. He stares at me imploringly, holding my luggage hostage.

"You don't have to go."

A fist squeezes my heart. "We both know this wasn't supposed to last. Fallon needs you, Aaron. Your baby needs you." I get in the car and close the door.

Aaron watches me through the window like he's committing me and this moment, this tsunami of feeling, to memory. It hurts too much to look at him, so I keep my eyes forward.

The driver opens the front passenger window. "Would you shut the trunk?" she asks.

"Meli," Aaron says one last time.

I shake my head and the tears come. I hear and feel Aaron stow the suitcase and shut the trunk, slamming the door on our future. The car pulls into traffic, but I don't feel the relief I expected. I only feel like the terrible person I told Emi that I was.

CHAPTER 22

HO'OPONOPONO

A few days later, Emi and I sit across from each other on the couch in my apartment. Blueberry has settled back into the familiar surroundings. After inspecting every corner in my bedroom and the living area, he hopped onto the couch and curled up to sleep, a furry croissant sinking into the backrest cushion. Other than to eat and use the litter box, he hasn't left his spot since we arrived. He won't even sleep with me, my punishment for taking him away from Aaron. I'm sure Blueberry is depressed and missing him. I know I am, which is probably why I share with Emi how Aaron and I met.

After I passed out from the champagne I'd drunk when I boarded, Aaron woke me from a buzzed slumber by poking me in the arm. At first, I felt a light touch, softer than the brush of hair against skin. He shook my shoulder next, then he poked his finger hard in my upper arm. I came fully awake with a start, kicking the seat in front of me as I looked around in a panic. I didn't remember why I was on a plane. But two pressing thoughts instantly rushed at me: I'd run scared from my own wedding, and I needed to pee.

Through folds of gossamer, I searched for the seat belt, unbuckling it and standing at the same time. I knocked into the opened tray table I hadn't noticed, and plates rattled.

"Whoa." My seatmate balanced my bottled water to keep it from toppling. "I woke you up, figuring you'd want dinner before it got cold."

I blinked at the chicken breast drowning in a mushroom cream sauce and the ungarnished mixed vegetables, trying to process what he was telling me. But I had to pee so bad, and I was still so foggy from sleep that I couldn't make sense of anything.

"If you're like my sister on her wedding day, you probably haven't eaten anything except the champagne when you boarded. I asked the attendant to leave you a tray. You need to eat."

I needed to pee.

"Move, please." I struggled to get out of my seat.

"Why?" His brows pulled to the center as if a seamstress sewed them together.

"I have to use the bathroom," I said with some urgency.

"Oh. *Ohhhh.*" He was out of his seat in an instant, taking our dinners with him and balancing the trays with a skill that under normal circumstances might have been admirable.

But nothing about that day had been normal. I was operating in new territory. For months, my wedding day had been planned down to the second. I'd woken that morning fully expecting to be married by evening. But I'd done the most spontaneous thing in my life, and my immediate future resided in a fog bank.

Gathering the skirt and train, I scooted from the row and up the aisle, squeezing into the narrow lavatory. I turned to close the door, and in my search for the latch, the train spilled into the aisle.

"Shit." I pulled the train back and shoved the bifold door. It didn't budge. I tried again. The door closed partially only to bounce back open. "Fuuuuuuck," I cursed through gritted teeth. The mountain of fabric blocked the door. Where was a bridesmaid when you needed one? I couldn't close the door on my own—impossible in that dress.

I poked my head into the aisle. The flight attendant was busy serving dinner. The nearest person out of their seat was my seatmate. He stood holding our trays, talking to the woman seated in the row across from us. If I'd overheard correctly when we boarded, she was traveling with her husband to Las Vegas for their fortieth wedding anniversary. They planned on taking in a show and gambling.

Good for them for having a long, successful marriage. I couldn't imagine Paul and I would have lasted for a fraction of that time, not if our marriage was as stifling as the months leading up to the wedding. Or as stifling as that dress.

"Hey," I said to get my seatmate's attention, wishing I'd had the forethought to ask him his name. "Hey you."

A front-row passenger curiously looked up at me, then back at my seatmate, who was chatting like he could stand there all day, holding our food.

"Guy with the trays," I said a little louder with more desperation.

"Excuse me, sir." The front row passenger tapped my seatmate's arm and pointed at me.

He finally looked over, his face pulled in confusion as if wondering what could I possibly want with him.

"Help."

He cocked his head. If his hands were free, he'd be pointing at himself and asking, "Me?"

I widened my eyes, hoping he caught on to my desperation. It took a second, but he clued in.

He set our food on our seat trays and came over. "What's up?"

"Can you push in the rest of my dress?"

"What? Oh. Sure." He looked down and picked up the errant layer I couldn't reach and handed it to me.

"Close the door, please."

He did and I fumbled to locate the latch. The door popped open a crack. I growled in frustration and toed the door fully open. He was headed back to our row. "Wait!"

He backed up to the lavatory doorway, his brows lifted in question.

"Hold the door closed, please."

"You want me to stand here while you . . ." He didn't finish that thought. And if my bladder hadn't been about to burst, I would have teased him about the deep blush smearing across his cheeks. His skin was like a mood ring.

"I can't reach the lock. You have to hold it closed from your side."

I didn't wait for his agreement. I shut the door with a huge sigh of gratitude when it didn't bounce open again. Thank goodness he held it from the other side because, through a miraculous feat of contortion, I was able to do my business. I even managed to wash and dry my hands.

Then I caught sight of my reflection. I looked haggard. Smudged mascara with hair as stiff as straw from the amount of hairspray the stylist had used, sticking up all over my head. There I was, on a plane to Vegas, of all god-awful places, because I had no plan after I'd run. All I'd known was that I had wanted out—out of my commitment to marry Paul and out of our relationship. I now wanted out of that dress.

Damn, it was scratchy.

And confining.

I struggled to catch my breath, trying to itch and scratch. But I couldn't reach that one spot between my shoulder blades that was driving me bonkers. When I did try, I lost control of the dress. The skirt exploded in the confined space as I went nuts with the scratching and itching and poking.

"Argh!"

"You okay in there?"

Right. My seatmate. The reluctant bridesman.

I threw open the door. "Undress me."

"Excuse me?" He lurched back.

I gave him my back. "Unbutton me." I did a frustrated little dance in an attempt to reach the buttons on my own.

"Can't somebody else help you? The flight attendant—"

"Is busy doing her job. Please," I begged, glancing at him over my shoulder. I was too anxious and antsy and unnerved to wait while he hailed someone else. He stared down the tube of the plane with a look of desperation that surely matched my own. I was asking a lot of this stranger.

"Please." I spoke low and frantic, and he looked at me. Our eyes briefly met, and I noticed how gray his were, how delightful they looked against his lavender button-down shirt. That was the artist in me, always cataloging color schemes. "Trust me, I'm decent underneath." I tried nudging him toward agreement, as if assuring him would make our situation any less embarrassing. "I just need to get out of this dress." I stared at the curved wall behind the toilet, waiting to feel the buttons popping, giving my ribs that extra luxurious inch to breathe.

"There's so many."

I squeezed my eyes shut. Thirty-three buttons in all. I'd counted when one of Paul's sisters buttoned me up earlier that afternoon.

"They're so tiny."

I held my breath. *Please.*

I felt a featherlight touch against the exposed skin above the dress's bodice and the soft press of fingers against my back as one button came undone, then another, and another. *Thank God.*

I sighed loudly, dropping my chin. I was so grateful for his assistance and patience with me.

The first few buttons he unfastened in an inept start and stall, but he quickly found a rhythm. Before I knew it, he murmured, "Done," and stepped back.

Finally, freedom. I shrugged the dress off my shoulders. The puffed sleeves slid down my arms, and the plethora of tulle and silk flowed down my body to reveal a long, white slip that looked more like a fashionable, modern wedding dress than Cheryl's gown ever could, no matter how much magic her seamstress had spun.

I turned around, the movement sudden, and my seatmate's eyes widened before he averted his face. He rubbed the back of his neck. "I'm going to . . ." He pointed toward our seats and headed over.

I gleefully scooped up the dress. After hours—make that months—of feeling stifled, I could breathe. I stuffed the dress into the first overhead bin, fitting it into the crevices around a couple of pieces of luggage. I shut the compartment and turned to my seat, bumping into my seatmate, who was back to standing in the aisle with our dinner trays.

"You're getting good at that." I chanced a smile and took my tray from him as I scooted into our row. He followed me in and we collapsed in our seats with mortified giggles.

"If I ever fantasized *how* I'd join the mile-high club, it did not go like that," he said.

"Technically, that did not get you into the club. Though it is the first time I've been undressed by a stranger."

He laughed. "It's a safe bet I've never had a day like yours, and I don't even know what happened."

"Jilting grooms at the altar isn't your thing?"

"Ouch. Marriage isn't my thing. I'm Aaron, by the way. I probably should have introduced myself before I undressed you."

I shook the hand he offered and an electrified zing shot up my arm. "Oh, wow." My eyes shot wide open, and I stole a glance at his face to see if he had a similar reaction.

A faint smile played on his lips. "That was something."

"Uh, yeah it was," I stammered, quickly brushing a hand through my hair. "Um, I'm Meli."

"Hi, Meli. Pleasure to officially meet you."

———

"And that," I now tell Emi, "was our meet-cute."

"I think that's when you started falling for him." Emi grasps my hand. Having moved since I started talking, Blueberry purrs next to me in a contented sleep.

"I think you're right." I can admit that now. Back then, I couldn't process what I felt for him. I'd just left Paul, whom I thought I'd been in love with. But what I'd felt for him doesn't compare to the cyclone of emotions for Aaron swirling through me now. Plus, it didn't feel right, nor had I been ready to acknowledge any feelings for Aaron given my frame of mind at the time.

There's an old Hawaiian saying: *ho'oponopono.* I saw it on a coffee mug while Aaron and I browsed the Shops at Wailea. When I asked the meaning, the store's owner, a native Hawaiian woman born and raised on the Big Island of Hawaii, explained *ho'oponopono* is the ancient Hawaiian practice of forgiveness and reconciliation, both with others and with ourselves. I looked it up on my phone after we'd left the store and learned the word roughly translates to "set things right" or "move things back into balance" by cleansing yourself of bad feelings through forgiveness to develop self-love and improve self-esteem, especially at a time when needed most.

I think that's what Aaron and I did during the five days we spent in Maui. We paused our lives, reevaluated our choices in life, and put ourselves back into balance. I had been a runaway bride who lost sight of her goals, and he had been at a crossroad with his family and career. For five days, we lived inside a bubble of our own making.

Anyone who knows me wouldn't have believed I flew to Maui with a man I'd met and married only twenty-four hours earlier, let alone that I didn't *sleep* with him during our entire stay, even though we'd shared a king bed for five nights. I was very attracted to Aaron from the moment we first met, and I had on firsthand authority that the feeling was mutual. We kissed at our impromptu wedding, and for show on the flight to Maui, then later at Logan International, where we'd said goodbye. But for our entire stay in Maui, we hadn't done anything more than hold hands or sleep wrapped around each other because our bodies sought one another in our sleep. In our own way, we had been healing as we tried to understand ourselves better along with some of the decisions we'd made in the past.

I'd woken each morning entangled in Aaron's embrace, his arm over my waist and his face tucked into my hair or the curve of my shoulder. As we watched the sky lighten through our window with the ocean view, I'd threaded my fingers through his and we'd talked about everything that had come to mind.

Well, almost everything.

He never confided about his brother. I can't blame him for not opening up to me then. I hadn't told him about Dad's arrest and Mom's drug addiction. Shame is the fallen tree that blocks the path, forcing you onto another trail, our conversations veering from one topic to another. And at the time, we didn't expect to ever see one another again after we returned to reality.

But there was one particular night—it had to have been around 2:00 a.m. as we lay in the dark—the subject of children had come up. I guess it was inevitable. As children raised by parents who'd been indifferent toward us to some degree, it made sense we'd question whether we'd be like them with our own kids. Since I'd been pretty set on not marrying again, I didn't see myself with children.

"But Aaron felt differently," I say, trying to explain to Emi why leaving him was the right thing to do.

In Maui he told me that even though he had no plans to marry, he hoped to have children one day. If he was fortunate to be blessed with one, he intended to be the one thing his parents hadn't been: present. Because of the demands of their company and Graham being an older father, they hadn't been actively involved in raising Aaron and his siblings. Kaye and Graham had left that up to nannies and coaches and boarding schools.

"He's going to be a great father. I can't take that from him."

"How does being married to him keep him from being a great father?" Emi challenges.

"For one, he can't marry Fallon if he's still married to me."

"You said he doesn't want to marry her, and he told you five years ago he has no interest in marrying anyone."

"He says that now, but people change their minds. Look at how different my parents are with me now than when I was a kid. Or Aaron.

For a guy once opposed to marriage, he was totally ready to stay married to me. He changed his mind."

"Because he was married to *you*."

"Look, I had just convinced myself that I could devote equal amounts of attention to woodworking, running a business with Aaron, and being married to him. Throw parenthood into the picture? That's an equation for disaster. Either I'll start resenting him for pulling me away from my work or he'll resent me for spending too much time at the shop. I know it, Emi."

"But you love him. That should be enough."

"I don't think it is." Not only that, I'm afraid it won't be.

"What are you going to do about Artisant, then? Will you still rent from him?"

I sink back into the cushions. "I don't know what I'm going to do." Without Aaron involved, I seem to have lost interest in the shop. I know it's because I'm upset and depressed, which keeps me from thinking clearly. But I honestly don't know right now if I'll keep Artisant running or tell Uncle Bear to shut it down.

"Either way," I continue, "Aaron needs to devote his full attention to his future family and not worry about me."

Emi sighs, and I can tell she doesn't agree with me. "I love you, Meli, but I think your nobility is misplaced. Was leaving better for him or for you?"

"Both of us."

Her eyes narrow. "Are you sure there isn't something more going on here?"

I pull back. "What do you mean?"

"I don't know," she says and studies me through narrowed eyes. "You were pretty quick to leave him. You didn't even give him a chance to hear what he thinks about all this. I'm wondering what you're afraid of, and I'm wondering if this has to do with your relationship with your parents."

"That's why I left. No way do I want to chance making Aaron or his kid feel like I'm pushing them aside because I'm focusing on something more important, like starting a new workshop," I answer almost too quickly. Because now that Emi mentioned it, I'm not sure I want to delve into it.

"I was thinking more the other way around," she clarifies and I shake my head. "Well, there's time to change your mind—you're still married. You might feel differently in a few weeks."

"It hurts." Losing him, walking away from him, even knowing I'm doing the right thing.

"I know." Emi squeezes my hand, and I hold on tight. A tear spills over and I roughly wipe my face. Emi plucks a tissue from the box. "Want to get coffee tomorrow morning?"

I nod, dabbing my eyes. I have to go into the shop, start winding down operations, and Isadora called. She's ready for her table. I have to coordinate the delivery.

As for still being married to Aaron, those days are numbered too. I emailed his attorney. He's drafting our divorce papers.

CHAPTER 23

So Long, Farewell

The following morning, I meet Emi in the elevator. She's wearing platform sandals with a lightweight paisley-print sundress that's sending all sorts of groovy '70s vibes. I'm decked out in my uniform of coveralls, cotton T-shirt, and boots. We'll pick up coffee on our way to the T. Emi will get off at her stop, and I'll continue on to mine, finishing my commute with the four-block walk to Artisant Designs, as I always did before I married Aaron and moved out. As if the prior couple of months never happened. As if the shop I grew up in and everything about my life isn't drastically altering by the hour.

In two weeks, maybe less, Artisant will close its doors and I'll be out of work. I'll also be twice divorced, or well on my way.

The elevator pings at my parents' floor and I nervously glance at Emi. The doors spread apart and there stands Mom. She looks up, our eyes meet, and her lips part slightly in a small "O" of surprise. 'Cause karma is the mom who's been ghosting you.

"Good morning, Meli." She greets me as if she didn't walk out on me and the shop. As if we all get along perfectly. She steps into the elevator. "Hello, Emi," she says with a smile before turning to face the closing doors.

"Hello, Mrs. Hynes. How are you?"

"Lovely, thank you."

We all face the doors. Me and Emi, with Mom between us.

Emi stares wide-eyed at me over Mom's head, goading me to say something. I really don't want to because I don't want to waste energy on someone who's intentionally making my life more difficult. Why am I always the one reaching out to her? Still wide-eyed, Emi juts her chin at Mom with a little shake of her head in a nonverbal nudge I can feel between my shoulder blades.

Fine. With an exasperated sigh, I hitch my backpack higher onto my shoulder. "Uh, morning, Mom."

She is quiet, then leans back to look askance at me. "Did you move back to your apartment?"

My brows shoot up into a peak, and there's a beat of frozen stillness. She wants to know about me.

Emi smiles broadly before pursing her lips and showing a sudden interest in an invisible speck of lint on her dress.

"I . . . I did."

I glance at Emi again, and she circles her hand, encouraging me to engage Mom in conversation. I switch my attention to Mom. She's dressed nicer this morning than she usually is. She wears a green linen blouse instead of her purple puffer vest, and she has on blue casual pants instead of her faded jeans.

"Where are you off to?" I ask her.

"Oh, to work."

Shock morphs into relieved delight. "You're going to the shop?" She didn't ditch me. Finally, she can show me Artisant's books. Maybe she can help me convince Uncle Bear to legally transfer ownership. Maybe if I can keep the shop open—somewhere, somehow—I can keep my family together.

"No, not the shop. I'm working temporarily at the library until something steadier comes along."

"But you already have a job, with me at Artisant."

"The shop is closing down once the building is sold, is it not? Your uncle hasn't officially transferred ownership, not on paper. If he has, he hasn't told me."

"I've been trying to reach him so he'll do exactly that. You guys have been ignoring my calls."

"I can't answer for your uncle, but I've been so busy."

The elevator pings for the first floor and the doors open.

"Have a lovely day, gals. Tootles." Mom waves and she's off.

"I have yet to figure her out," Emi quips as we leave the building.

"She definitely marches to the beat of her own drum," I say, wondering what happened to the woman who used to chase fireflies through the woods and sing lullabies to me. I should be used to her emotional unavailability, but I'm not.

When I arrive at the shop, the building feels cavernous and still. The familiar scents of sawdust and resin that used to motivate me through a productive day now make me sad. I'll forever associate these smells with a period of my life when I felt like part of something larger than myself, despite how toxic my family is.

I drop my backpack on a workbench and make a call to the local pickup-and-delivery service we use for our larger pieces; Isadora's table is one of the largest I've built. I schedule her delivery for the following Friday, then I arrange for Artisant's equipment and tools to be packed and moved to a storage unit I leased yesterday. By the end of the weekend after next, this building will be empty. It will also belong to the Savant House.

Next, I put in a few hours of work on the chair for Uncle Bear's client, prepping the piece for staining. It, too, will be delivered next week, and I schedule that. I get more work done on the tables for my last two clients and cancel new orders that have come in. I don't have the means or desire to fill them. After I update Artisant's website with a message to our customers that we're closing for business and take down the online order form, I call Dad. For once, he answers the phone.

"Hey there, Meli-pie."

My lungs inflate on a sharp breath. I haven't heard that nickname since I was ten. "Hi, Dad."

"How are you holding up?"

I give my phone a sideward glance, shocked at his sudden interest in my well-being. "Why are you asking?"

"I haven't seen you around since you moved out of your apartment, that's all."

"Didn't Mom tell you? I moved back in."

"She's not speaking to me. I've been living at your uncle's."

"Oh. Since when?"

"A month or so. I haven't really kept track. So, you still married to that Aaron guy?"

"At the moment."

"Hmm."

"What?"

"Oh, nothing. Nothing."

"Are you and Mom still married?"

"Yeah, we are. Though I don't think she wants to be. What did you call for?"

"Oh, ah . . ." I stumble to collect my thoughts.

My parents are separated? This has been a long time coming, and I shouldn't be surprised. Dad's imprisonment and Mom's stint in rehab had been a huge strain. They were never the same after that. And then working and living together put even more strain on their marriage. I'm just shocked it took them this long—that they suddenly aren't together after all this time.

"The desk you're building," I say, eyeballing the stunning live-edge piece. Dad's woodworking skill far exceeds Uncle Bear's when he puts his mind to it. But getting the guy to focus long enough to finish a complex job is a whole other feat. I'm sure years of drugs and depression contribute to his short attention span. There might be some undiagnosed ADHD in the picture. But he always chose simpler projects on incoming orders.

This piece is a whole different animal for him. It's built to last, optimized for peak efficiency with nooks for data and power integration, and a design that bridges luxury with style and function. I'm jealous of the person who gets to use it. The desk will surely be the centerpiece in someone's upscale office in downtown Boston. "I can't find the job specs so I can't finish it for you, and I don't know who it's going to since I can't locate the invoice. What do you want me to do with it?"

"Nothing. I'll come get it."

"Are you sure?" Moving the desk is a two-person job. "You don't want to finish working on it here?" I wondered where he planned to move it.

"Yeah. When do you need it out of there?"

"Any time before next Friday."

"Got it. I'll take care of it."

"Thanks, Dad."

"No problem." He hangs up.

I stare at the desk with a frown. Those were the most words he's spoken to me at once in years.

My phone rings. Aaron's attorney is calling. I feel a quiver of dread. "Hello?"

"Meli, hi. It's Nash. Your papers are ready. Lauren emailed them for your review." His assistant.

"Are they ready to sign?"

"If everything looks all right to you, then yes, go ahead and sign. Aaron's already read through them."

My traitorous heart thrums at the mention of my soon-to-be-ex's name. "So once we both sign, we're divorced, just like last time."

"After the mandatory ninety-day cooling-off period, yes, it's final. Here's the thing: Aaron won't sign unless you personally serve the papers."

He wants to change my mind.

"He promised he wouldn't contest."

"He's not contesting. But I advised him that you have every right to refuse. If you in any way feel threatened or aren't comfortable doing so—"

"I'll do it."

I close my eyes and take a breath. It won't be easy, seeing him in person, but I need to finish what I started. If my serving Aaron with our divorce papers is his only demand, I'll grant it.

"We're all set, then," Nash says. "I'll have Lauren email you to get a couple dates, and she'll coordinate a meetup between you and Aaron. Any location requests?"

That's a no-brainer.

"Perkatory."

The name of our favorite coffee shop couldn't be more apt. Purgatory, itself, is a state of transition, exactly where I've been stuck.

———

A few days later, I'm back in Aaron's neighborhood, wishing the weather reflected my mood as it does in movies and books when the protagonist is on the cusp of a monumental change. Dour clouds and sheets of rain would be suitable given how I'm feeling. A thunderstorm would be fitting for what I'm about to do. I deserve a good drenching for breaking my promise to Aaron. But the clear sky, so bright it's almost cartoonish blue, speckled with wisps of clouds that look like a pastry chef flicked globs of whipped cream on a wedding cake, seems out of place. This is beach weather. I should be at the Cape under a canvas umbrella, reading the latest Camille Pagán novel instead of thirty seconds and ten yards away from serving my husband with divorce papers.

But here I am, standing across the narrow road, watching through the picture window as he makes his way from the counter to our table inside Perkatory. Divorce was my idea, after all. I'm the one insisting. Then again, he changed the terms of our marriage of convenience. I could argue he broke our deal first. He made me fall in love with him. And I did, even though I swore to myself I wouldn't.

Aaron settles into his chair at our table and slouches over a ceramic mug he doesn't touch. He's probably ordered his usual Americano; no sweeteners for him. And the seat across from him—my chair—probably won't be empty for long. Not that I don't plan to sit with him when I motivate myself to get over there. I'll sit with him, briefly, assuming he wants to talk before he signs the paperwork. He'll try to convince me in that unsubtle, nonconfrontational way of his to change my mind. But I tell myself that Fallon will soon replace me, accompanying him every morning for coffee as she should. She is the mother of their child.

I study him while I wait for the light to change. His hair is mussed and in need of a trim. Even from this distance, I can tell he hasn't shaved in several days. He isn't dressed in his daily uniform of slacks and a long-sleeve button-down; no need to since his mom fired him from the Savant House. But he's not even wearing the jeans or boots he would at his woodshop. Instead, a rumpled shirt I suspect he's slept in and navy joggers have replaced his workday finery. Seeing him so down squeezes the breath from my lungs. My leaving has really messed him up.

But I'm determined to stay the course. Divorcing him before we have a chance to hurt or further disappoint each other is the right thing to do.

I then notice the second mug on the table. It'll be an oat-milk caramel macchiato with two raw sugars on the side. My Perkatory usual.

A pang of sadness stabs my ribs. Why does he have to be so nice? So *perfect*? I remind myself again I'm doing us a favor.

"Gorgeous day, isn't it?"

I glance at the shorter woman waiting on the curb beside me. She's looking at the sky.

"Not too humid yet," she says.

"I wish it was pouring."

Before the woman can comment, the light changes and we're moving across the road among a gelatinous mass of people rushing to work. The woman disappears into the crowd, and I angle toward the coffee shop, my eyes meeting Aaron's when I pass the window. He lifts a hand in a listless wave. I wave back, but I do so with the hand holding our divorce papers. The movement is infinitesimal, but Aaron physically deflates. His eyes, his mouth, his shoulders . . . Everything sags. His hand flops onto the table like a dead fish.

A cheery bell tinkles a welcome when I open the door. I cross the café to Aaron. He stands and pulls me into a full-body hug, his arms surrounding me. I'm not expecting this, or how my head naturally tucks under his chin where it's a splendid fit. I can feel him from cheek to knees. I think I even sigh.

"I've missed you," he whispers into my hair.

From habit, I lift my arms to return his hug, then remember myself. I step back. He folds his arms tightly over his chest. "That was weird. Was that weird?"

I glance down at the envelope I'm carrying.

"I shouldn't have done that. Said that . . ." His voice trails off.

"It's fine. Let's just . . ." I gesture at the table, again with the envelope.

"I bought you coffee," he says as we sit. He's nervous. He doesn't know what to do with his hands. He picks up his mug with enough force to dribble on his shirt. "Shit." He wipes his hand down his chest, spreading the stain into the cotton to blend with specks of sawdust he picked up from my coveralls when we hugged.

Any other day, I'd rip open the sugar packets and simultaneously pour them into my coffee. But I can't stomach caffeine right now. Aaron isn't the only one who's nervous. Our first divorce was much easier than this.

I leave the coffee untouched and slide the envelope across the table. He stares at it like it'll leap up and bite off his nose.

"How's the shop? Did you find a new location?"

I shake my head. "It's closing. Uncle Bear's been avoiding me. He won't transfer ownership."

"Is there anything I can do?"

"No. If you don't mind signing." I nudge the envelope.

"What are you going to do? Where are you going to work?"

"Stone & Bloom, probably. Emi says they have a senior cabinetmaker position opening up soon."

His brows furrow deeply. "That's the last thing you want to do."

"I don't have much choice. I need to work and it saves me time looking for a job at another shop." And working at the same company as Emi, Shae, and Tam is a bonus. They'll keep me distracted and my mind off the man sitting across from me.

"Work with me, Meli. Let's go into business like we talked about. We could do amazing things together."

I imagine we could. But how long would it last before I grow frustrated because his focus is on his new baby and not our business? As selfish as that makes me sound, I don't want to feel like I'm competing for his attention. I was on the receiving end of that resentment and envy with Paul.

"Please sign." I put a pen on the envelope.

"Meli . . ."

I shake my head, looking down at the table, bouncing my knee.

He doesn't reach for either the pen or envelope.

"You look good," he says, and I realize what he's doing. He won't outright try to change my mind or manipulate me into a decision I might disagree with. Not again. No, he'll just sit here with me, reminding me how magnetic we are together. "How are you?"

"Aaron, don't."

"Don't what? Ask how you're doing? Let you know I still care? I care so much," he says, impassioned.

I shake my head. I don't want to hear this because I know he won't always feel that way.

"It doesn't have to be like this. We can make it work. She isn't asking me to marry her."

Not yet, but I'm sure Kaye will make it her mission to change Fallon's mind.

I lift my hand. "Please stop."

He stares at me, his cheek flexing in anger. Then his nostrils flare. He grabs the pen and yanks out the papers. He doesn't bother reading the document. Nash said he already had. Aaron signs where it's marked and returns the papers to the envelope, drops the pen on top, and pushes the envelope to my side of the table.

The relief I expected to feel doesn't come, remaining offshore.

"Thank you," I mumble.

He doesn't say anything back. He doesn't look at me either. He just stares out the window, his eyes hard and jaw clenched.

That's it, I guess. The end of us. Again.

I push down the words that surface from habit. *See you later. Text me when you get home.* And the ones that come that aren't from habit. The ones I'm not brave enough to say, even though I would really mean them. *I love you.*

I put the pen away and pick up the envelope, push back my chair, and stand.

"Meli." Aaron's head lifts. His eyes bore into mine and my heart jumps hurdles. "I'll never stop thinking about you."

My breath hitches.

He said those exact words right before our first divorce.

Like the first time, I don't repeat them back.

Unlike the first time, walking away is immensely difficult. But I do, and on my way out, the cheery little bell above the door rings out as a hollow thud. And when I step outside from under the awning, a seagull poops on my shoulder. Turd oozes over the swell of my boob.

"Great," I mutter.

The weather didn't clue in, but somebody above understands exactly how I feel right now. Like crap.

CHAPTER 24

THE RHYTHM OF FALLING LEAVES

I direct Emmett and Vincent to shift Isadora's 92-inch live-edge walnut dining table a few inches more to the right until the piece is perfectly centered between her remodeled kitchen and great room. There is enough space on all sides for her large family of siblings, nieces, and nephews to gather round for holiday dinners and family celebrations, exactly how Isadora imagined when I first showed her the design.

Emi did a spectacular job designing Isadora's open-concept kitchen with its brushed-gold hardware, wide-plank flooring, and stained, rustic beams exposed overhead that complement the repurposed wood in the fireplace mantel as well as the kitchen cabinets. The table's arrival adds the finishing touch by pulling the three spaces together: kitchen, dining, and great room. The entire living area opens to a backyard bursting with color that spills down to the edge of the Charles River.

Outside, Isadora's Italian greyhounds, Sophia and Loren, jump on hind legs, their nails scratching at the glass door as they bark exuberantly at me and my moving team. Isadora snaps her fingers and issues a harsh command in Italian. The dogs promptly sit, whining their frustration over being excluded from the excitement inside.

"Anything else, Meli?" Vincent asks, rubbing his large hands together.

I glance at Isadora for confirmation that we've placed the table exactly where she wants it. *"Perfetto,"* she announces, pleased, and I say to Vincent, "I think we're good. Thanks, guys. I'll see you at the shop tomorrow." I've hired them to help move our tools into storage.

"You got it." Emmett shakes my hand, and with a wave from Vincent, they leave the house.

I wipe the table of dust collected during transport and polish the entire surface of fingerprint smudges while Isadora arranges the dining chairs she ordered around the table.

"You have outdone yourself, Meli," she praises in a thick Italian accent. "Your table is more beautiful than I imagined."

"It's your table now."

"I'm so pleased Emi referred you."

"I'm sure you'll hear from her soon. When you're ready, she wants to send over her team to take photos for Stone & Bloom's portfolio. Shae and Tam are excellent. You'll love their work, so make sure you get copies of the pictures."

"I'll call Emi right after this. I'm looking forward to hosting my first dinner party."

She positions the last chair when I finish polishing, and I step back to take a look. The chairs, fully upholstered in a sand deco weave, are beautiful. Their fresh style and curved-back silhouettes coordinate well with the sitting area. But their wide bodies dominate the visual space. They also look vaguely familiar. I feign dropping my soiled rag and sneak a peek under the seat when I pick it up, and I feel a sharp burn of longing in my chest. Of course they're from the Savant House. I guess Aaron will haunt me the rest of my life. There will always be reminders of him around me. I wonder, as I often have these past days, if I'll ever get over him. Will I stop feeling that ache inside whenever he comes to mind, as he constantly does?

Isadora dramatically wipes her hands and steps back to take in the room with her new table and chairs. Her face pulls in tight. "No, no, no. This won't do. The chairs don't go at all. Do you not agree?"

"They do go. They're beautiful. They're just"—How to put this delicately?—"overpowering." I might be biased, but the table is a work of art. It should be the room's focal point. But it's lost among all the fine upholstery.

"Exactly what I was thinking. I thought this would be the case, and I hoped I was wrong. I must remember I'm never wrong." She wags a bejeweled finger, laughing at herself. "I do love these chairs, but no. They don't work. They must go. All of them." She throws out her arms with the announcement.

"Not all of them. Keep the end chairs. Just get side chairs that match the stain and style but aren't upholstered."

Isadora gives me a look. "We both know I'll never find a perfect match to your custom table. That's only possible if you make them. I need ten. How soon can you have them for me?"

The rush of excited anticipation of creating something new bursts inside me. I can already picture the chairs, sketching the design in my head. The lines will match the upholstered end chairs but with a narrower silhouette, and I selfishly feel a twinge of satisfaction that she'd replace Savant's chairs with mine. Mine, of course, would be better made and of higher quality. They'd survive spilled grape juice and splattered spaghetti sauce from dinners with rambunctious children.

Then I wake up.

I don't have a shop anymore.

With reluctant disappointment, I say, "Thank you for the opportunity, but I have to decline."

"What? Why?"

"As of this weekend, Artisant Designs is closed for business."

"Whatever for?"

"My uncle sold the building."

"Can't you relocate?"

"I would if I could, but my uncle owns the shop. It's up to him."

"Convince him to change his mind," she orders with a flourished wave of her hand, each finger encumbered with stones and gems.

Bangles jangle on her wrist. Isadora loves her jewelry. "Tell him to sell you the shop. You can't go out of business. Your pieces are exceptional, your work too good. It must be shared with the world." She dramatically swings her arms, the open ends of the sheer brightly patterned robe she wears over her linen pencil pants and silk camisole billowing outward.

"Believe me, I've tried. He won't return my calls or answer the door when I've gone by his place." To my consternation, my eyes unexpectedly fill with tears, and Isadora notices. I itch my eyes, trying to pass the dampness off as allergies.

She *tsks*, fluttering about me. "*Oh, cara. Tesoro. Figlia mia.* Sit, sit, sit on this dreadful chair." She pulls one of the Savant chairs from the table and pats the seat. "I'll make us tea."

Laughter bubbles, making me snort since I'm crying, which makes me cry-laugh. Then I just cry.

Isadora's expression turns horrified. "What is it? What did I say?"

"The chairs." I point at them, crying harder. "They're from the Savant House." And now I'm utterly mortified because the darn tears won't stop. Probably because I've been fighting them since Aaron signed our divorce papers. It's really over.

Isadora frowns. "*Sì.* Is that a problem? I know they must go. You don't need to worry. I'm returning them."

"It's not that. It's . . . They remind me of my husband."

"You're married? When did you get married?"

"A couple of months ago. But no, we're not married anymore. We're divorcing, and this is the second time we've gotten divorced."

"From each other?"

I nod. "It's so much harder this time around. It's really hitting me how much I love him."

"Mamma mia! Forget the tea. This calls for something stronger." She buzzes over to the bar cart, her robe flowing behind her.

"I can't drink. I have to drive." I followed Emmett and Vincent's delivery truck here in the shop's old U-Haul truck.

"Not for you, for me." She turns back to me. "But I insist you do not let me drink alone. You'll stay here as long as you need to. Come, come." She takes my hand and pulls me over to the sofa. "Sit."

I look at the cushions' pristine oatmeal weave. "I can't." My coveralls are dirty and stained.

"You can. I have two dogs," she says, reading my hesitation. At the mention of her dogs, she heads for the patio door. "Sofas are meant to be sat on. Now, please tell me everything." She lets in the dogs who run circles around the new table, sniffing madly, their toenails clicking wildly. After the table passes inspection, Sophia and Loren rush over to me and happily greet me with friendly sniffs and licks, which will only make Blueberry hiss and spit at me when I get home. But I relish the affection they lavish on me. They leap onto the couch and curl up beside me while Isadora pours us each two fingers of Macallan. She gives me a cut-crystal glass, clicks hers to mine, and settles on the couch beside me, opposite her dogs. Sophia, or maybe it's Loren, notices. She wiggles her way onto Isadora's lap. Isadora pets the dog's smooth head and sips her whiskey. She circles her hand at me. "Talk, *cara*. Let it all out."

And I do. I tell her everything that's happened since she ordered her table and more, from being a runaway bride to my first marriage to Aaron, from Uncle Bear arranging the shop's acquisition without involving me to my family ghosting me, leaving me to shut down the shop on my own in retribution for me marrying Aaron to manipulate the Savant House into retracting their acquisition offer. I explain that starting next week, I'll work with Emi, Shae, and Tam at Stone & Bloom because now that I remember I no longer have a shop, I don't have the desire to craft anything more creative than precut cabinet boxes.

When I finish, Isadora, who didn't interrupt once as I poured my heart out, purses her lips. Then her head tilts back and she cackles. And cackles and cackles until both her dogs nervously glance from her to me as I shift uncomfortably on the couch. She claps her hands loudly, her applause slowly easing with her laughter until she sighs heavily and grins.

"What's so funny?" I ask, feeling like I should be offended but I don't have the energy in me.

"I've been married four times, *cara*, one of them to a gorgeous man more than twice my age who descended from Italian royalty, whom I met while bathing topless in Monaco when I was eighteen, and none of my marriages—not a single one—tops your story. You make all mine seem so dull."

"And that's funny?"

"It's delightful. Men are capricious creatures, and some of us women are better off on our own. It took me four husbands to realize I loved myself better than they ever could, and that I am a better person on my own than with any one of them. You also don't need to be married to be committed to each other, so don't believe that since you're now twice divorced, it proves marriage isn't for someone like you, as your uncle not so eloquently put it. Or that you aren't marriage material, as your ex-fiancé believes. Good thing you didn't end up with him. Any man who says that to a woman doesn't deserve that woman. Nothing your uncle has told you proves that you can't be in a committed relationship, that you can't love and have your work, and even work together. Sometimes I think the kids these days who forgo marriage and live together as partners have it right. The whole act of legally binding yourself to another person complicates relationships, and life is already complicated enough. But please, *cara*, for the love of God, tell me why you left Aaron when you are so obviously in love with him."

"It's complicated."

"*Questa è una stronzata.* Excuses, excuses. This isn't a status update on social media. This is your life."

I sigh and stare down at the whiskey in the cut-crystal glass cupped in my hands. Maybe it's because Isadora is more of a stranger than a friend, making it somewhat easier to talk with her without the fear of being judged, that I finally share out loud what's really bothering me.

What I've been mulling over since Emi first mentioned it. "I don't want to feel unimportant to him," I admit.

"Because he has a baby on the way?"

"Aaron needs to focus on his new family. I'll only be a distraction. We were never meant to be long term anyway. It was just supposed to be a marriage of convenience. I was the one who said no sex."

Isadora leans forward. "How well did that one work out for you?"

I roll my eyes and she laughs.

"But he loves you and he said he wanted your marriage of convenience to be something more," she argues. "He even told you he doesn't want to marry that Fallon woman."

"You sound like Emi."

"Emi is smart."

"And I'm not?" I ask with a mirthful smirk, mildly affronted.

"Of course you are. But sometimes when you're in love, it's hard to see clearly. It's also hard not to be afraid of losing that love once you have it. That's perfectly normal. But let's get back to this fear of feeling unimportant. Where is this coming from?"

"I'm sure it stems from my own relationship with my parents." I tell her about my childhood, and despite the drugs and alcohol, how I'd been the center of my parents' world. Then I share how things changed upon their return, my anger toward them and their disinterest in me, and the gaping chasm that's now between us.

"Be honest," Isadora says when I finish. "If you had been the center of your parents' world, the drugs and alcohol wouldn't have been in the picture. They wouldn't be a part of those idyllic childhood memories you've latched on to."

"The drugs and alcohol aren't in those memories. It was only us digging up clams on the beach, playing princess in the park, and reading books among the stacks in the library. They weren't intoxicated when we chased fireflies. They were sober. They were themselves."

"Are you sure? Is it possible your mind chose to ignore it? Is it possible your memories are nothing more than fantasies?"

My frown deepens as I sink further into my head, my memories splintering as cracks begin to form. And then I see it, the truth hiding under the sparkling happiness and glittering love. Mom slipping a pill onto her tongue in the library when she didn't think I was looking. Dad giving me his back to drain a flask at the park. The two of them sharing a joint at the beach, passing the smoldering flint above my head. And I sink further into my sadness. I was never important enough to them to care about what they were truly doing to me, the risks they were taking with me around. No wonder Uncle Bear took custody of me.

"I want to share something with you, but I don't think you'll want to hear it," she says gently. "You'll think I'm overstepping."

"No, say it. I want to hear it." As much as the truth hurts, I admire Isadora for actually caring. Her interest in me is more than my parents have shown me.

"All right. I think your desire to be close with your family is rooted in an emotional need for connection and acceptance."

"We're going deep here."

"We are. From what you've told me, I think you harbor a belief that you're not enough to be truly loved and valued. And I think witnessing Aaron potentially have a family so much like what you crave, with a woman other than yourself, triggered your fears of inadequacy, which, as you say, stems from your parents' lack of interest and affection. They have done quite a number on you over the years, making you believe you're less than you really are or deserve to be. You might even believe you aren't good enough to be a mother to his child because you're terrified of re-creating your own family's dysfunctional dynamic. This fear manifested in you making a self-sacrificing decision to step aside because you're convinced you aren't the right person for him in the long run. Because wasn't all of this with him supposed to be pretend?"

I inhale a deep, shuddering breath. "Whoa, okay. You went right for the heart."

"The only rule in pool that matters, I say, is to aim straight for the pocket."

I laugh dryly. "That's a lot to absorb."

"It is. I tend to get carried away with my advice, but I'm old. Beating around the bush is a waste of time, and I don't have much of that left either. Why waste a perfectly good minute? So I'll tell you this too: nobody, and I mean nobody, can tell Aaron who the right person for him is but him. And it sounds like he's already told you it's you. One more thing, since I'm on a roll: it's a shame Artisant Designs is closing. But it's even more of a shame you don't intend to exercise your craft. You are so skilled."

"My heart just isn't into it. The spark is waning."

"But it's not completely out, now is it? Take a break; clear your head. But don't do yourself a disservice. Listen to the rhythm of falling leaves."

I frown. "The rhythm of falling leaves?"

"Every moment in life is a chance to create something beautiful, with someone or for someone. Even for yourself. Embrace the impermanence of life, like falling leaves. What you're going through right now is but one of many seasons for you. Use these moments to prepare your masterpiece. In other words, your creativity won't be sequestered for long. It will resurface, and when it does, you'll be ready to find an appropriate outlet. This time, it'll be what's right for you, not what anyone—your uncle, your parents, that blockhead ex-fiancé of yours, even Aaron—tell you."

I slowly nod along to her advice and wipe the moisture from my face when she finishes. "Thank you," I whisper.

"Well." She leans back with a sigh. "I bet you didn't expect this conversation to be part of your delivery package."

I laugh. "No, but I think I needed to have it."

"Because you were ready to have it. What you do with what I said is up to you. But please, stay for dinner. I'd love the company. After spending weeks abroad with my loud family, this house is too quiet."

The thought of returning to an empty, dark apartment (kitty cat aside) fills me with dread and a longing for a specific someone to be waiting for me at home.

"I would love to join you for dinner. Thank you."

Isadora cooks us a delectable meal of mushroom raviolis in a buttery sauce with fresh Parmesan and a fine Italian red wine while sharing stories of her trip to Italy and reminiscing about growing up with her older brother who passed away. It's after 10:00 p.m. when I leave her house. I park the truck in front of my apartment since I'm driving in to work tomorrow. There will be lots of back-and-forth between the shop and storage as I clean out Uncle Bear's building.

On my way inside, I text Dad a reminder to pick up his desk tomorrow. I'm looking down at my phone and don't notice Mom until we're standing beside each other, waiting for the elevator.

I put my phone away. "Hello, Mom. You're out late."

"I went for a walk," she says in a shaky voice. Her bottom lip wobbles and she glances away.

I frown. It's not unusual for her to walk alone, but it is at this late hour. Then I remember Dad moved out.

"Is everything all right?"

She opens her purse, interested in something inside. "Yes, it's fine. I'm fine."

She is clearly not fine.

The elevator arrives and we get on. We turn to face the doors as they close. Maybe it's because we're once again sharing an elevator and not saying a word. Maybe it's because I'm feeling emotionally drained after visiting with Isadora. Or maybe it's because the talking-to I've wanted—the one I needed to hear—didn't come from Mom but a client with a heart big enough to care. Someone who wasn't my mom or dad or uncle who realized that *I* was not all right. I turn to face her. "Why don't you ever talk to me?"

"What?" She looks up, surprised.

"Why do you act like you don't care? Other than when we're at the shop or hanging out at Uncle Bear's on holidays and birthdays, you treat me like I'm nobody to you, like you could care less about me or what I do. You treat me like an outsider in my own family. All of you do! I'm your daughter, for Pete's sake. You used to love me so much. When did you stop? What did I do to make you and Dad hate me? I'm so sick of holding on to this stupid fantasy of us ever being a close-knit family again." And because my emotions are riding high, I once again burst into tears. I haven't cried this much since I was a child. I haven't cried in front of Mom since she left when I was ten.

Mom looks seriously uncomfortable, her eyes darting about the elevator while I speak. But when I start crying, she haltingly touches my face. It's a motherly touch, light, tender . . . loving, and I go very still, my breath held captive in my throat.

"Meli. Honey. We never stopped loving you. If anything, we love you too much."

"That makes absolutely no sense. How is that possible?"

The way she bites her bottom lip reminds me so much of myself.

"I wish I could explain," she says.

"Please do. I need to know. Tell me what I did wrong."

"You've done nothing wrong. It's us, Meli. It's always been us."

Mom plucks a fresh tissue from her purse for me. The elevator dings for her floor and the doors open. Panicked, desperate for answers, I look at the open doors, then to Mom with a sinking feeling that once she steps off the elevator, she'll go back to avoiding me and I will never get those answers.

But Mom surprises me. She presses the button that holds the doors open. Then she turns back to me. "Do you want to come home with me?"

My mouth turns down at the corners as I struggle not to cry harder. I nod. "Yes, I want to come home."

CHAPTER 25

HEART TO HEART

Mom asks if I'd like a cup of chamomile tea, and even though I don't want one, I don't decline. Because she's my mom, and she's invited me back to her apartment.

She busies herself in the kitchen, steeping our tea. I feel like she's procrastinating. She isn't much of a conversationalist, and as I sort through a multitude of questions to get her talking, I'm also wondering whether she's always been this reserved. It almost seems like she has a fear of talking if she's not in a familiar setting like the shop. My being here in her apartment is highly irregular, and that alone might have her withdrawing into herself. So I occupy myself looking around the apartment, letting her warm up to me.

The apartment isn't the same unit we lived in before my parents left. The floor plans are similar—two beds and baths. All the windows in this apartment face the street in front as opposed to the building in back. I recall many evenings sitting at my window, watching the neighbors watch TV, prepare for bed, kiss, argue, live.

The furniture is also different, though I do recognize a few pieces, like the short, circular coffee table and the square dining table Dad built. I didn't realize he crafted his own furniture. I always thought he'd made these pieces for clients. But it makes sense they'd need new furniture when they returned. Uncle Bear had sold off what he hadn't put in storage. Their lease ended while Dad was still imprisoned and Mom was off living elsewhere. I spot another one of his tables by the door and a media console, all beautiful pieces of elegant craftsmanship intermixed with the bold purples and blues of the sofas and pillows and artwork on the walls. Mom never was one for monochrome and neutral-toned aesthetics. She always gravitated to vivid colors, which could explain why I remember so much color in my childhood, now that I think on it.

I wander down the hallway, the wood flooring settling under my weight, to the room that would have been my room in the other apartment. I almost expect to see an explosion of teals and yellows, ruffles and bows from my youth. It now holds a hodgepodge of hobby supplies and household items. There's a laptop on a desk buried under magazines and files. A blue sofa bed I doubt ever gets used as a bed. I don't know if my parents host guests, not like they did before. Who would they have over? The only friends I know of are Dad's and Uncle Bear's bowling teammates. If Mom and Dad have a life outside of Artisant, I haven't been privy to it.

My parents' room at the end of the hall is simple, neatly furnished with Dad's pieces: bedside tables, headboard, armoire, and dresser. Together they would have cost close to twenty grand had they purchased the items through Artisant's website like any other client. As for the queen bed, I no longer know the people who sleep there.

I return to the living room. Mom sits at the table with our tea. Both hands hug her mug. I'm about to join her when I notice the one photo album we had from my childhood on the shelf. I pick it up.

"Do you still take pictures?" Mom used to enjoy photography. I haven't seen her with a camera in years.

"Sometimes. I take pictures mostly of birds and flowers now. I've gone to the park on occasion and taken pictures of the dogs there. If their owners say okay. I always ask."

I join her at the table and open the album. There is infant me, my little feet, button toes. Dad cradles me in one picture. Mom breastfeeds me in another. We look perfectly normal, loving. I wonder when it went downhill.

I flip through the pages and stop at my first trip to the beach. I couldn't be older than one, and I'm naked as the day I was born, sitting in the sand between Mom's legs. A wave tickles my toes. Mom sits behind me, keeping me balanced. Her eyes are closed and her head thrown back in laughter. We're both laughing. I can almost hear my squeals of delight. It strikes me how Mom is in a lot of these photos.

"Your dad was good with the camera too," she says as if reading my thoughts. "He used to be good with a lot of things." Her tone is bitter with regret.

I am loaded with questions. I've been collecting them over the years as one would store positive affirmations in a glass jar. But I ask the most recent one that's bewildered me.

"Why did you ask Dad to move out? It's obvious you haven't been getting along for a long time. You guys bicker all the time, and Dad's always testing your patience. But why now? Is it because Uncle Bear sold the building?"

Mom sighs. "Not entirely. There are so many factors, Meli, so many reasons. I don't know where to begin."

"How about the beginning? Or with one factor? Start with that." I'm willing to stay up all night if it means finally getting my answers.

Mom sips her tea, sets down the mug. Pauses. "I needed a break. Your dad keeps making stupid mistakes, and that uncle of yours keeps bailing him out. They never learn."

I close the album and nudge the book aside. "Maybe you should start at the beginning instead."

"You're right. I never wanted you to hear this because your uncle was your legal guardian and you looked up to him. After your dad and I . . ." She stops. "We really messed up, Meli. But your uncle, he loved you very much and you adored him and . . ." Her gaze darts from me to her tea.

"Mom, if the past couple months have proved anything, it's that Uncle Bear is far from perfect. I get that. Whatever you have to say won't distort any glorified view you think I have of him. That's gone."

Mom grumbles something under her breath. "You didn't think that when you were young, and we didn't want you to look at him any other way. You already hated us."

"I never hated you. Was I angry? Absolutely. Did I have a hard time getting why you guys left? Of course. I was ten. But I got over that. Not right away, but when I did, there was this huge chasm between us. Nothing I said or did seemed to fix that. You guys just shut me out, and I don't understand why. Is it because you thought I hated you?"

Mom hedges. "Like I said, there were a lot of reasons."

I drag a hand down my face, feeling my frustration rising. I take a few beats to gather my cool. If I start snapping at her, she'll stop talking. "Let's go back to the beginning."

Mom nods, and she goes way back. "Your grandmother passed away when Bear and your dad were young. They were raised in the shop pretty much like you were. Grandpa Walt did the best he could, working full-time, managing the shop, and raising two boys. Bear met Aria about the same time your dad and I met."

"Who's Aria?"

"Your aunt—or she *was*."

I put my hands on the table and lean forward. "Wait . . . Uncle Bear was married?"

"For a short time. He and Aria were very much in love. Bear would have done anything for her, to a point. When your grandfather died, he left the building to Bear and your dad, but Bear got the shop and he brought Aria on as a partner. The books were a mess and business slowed, and your uncle struggled to keep it afloat. He and Aria had to spend a lot of late nights and weekends at the shop rather than time with each other, and as much as Aria loved your uncle, she was young and selfish. She wanted to sell. And when your uncle wouldn't give up the shop for her, she left him. It hit him hard and he started using to cope. And since he and your dad are close . . ." She flips open her hands and shrugs.

"That's when you and Dad started using."

"You were only a few months old. I was stressed about raising a newborn, and we didn't know if we could keep the shop from going under. It was touch-and-go there for a while. It was so easy to take a pill and forget."

Anger boils in my stomach. "I was a baby."

"I know," Mom says, nodding. "I shouldn't have put you through that. Neither your father nor I should have."

I lean back, fighting off bitter tears. How could she have been so selfish? All of them!

"Continue," I say in a flat tone, trying not to get worked up. It's in the past. I can't change what happened. But I need to hear it, as difficult as it is.

"Your uncle cleaned up, got his act together. But your dad and I . . ." She shakes her head as if she's still in denial.

"Tell me, whatever it is. I need to know."

"Bear feels responsible for what happened to us: you, me, your dad. He's the one who called the cops on your dad. Bear tried to get us off the drugs, tried to intervene, but at the time, your dad had also started dealing. He liked the extra cash. You know how stubborn he can be. Your uncle even more so. He became your guardian when we couldn't take care of you, and he told me to stay away until I got clean and could prove that I could stay clean."

"That's why you didn't move back until Dad got released."

"Your uncle did the right thing to keep me away. I wasn't fit to be a mom. I question if I ever was."

"So, what? You cleaned up and Dad served his sentence. You came back and decided you didn't need to be my parents because Uncle Bear said so? Did you think that because he was my legal guardian you were free from caring about me? Loving me? Showing any interest at all in me?" I ask, my voice rising. Now I'm getting worked up.

"No, no, no." Mom shakes her head. "It was nothing like that."

"Then what was it?" I smack my hand on the table.

"We felt so ashamed for deserting you. We didn't deserve to be your parents anymore. Bear was your parent now. There were legal restrictions, yes, but we all were afraid to uproot you to come live with us after you'd been with your uncle for so long. But more than that, you were just so angry with us, so we gave you space. I guess we took it too far, because when we tried to close the distance, we just didn't know how. I think we felt too guilty. And please, Meli, please don't take this the wrong way, but part of that reason was because we had to prioritize rebuilding and recovering our lives. We had to focus on us."

"Well, excuse me for being too much for you to handle." I abruptly push back from the table to stand up. I pace away, shaking my arms to let off steam.

"You're right, we shouldn't have taken it to such an extreme." Mom cowers at the table, not looking at me. "It didn't work anyway."

I turn back. "What do you mean?"

"Your dad. Before it was drugs and alcohol. Now . . . now it's gambling."

"Gambling?"

Mom nods, and snippets of things that once didn't make sense start to form a solid picture.

"Those large, uncategorized withdrawals in Artisant's accounts. What were they for?"

"You saw those?"

"Dad gave me copies of the ledgers when I was trying to pitch Uncle Bear to sell me the shop," I say, returning to my seat.

"Bear has been paying off your dad's gambling debts."

Because my uncle will always bail out his little brother. He feels responsible for the problems Dad has now.

Mom fidgets with the tea-bag string. "I didn't realize how bad his addiction was until six months ago when we took that long weekend to Las Vegas."

I remember their trip. It was the first vacation I believe they'd ever taken. Mom wanted to see Adele in concert. Dad had bought her tickets. Whatever had happened on that trip, Mom wasn't speaking to Dad when they returned. It took weeks before she looked his way or gave him anything more than single-word answers to his questions.

"He lost a lot of money—like, a lot. The casino put a marker on him. He couldn't pay within their thirty-day time frame, and an arrest warrant was issued. We've been paying off little chunks here and there, just to keep him out of jail until . . ." Mom's gaze anxiously darts my way.

"No." I cup my hands over my mouth. "Please tell me that's not why Uncle Bear sold the building."

Mom nods.

"How much does Dad owe?"

"One point eight."

"Million?" I shriek, and she nods, eyes squeezed shut. "Holy shit, Mom. What the hell?"

"I know, I know."

I don't know much about gambling, but apparently the casino extended a marker for the value of Dad's portion, Mom explains to me. But with taxes on the property's sale, Bear had to contribute a portion of his share to fully pay off the debt. In one weekend, Dad wiped out their portfolio.

"Bear didn't want you to know, and frankly, neither did I. You think so little of us already. This is just one more way we've disappointed you. I was so fed up with him. I mean, how could he make things worse than they already were between us? I couldn't deal with him anymore. I told him to leave."

"After all that, Uncle Bear is letting Dad live with him?"

"Your dad has a key to your uncle's apartment. Bear doesn't know he's staying there."

"Where's Uncle Bear?"

"Gone. We don't know where. It's probably best. It's hard enough as it is for him to see the shop go."

Mom sips her tea and goes quiet. I sit silently beside her, reeling, not quite sure what to think about any of this, and I express that to Mom. Her bottom lip trembles, and as angry and confused and betrayed and disheartened as I feel, it doesn't prevent me from clearly seeing what's going on with Mom. For the first time in her life, other than when Dad was imprisoned, she is alone. She must be scared, stressed, and nervous too. She lost her job at the shop and her retirement.

"I am really angry with all of you," I say. "But I'm sorry things worked out the way they have. I'm sorry Uncle Bear sold the building and Dad did what he did."

"Me too, Meli."

"It's going to take a long time to forgive you guys. There's a lot I need to process. But if you ever want company on your walks, I'd love to join you, if you'll have me."

"I'd love that too."

A shy, fleeting smile touches her lips, and I smile back, neither of us making a move to leave the table.

Several hours later, I'm lying alone in bed in the dark and staring at the ceiling. Blueberry sprawls, belly-up, beside me. I can't sleep after so much input today, between Isadora's advice and my talk with Mom. But I'm not thinking about them, or Dad. I'm thinking about Uncle Bear and the ripple effect through our family from his reaction to Aria's leaving. How distraught and in love and lonely he must have been to believe that turning to drugs was the only way to cope. Then to feel responsible for what happened to us because of his actions. In his own way, he's been protecting, supporting, and holding our family together ever since.

I don't agree with his methods—the poor communication and some of his decisions surrounding my well-being. But I can't imagine the loneliness he must have felt over the years. To forsake love because he had lost Aria. To be unwilling to take another chance on love because of the devastating choice he made after Aria deserted him. All this time, I believed he and my parents couldn't manage living and loving and working together successfully because of the impossibility of balancing their passions in work and life, when it really came down to them just making one mistake after another.

I don't want to live like them, a half-life, too afraid to go after what they want. Where self-preservation keeps them self-focused to the point of selfishness, remaining stuck in the past and building boundaries around themselves so high because of their fear of rejection. They not only push people away—push *me* away—but also keep people out. Like they have kept me out.

I'm starting to see what Emi and Isadora were trying to show me. Leaving Aaron so abruptly—pushing him away—is wrong. It's me mirroring my uncle and parents.

As if my thoughts found him across the city, my phone pings with a text from Aaron. I haven't heard from him since I saw him last week at Perkatory.

I miss you.

I hug the phone to my chest. Then I text back.

I miss you too.

CHAPTER 26

GOOD TO US

Emi is at my door first thing in the morning with two to-go cups of coffee, looking as put together as ever in court sneakers, tube socks, cuffed jean shorts, a baseball tee, and a head scarf. "Ready to go to work?"

"Ready as I'll ever be." With my hair in a high pony, I ditched my coveralls for loose, ripped jeans cuffed at the ankle, an old AC/DC concert shirt I snagged from Uncle Bear when I was a teen, and black Pumas. I swipe up my keys and Uncle Bear's master keys for the shop and take one of the coffees as I join Emi in the hallway.

"Shae and Tam said they'd meet us there. They're picking up doughnuts. Oh! How did Isadora's delivery go yesterday?"

Emi is too chipper for me this morning. I woke up drained from yesterday and I'm dragging.

"Interesting." I cover a yawn as we step into the elevator. "I'll tell you about it on the ride over."

The elevator stops at my parents' floor. When the doors open, Mom is waiting there in jeans, purple sneakers, and the infamous purple puffer vest zipped over a short-sleeve light-blue tee.

"Good morning, Meli, Emi," she says, boarding the elevator.

Emi and I exchange a surprised glance.

"Good morning, Mrs. Hynes."

"Hi, Mom," I say with genuine enthusiasm at seeing her, and Emi gives me a double take. "What's got you up so early this morning?" It's Saturday. If she has a shift, the library doesn't open for several hours.

"I thought I'd help you gals pack up the shop. Do you have room for me in the truck?"

Emi's mouth falls open.

"Absolutely. We'd love to have your help." I grin broadly so I don't tear up.

"And, Emi, dear," Mom says with a glance at her, "when are you going to stop calling me Mrs. Hynes? It's Gemma."

Emi sputters her astonishment and nods. "You got it, Gemma. Nice to have you along." She leans around Mom and mouths "Oh my God" to me.

"I can see your reflection in the door, Emi."

Emi straightens and schools her face like she's been reprimanded by her teacher, and I laugh. It feels really good to laugh, especially when Mom's mouth twitches with a smile.

I don't get the chance to catch Emi up about yesterday with Isadora and my mom since Mom sits between us on the old bench seat on the drive over. I know Emi's dying to know what brought on this change in Mom and our relationship. But we'll have time to talk later. Emmett and Vincent are waiting in the alley like two stealthy cats with the transport truck when we arrive. I open the shop's back door, probably for the last time, then I lift up the big roll door, also probably for the last time. I flick on the lights and ceiling fans. I go to unlock the front entrance and find Shae and Tam waiting there with big disposable coffee carafes, a couple of boxes of doughnuts, and their video equipment.

"It's the end of an era," Shae announces, greeting me with a hug.

"We're going to document the entire day," Tam says.

"You guys. You're going to make me cry." I hug Tam, then help them bring everything inside.

The crew gathers around my workstation where I spent years designing furniture for countless clients. Shae already has the video camera rolling, and Tam gives her wife a *hang loose* sign when Shae aims the lens at her partner.

My lungs have been burning since the drive over, and I take a deep breath to ease the discomfort.

Emi nudges me. "What's wrong?"

"Nothing, everything."

Emi gives me a warm smile. Today is bittersweet. Mom rubs my back, but as much as I relish her reassurance and am thrilled she's here and finally taking some interest in me, I tell her that I'll be okay. If she shows me any more affection, I'll burst into tears and not get any work done.

"Thank you for coming today," I tell everyone. "I couldn't do this without you."

Emmett smirks. "No, you couldn't. I'd like to see you move that table saw on your own."

"Har-har. Seriously, thank you. So . . ." I look at each of their expectant faces. "Who's ready to get to work?"

Emi whoops, and Vincent claps his big hands, saying, "Let's do this."

I bring up the playlist I created specifically for today and plug it into the shop's stereo system. Chappell Roan's campy synth-pop gets us started. We load equipment onto the truck and pack the tools, labeling the boxes. Everything goes into storage since, technically, everything still belongs to Uncle Bear. What he does with this stuff is up to him.

Several hours later when we're well into the shop's cleanup, I'm ready to order us pizzas. Mom is standing at her desk, staring off into space. She's spent the morning organizing years' worth of paperwork, shredding some files and packing others.

"Everything all right, Mom?" I ask.

Mom snaps out of her zone and smiles at me. "Oh yes. I was just thinking. This building was such a big part of our lives."

"It was." I look up at the cobwebs in the rafters and water stains on the metal roof. "I wish Dad and Uncle Bear were here. They need to say goodbye too."

"We wouldn't get any work done with those lazy asses hanging around."

I laugh. She speaks the truth. Uncle Bear would question how everything was being packed, slowing our progress. Dad would excuse himself every half hour to take a smoke break.

"Where's your husband?"

Mom's question startles me. I blink. "My . . . husband?"

"Yes. Aaron. Aren't you two married? I thought he'd be here helping. I wanted to meet him."

"You did?"

"Doesn't every mom want to meet their son-in-law?"

"Oh. Well . . . we're divorced." Mom's eyes widen. "It's not final yet, but it will be," I say, a little glum.

Mom frowns. "Do you want the divorce?"

"I did ask for it. But at this point, it might not matter what I want," I say, thinking of how abruptly I'd left him.

Mom touches my arm, and I'm reminded of how affectionate she once was toward me. "Of course it matters."

I attempt to smile. "We'll see." For now I need to focus on clearing the shop. With such big changes ahead for me, I can take this only one step at a time.

It's almost the evening when we've boxed the last of the tools and loaded the lumber supply onto the truck. The only thing left is Dad's unfinished desk. And the dirt and trash on the floor from our flurry of activity. Vincent and Emmett leave for the storage unit. I'll meet them there later since I need to wait for my dad before locking up. Tam takes out the trash, and after hugging me goodbye, Mom leaves. She wants to visit the library before it closes and be gone before Dad arrives. I also don't think she wants to be the last one here at the shop. She's seen enough. And when I notice her choke up, I let her go, telling her I'll check in with her when I get home. Maybe we can go for a walk tonight. I think we'll both be in the mood for some fresh air.

Shae wraps up filming and packs her camera equipment. "Well, Meli, it's been fun."

"Actually, today was sort of fun." Surprisingly uplifting, albeit bittersweet. A burden I didn't realize had been one has lifted. I feel like I can now fully focus on this new phase of my life.

"Incoming!" Emi flies in to deliver a big hug. "Proud of you, girl."

"Thank you."

She leans back to look at me. "I know you. Today wasn't as easy as you're letting on."

I grab the broom and start sweeping.

"You don't need to sweep the floor. Nobody is moving in."

I shush her, bouncing my hand for her to keep it down. Let me be in denial. No, the floor doesn't need to be swept. Savant will tear down the building. But sweeping was my first job at the shop, and doing this now feels cathartic. Full circle. It makes sense this is my last task here. Artisant Designs was more of a home than my apartment. Before I turn the lights off one final time, it only feels right to take care of her when she took such good care of me.

"Waffle brunch at my place tomorrow. Ten a.m.," Emi reminds us.

"We'll be there," Tam says.

"Anything we can bring?" Shae asks.

"Nope, I got it covered. But you can give me a ride to the store."

Emi leaves with Shae and Tam, and I text Dad one last reminder to pick up his desk before I lock up and leave with the truck. But before I can send it off, the front door opens.

"Wow," Dad says, coming inside to look around. "This place is empty."

I lean on the broom. "Nice of you to show up."

"Yeah, well, I was giving your mom space."

"Mom told me what happened."

His shaggy brows leap to his hairline. "Everything?"

I nod, and he releases a long sigh. He looks at the floor. "I called the gambling hotline last night," he says after a bit. "I'm getting help."

"I'm sure asking wasn't easy." I can tell it was difficult for him to share this with me let alone make that call.

Dad goes quiet. He looks like he has something to say but doesn't know how or where to start. I decide to put him out of his misery. Without the shop or Uncle Bear holding our family together, someone needs to step up.

"What you did to us, gambling away the building, I should hate you for it. I'm sure Uncle Bear does. But I don't." Dad looks up, shocked. His expression asks me why, so I confess something I've only begun to realize myself. "If you hadn't gambled it away, I never would have let go of Artisant and tried something different or new. I was too stuck on the idea that it was the shop that kept us together when it's been Uncle Bear all along. Now, he's kind of done a crap job at it." Dad laughs and the side of my mouth pulls up into a half grin. "I guess what I'm trying to say is that if you ever want to come over and hang out with your daughter, the door's open."

Dad's face pulls tight. He glances away. "Thanks, Meli-pie. I don't deserve that."

"Probably not, but we all deserve a third chance."

Dad barks a laugh. "Guess the third time is a charm."

"It will be." I smile.

"What's next for you?" he asks.

"I'm not sure yet, but I have ideas. What do you say we get your desk into storage and get the hell out of here?"

"You've done enough for the day. Give me the keys. I'll take the truck. You go home and rest."

Good, because I had no idea where I was going to park that truck. Without the shop, the truck lost its parking spot. I gladly drop the keys in his palm. Let him figure that out.

Dad heads for the alley to open the back of the truck but stops. He looks up and around. Then he looks at me, finally making eye contact.

Underneath the shock, I feel a jolt of love and relief, a sense of truly being seen by him again.

He smiles easily, knowingly. "She was good to us."

"She was."

He nods slowly and continues his way out back.

The desk is a solid beast, but we load it up. Within a half hour, Dad is gone.

I finish sweeping, taking my time, clearing each corner. I dump the trash and pull down the roll door for the last time. I lock the rear door, turn off the ceiling fans and HVAC, and slowly make my way to the front entrance, lingering there, saying goodbye. I go to turn off the lights one last time when the door swings open. Uncle Bear pops in.

"Hey, Melisaurus," he says as if it's just another day at the shop. "Glad I caught you. How's it going?"

I gape at him. "Seriously? You dump the shop on me, ghost the family, then have the nerve to show up *after* we've finished cleaning? And you want to know how it's going? *For real?*"

He swipes his hand in the air and scoffs. "Yeah, I know. But after what Dean did, then you go off and get married and screw up my deal, I figured you all deserved it."

My mouth falls open.

"But you're right. It was a shit move. I should have been here for you."

I sputter, my argument wilting on my tongue with his apology.

"Where have you been?" I ask.

Uncle Bear's cheeks brighten to a ruddy red. He clears his throat and drags a hand over his jaw. "I was at the Cape."

"Alone?"

"Not exactly," he hedges. I wait. He sighs, annoyed. "Remember that delivery to the Cape your dad and I did a month back? It was for a woman, a retired banker. Lovely lady who lost her husband a few years back." He stalls.

"And?"

230

He shrugs. "And we hit it off."

Uncle Bear has a girlfriend? I could tease him but I won't. This is a big step for him, to take a risk with his emotions.

"I'm happy for you."

"You'd like her, Meli."

"I look forward to meeting her."

A fleeting smile appears on his face that I now notice is quite tan. He's been spending time in the sun with his lady friend.

Uncle Bear is quiet and contemplative when he takes his last lap around the shop. He stops, touches a wall. Then he abruptly turns and walks my way. "Ready?"

"Are you?"

"Yep. Been ready for a long time."

I study him, wondering if he feels the same as me. Like the weight of the past has finally lifted, leaving room for a fresh start and new beginnings.

"Want to get the lights?" I ask, my hand on the door.

"Nah. You do the honors."

"All right." I hold my hand over the switch. "Three, two, one." I flick off the lights, and Artisant Designs goes dark. We leave the building.

"Nice shirt." Uncle Bear nods over at me as we walk toward the T station.

I look down at myself. "Thanks. Found it in my uncle's closet."

Uncle Bear grumbles his displeasure under his breath. "I always wondered where it went."

I grin.

"Want to grab chowder and beers?"

I hook my arm with his. "I'd love to."

"Always leave a lasting finish," he muses.

My brows bounce. "Is that a new Bearism?"

"With the warmth of your company, this evening is bound to become a memory that will linger like a beautiful, hand-rubbed finish. Yep, I guess it is."

"I've missed those, your little life lessons," I say, and take a deep breath. "I'm sorry I doubted you. I should have known you weren't selling to intentionally hurt me."

"I'm sorry I didn't trust you enough to tell you the truth. We both have some sanding to do, don't we?"

I laugh softly. "Another Bearism?" He shrugs, a slight smile appearing, and I say, "Despite everything, I wouldn't trade our family for anything. We're like a piece of knotty pine—full of character."

"And just as sturdy. We bend, but we don't break."

I bark a laugh and he chuckles, and I rest my head on his shoulder. "I think I'm ready to focus on building something new out of the ashes of the old."

My uncle nods approvingly. "That's my girl. Some of the most beautiful creations often come from repurposed materials."

I lift my head to look at him, feeling my eyes soften. "Love you, Uncle Bear."

He pats the hand hooked in his elbow. "Love you too, Melisaurus."

CHAPTER 27

WAFFLY GOOD TO HAVE FRIENDS

Emi has outdone herself. Her waffle bar is an explosion of festive colors and syrupy sweetness, from jellies to nuts and an assortment of sugary toppings with flavored whipped creams.

"What are we celebrating?" I ask.

"New adventures!" Emi slides a platter of waffles that were warming in the oven onto the counter.

"I'll eat to that," Shae chimes in.

We load our plates and take our waffle mountains to the table. Tam pours a round of strawberry mimosas. We toast to our hard work yesterday. We're all sore in super odd places from pushing and pulling and lifting. I woke with a stitch between my shoulder blades and a pain in my hip flexor.

I thank the gals over and over as we stuff our faces, and I get emotional, explaining that, yes, Mom and I are working on our mother-daughter relationship, and surprise! Uncle Bear showed up at the last minute yesterday after they'd all left. I catch them up on what happened between me and my parents and how my uncle had to give up the shop because of my dad, and that later over chowder and beers, Uncle Bear made a confession. He'd taken a long sip of beer and said to me, "I'm not sorry to see the shop go. Truth is, I've been more ready to retire than I realized."

The admission caught me off guard. "But Artisant was your life's work."

He chuckled, shaking his head. "It was a chapter, Meli. A long one, sure, but still just a chapter. It was time to start a new one."

"So you're not upset with Dad?"

"I didn't say that." He paused, staring at the wall over my shoulder as he reflected. "I'm not happy with how it happened or that he and your mother lost their portion of the investment. I think she's mad enough at him for both of us. I'm just going to let him stew awhile and let him think I don't want anything to do with him. He'll think twice before he does something stupid again," he said with a wink at me.

While I had been out to dinner with Uncle Bear, Shae and Tam edited some of the video they'd taken yesterday and made me a few goodbye reels I can post to Artisant Design's social media handles before I close those too. We watch them as we devour our waffles, and I'm crying again.

"How is there anything left?" I ask of my tears, laughing into my hands as I wipe my face.

We all laugh and Emi tops off our mimosas.

Shae pours coconut syrup over vanilla-flavored whipped cream. "When do you start at Stone & Bloom?"

"Tomorrow," Tam answers for me. "Are you sure building kitchen cabinets is what you want to do?"

"No," I say. "It's only temporary."

"Actually, she isn't starting in cabinetmaking. She's coming to work with me." Emi takes the syrup from Shae and pours it over her plate until it puddles around her waffles.

"You're designing kitchens?" Tam asks me.

"Attempting to."

"Heidi quit on Friday," Emi says. "I need someone to stand in who knows AutoCAD, so she's starting a week early. She'll pick up Kitchen CAD pretty quick."

"I'm surprised you aren't taking time off," Shae says. "You should go on vacation."

"I can't afford to." I'm not getting the money from the shop's sale that Uncle Bear would have put in trust for me since the Savant House never acquired Artisant, and I won't receive a single dollar from the property sale. What I currently have in savings I would like to keep there. "The work will keep me busy." And from moping around my apartment.

"What would you rather be doing if you weren't coming to work with us?"

"She wants to launch her own woodshop but needs to work up the courage to strike out on her own first," Emi answers for me when I hedge. I glare at her. She glares back.

"How cool is that?" Shae's excited for me. "What are you waiting for?"

"She doesn't know if she wants to open her own shop or go into business with Aaron."

"Oh my God, Emi, would you stop?" I glare at her again, and she gives me a smug, close-lipped grin.

"I haven't decided if I want to open my own shop or partner with Aaron," I repeat flatly.

The three of them laugh.

Stuffed, Tam pushes her plate away. "Does Aaron know you want to partner with him?"

"I haven't decided yet if I'm going to partner with him. And no, he doesn't know." Not after the way I left him. But before I dive into anything, I need to decide if I can live with just being his business partner and nothing more.

"Stone & Bloom is lucky to have you however long you'll give us," Shae says.

"Thank you."

It's late afternoon when we leave Emi's apartment, buzzed and overly full. I flop onto the couch in my apartment with Blueberry snuggled in the crook of my arm and turn on the TV. An episode of *Bridgerton* is cued up. I groan. I can't watch anything remotely romantic right now.

I turn off the TV and pick up my phone. I stare at the screen, then give in. I text Aaron.

I still miss you.

I wait for the bubbles, for his reply to come as quick as I sent mine the other night, but his response doesn't come. He doesn't even read the text.

When I wake the next morning, my text is still unread.

It's too late to unsend my message, but just as well he hasn't read it. We shouldn't be texting that we miss each other when I was the one who left so abruptly. I have no business flirting with him or even missing him after hurting him the way I did.

Before work, I meet Emi in the hallway like usual. This time I'm styling with a slim-fit navy vest, coordinating wide-leg trousers, and off-white mules.

"You look fantastic," Emi compliments. She has on a cozy sleeveless khaki one-piece jumpsuit with white platform sneakers.

"You look amazing, as usual," I say, feeling more anxious than I usually do in the morning. I haven't worked anywhere but Artisant Designs. I haven't worked with anyone other than my family and the occasional intern like Kidder. As we walk to Bean There, Done That, I ask Emi what I should expect from working at Stone & Bloom. What will her team expect of me?

"They are going to love you, Meli, so stop worrying. You're good at what you do, and you have a keen, creative eye. Lots of people say they're artsy and just aren't. That's not you."

"Tell me about the people I'll be working with," I ask to keep her talking and me from worrying.

"There's Piper; she's amazing. She's our project coordinator. If you need to reschedule appointments, she's your gal. She manages all client communications. Then there's Arlo, our procurement specialist. He orders our materials and tracks inventory. He also taps every countertop he encounters. He says he's judging its solidity, but it's super annoying. Max is the guy who . . ."

I can't help it; my mind wanders. Emi loves her job. She's stellar at it. But even knowing my position is temporary, I'm realizing it's not where I want to be right now. Stone & Bloom is not where I want to go.

I grow more antsy as we enter Bean There, Done That and place our orders. As we wait, Emi keeps chatting away. The couple waiting beside us catches my attention, and I feel a jolt of recognition. It's Aaron's dad. He's with a young woman who must be his wife. Oriana, the twat, as Kaye Borland called her.

"Excuse me for a second." I interrupt Emi midsentence and approach Graham. "Mr. Borland," I introduce myself. "I'm Melissa Hynes. We met at the Savant House's gala a couple of months back."

Oriana looks at me with curious interest when Graham's face brightens at the mention of my name. He takes my hand. "Yes, Melissa. I do remember you. You're Aaron's wife."

A surprised cough escapes me at his warm reception. Oriana's slightly raised brows lift even farther as she turns more fully toward me.

"Oriana, honey," Graham says. "This is Meli . . . Is it all right if I call you Meli?"

"Of course."

He smiles. "She's Aaron's wife. Surprised us all when he told us, didn't he?"

"He sure did," Oriana agrees, and Graham winks at me.

I feel a gentle upturn of the corners of my mouth in response to his ease at using the familiar version of my name and introducing me as his son's wife. After Kaye's cold welcome into the family, Graham's acknowledgment—and dare I say, acceptance—of my status doesn't make me feel like the temporary fixture in Aaron's life I'd started out as.

"Meli," Graham says with a smile that is both proud and full of love, "this is my wife, Oriana."

She extends her hand. "Nice to meet you, Meli." Her voice is crisp, her handshake firm, and she has great eye contact. She's wearing an expensive pantsuit with heels. I immediately judge her as a highly educated woman. I'd put my finger on Oxford or Cambridge given her accent.

Feeling slightly intimidated, I say, "Nice to meet you too. And, well, Aaron and I aren't married anymore. We're getting divorced."

Graham looks astounded. "He didn't tell us. That's a shame. He so admired you. I admit, it was certainly a shock when he told us he married and why." He gives me a knowing grin and looks at his wife. "He really stuck it to Kaye, didn't he? He showed her. The way he got her to fire him. Brilliant. Always has been a clever boy. He would have made a superb president for Savant, but Charlie has a good handle on things. Plus, I think Aaron's happier not working with his mother. She can be a real pain in the ass," he says to me, and Oriana smirks.

"You're being too kind, Graham."

He grunts. "I'm disappointed to see him go but admire his guts. He knows what he wants, which isn't working ten- and twelve-hour days as Kaye expected of him. In retrospect, I wish I'd taken more time off to be with the family."

"I admire Aaron too," I hear myself say. "He recognized what had been a perfect career for you and Kaye, and may be for Charlie, isn't right for him." Just as continuing Artisant Designs wasn't right for me. Even without my uncle and parents, I'd still be working in their shadows. If I want to grow, I must seek out the sunlight. "We need to follow our own paths."

Oriana turns to me with a widening smile. "I couldn't have said that better myself. My parents wanted me to follow in their footsteps. They're both genetic scientists. Research bores me."

"What do you do?" I ask, genuinely curious.

"I'm an attorney. I specialize in international law and human rights."

Now I'm smirking. Oriana is more of an Amal Clooney and far less the twat Kaye considers her. No wonder Kaye doesn't want Oriana anywhere near the Savant House. She'd probably end up running it.

"Graham, darling." Oriana rests a hand on his forearm. "No regrets. You can't change the past. You spend a lot of time with me and my family, and you're very good at letting me know when I'm working too much."

"I am now. I didn't used to be. Took me most of my life, Meli, to learn how to prioritize my personal life without sacrificing my goals for Savant."

"Communication has helped us when it comes to time management," Oriana points out.

"It certainly does, as does supporting each other's endeavors," Graham countered.

"And you're very good at that with me. You're also good at giving me personal space when I need it." Oriana gives his forearm a gentle pat, and I'm reminded of the Marriage-Material List Aaron and I drafted years ago on the plane. Graham and Oriana's exchange echoes what we wrote: Someone who supports your passions. Someone who will stand behind you. Someone who understands "me time" doesn't mean you don't want to be with them.

Their conversation is a stark contrast to what I've observed in my parents' relationship, my own past experiences, and what I know of Uncle Bear's marriage to Aria. But Aaron and I unknowingly outlined a blueprint for our ideal balanced and supportive relationship. And for the past couple of months, we lived by those guidelines because we knew what we've wanted all along in a marriage. We—I—already understand what it'll take to make my relationship with Aaron work alongside my passion for woodworking.

I've been so determined to adhere to Uncle Bear's advice so I wouldn't repeat his or my parents' mistakes, or risk losing myself in a relationship, or neglect it for my work. But Aaron and I created a vision of a partnership where we can both thrive. I don't have to choose between loving him and loving my craft, while wondering how I fit into helping him and Fallon raise their child. I can have it all, and I can do it all, because Aaron and I are true partners. We'll help each other prioritize what's important. We'll help each other find balance.

Oriana glances at her watch. "I'm running late. I have to get to court. It's been a pleasure, Meli. I hope we can meet up again. I'll see you at home this evening, dear." Oriana kisses Graham's cheek.

"Aren't you waiting for your coffee?" I ask.

"I don't drink coffee. I was just keeping Graham company. Have a good day." Oriana waves and she's off, leaving me basking in and slightly envious of the affection, admiration, and respect I witnessed between her and Graham. Almost too easily, I can picture Aaron and me doing the same, grabbing coffee in the morning and sending each other off for the day with a kiss. In fact, we did that on quite a few occasions when we were together.

I miss spending mornings with him. I also don't want to go to work in the opposite direction of him. I want to be with him *and* go to work with him.

The barista calls Graham's name. His order is ready.

He smiles at me. "That's my cue. Let me know if you and Aaron work things out. We'd love to meet you for dinner some night."

"Thank you. I'd like that," I say, realizing how much I do want that to happen.

I return to Emi's side, hoping there's a chance it will. I like Graham, and I would like to know Oriana better.

"Who was that?" she asks.

"Aaron's dad."

She hums. "I thought I recognized him."

Graham nods at us as he passes on his way to the door, and we watch him leave.

I retreat into my head and find myself sitting on the beach beside Aaron, our toes dipped in the water where the waves meet the sand. It was our last night in Maui and we were watching the sunset. At the time, I was feeling melancholy about returning home and not looking forward to reaching out to Paul and his family, not only to apologize for ruining the wedding but also to explain why I'd run away. I could blame him for demanding I give up my craft, but I was just as much at fault. I should have stood up for myself. I should have communicated what I wanted.

But despite that, I felt excited while on the island, and for the first time in a while, truly happy. I was happy with myself, and I was happy being with Aaron.

Through an unusual sequence of circumstances, I'd met this stranger who, by the end of our getaway, I considered a friend. I felt that way, even knowing we'd agreed to part ways and not see one another again. We had lives to return to. Goals to pursue. Futures waiting for us.

But I never forgot him, and I never stopped thinking about him or what he had said to me on the beach that last evening.

"I still don't see myself ever marrying—for real next time," he clarified, and we chuckled. "But if I do, I hope I marry someone like you."

"Maybe it will be me," I said good-naturedly.

"Maybe," he murmured.

We watched each other for a long moment with slight smiles that might have been full of secrets. Then the sun disappeared below the horizon, and we gasped at the sky's dazzling color palette.

Wishes are usually made on the rising sun or shooting stars. But I made a wish right then that if Aaron and I were meant to be, perhaps we'd find our way back to one another.

Maybe, not so surprisingly, we had.

And maybe, not so surprisingly, we've grown since then because we support each other's dreams and give each other space and are willing to try new things together. Going into business with him and being in a romantic relationship with him isn't a risk. It's an opportunity for us to build something amazing. Something as sturdy, beautiful, and lasting as the furniture I create.

I turn to Emi. "I can't do it. I can't go to work with you."

Startled, Emi blinks. "Why?"

"There's something I need to do. I'm sorry. You went out of your way to get me this job. Please don't be mad."

"How could I be mad? I'm relieved. You saved me from firing your ass."

"Excuse me?"

"If you didn't figure out working at Stone & Bloom is the worst thing for you by the end of the day, I was going to fire you."

"You bitch." I say this to her with the utmost love and respect.

Emi laughs, shoving me toward the door. "Go. Get out of here. I'll see you tonight. Oh, and I want a full report. Details, woman." She snaps her fingers.

"Thank you," I shout and run out of the coffee shop, totally forgetting my coffee.

I sought out Aaron a couple of months ago because my family had been meddling with my future. They'd taken it upon themselves to decide what was best for me and had tried to control my destiny. That's my job, and mine alone. Just as Isadora advised the other day that the only person who can tell Aaron who is best for him, is Aaron.

I'm hoping he still thinks it's me.

I race back to my apartment ready to shape my destiny, to grab hold of my future, and to let Aaron know that I wholeheartedly agree with him. I am the right one for him, as he is for me.

CHAPTER 28

BETTER TOGETHER

I stand in the front office area of the building Aaron showed me a few weeks back, cracking my knuckles. I'm nervous, more so than I was this morning when I'd planned to go work at Stone & Bloom. Fear of rejection does that to you. But I need to be honest with myself. I've known all along a job at the kitchen-and-bath showroom was not meant to be, even if it was temporary. I don't know why I tried to convince myself I could work there.

The barren conference room with the threadbare, low-profile industrial carpeting is set up with the laptop and portable projector on the floor. After verifying my calculations and projections with Mom, who tracked industry numbers and managed Artisant Design's finances for almost three decades, and after taking another quick errand across town, I came straight over. I figured Aaron has been spending his days here. His car is parked in front and the entrance was unlocked, so I came inside and made myself at home. I just texted him I'm here, waiting for him in front.

Seconds later the door into the woodshop in back swings open and closes behind Aaron and on the loud whine of a table saw. He isn't here alone.

I push down a lump in my tight throat and fold my hands as a wave of longing washes over me. A flicker of anticipation runs through me as Aaron approaches, his expression a blend of confusion and something that might be hope. He looks like he can't believe I'm here. Like he yearns for me. Like he can't hide the pain that my leaving caused him, and I feel a slight, uncomfortable pressure in my chest. I don't want to be the Aria to his Bear. I ache to put him at ease, make right my wrong and hold him.

That will have to wait.

I give him a tentative smile.

"Hey, Meli," he says cautiously when he reaches me. "What are you doing here?"

My heart rate skyrockets. I crack a knuckle. "I have a proposal for you."

The corner of his mouth twitches. Some of the tension he's carrying visibly eases. "Is that wise given our history with proposals?"

He's making jokes. I'll take that as a good sign. My smile briefly widens. "Do you have a moment?"

"Meli, I'll give you all the moments in the world. All you have to do is ask."

My heart. This man.

The air shudders out of me. I rub the side of my neck and with a shy smile, gesture at the barren conference room. "I'm set up in there."

"Oh." He looks in that direction, surprised. "All right. Lead the way."

He follows me into the room.

"Do you mind sitting on the floor? You don't have a table yet."

"Because I don't know if the artisan I want to hire is still taking on clients." His gaze is piercing, and I feel a fluttering low inside me.

"Oh. Right. About that, I might have an answer for you. Let's sit."

I settle cross-legged on the floor. Aaron sits next to me but not directly beside me, which I appreciate. I'm already having a hard enough time concentrating with him in the same room.

I turn on the projector and glide my finger on the mouse pad to wake up my laptop. It displays on the wall the opening slide to the presentation I'd put together in hopes of pitching Uncle Bear to sell me Artisant Designs. The title slide is Artisant's logo.

A slight frown pulls Aaron's brows together at the center. "Didn't you show me this before?"

Seems like eons ago when I practiced the presentation on him in his kitchen.

"Yes and no. Bear with me. Pun not intended." I didn't want to waste time revising the slide show after already spending two hours with Mom this morning.

A ghost of a smile appears. "Show me what you've got." He gestures at the wall and leans back on his hands, stretching out his legs, keeping them crossed at the ankles.

I mentally groan at the image he makes in his worn jeans and the black tee stretched tight across his chest. I'm sorely tempted to push him onto his back and straddle him. At the thought, warmth spreads through me, and I feel my cheeks flush. Aaron cocks his brows. "Feeling okay?"

I clear my throat and glance away. "Yes. Well, then. Let's get started."

I'm a bundle of nerves and too animated to stay seated so I stand back up and launch into my presentation. As I speak, I replace "Artisant Designs" with "our company," and when I get to the offerings I wanted to launch through Artisant, I weave in the ideas we brainstormed when he asked to go into business with me, like the online catalog and, someday, retail stores. He'd manage the sales and marketing and financing side of this venture, and I'd head up product development and oversee our portfolio of revenue-generating services. I pitch expansion plans and highlight competitive strategies. I emphasize partnership and teamwork and giving back to the community. We'd create a company culture that stimulates innovation and the imagination to set new trends in high-end, artisan-crafted wood furniture.

When I finish, I feel inspired and hopeful. But apprehension threads through me as I look down at Aaron. He didn't say one word throughout the entire presentation. He didn't ask a single question, whereas last time he regularly interrupted me to clarify a point or challenge a strategy, testing their potential success.

A knuckle pops. "What are you thinking?" I ask.

Aaron sits upright, pulling his legs in, and looks up at me. "What are you asking of me, Meli? I think I need to hear you say it straight so there is no doubt in my mind."

I drop to my knees in front of him, pretty sure my expression reflects the same hope I saw on his face moments ago. My fears of a real marriage with Aaron were unfounded. We have already laid the groundwork for a balanced and supportive relationship that encompasses both our personal and professional lives. "I want to be your partner, in business and in life. If you'll have me."

Aaron's throat ripples and I catch the briefest tremor in his hands before he manages to speak, his voice carrying a hint of wonder. "You want both? Are you sure about that?"

"I am." From my pants pocket, I carefully remove and unfold the worn napkin I picked up from his house on my way here. I don't want to tear it. In fact, I want to frame this napkin and hang it in our kitchen where we'll see it at the beginning and end of each day.

Aaron's eyes widen with surprise when he realizes what I have. "When did you take that?"

"I stopped at the house on my way over. I still have a key." And he didn't change the alarm code.

"What are you doing with it?" He isn't angry. He's curious.

"I'm answering your question. Aaron, you are someone I want to wake up with every morning. Since the moment we met, you have prioritized us. You love to dance with me. Your singing voice leaves something to be desired, but it hasn't stopped you from singing to me."

He barks a laugh.

"You have supported my passions since day one. I don't know anyone who's been more of a cheerleader for me than you."

"Rah-rah." He pumps a fist and I try not to laugh.

"I'm not done," I warn him, trying to sound serious. "You have never resented me because of my work, and I've never resented you. You understand 'me time' doesn't mean I don't want to be with you."

"And I'll be here when you're ready to come back to me," he says.

I nod, tight-lipped, emotion welling up my throat. "I know when you're ready to say 'I love you' that you'll mean it."

"It'll be from my heart," he says with reverence.

I exhale a long stream of air to relieve the pressure building in my chest. It's a moment before I continue reading. "We are fun and playful together. We try new things with each other. You are compassionate, kind, and respectful."

"It goes both ways, Meli."

"It does?" I'm not so confident after leaving him so abruptly.

"It does."

"Thank you," I silently mouth. There's too much burning pressure building in me to say the words out loud. I take another breath. "You are not afraid to stand up to me. You have always stood behind me. And you stood up for me to your mom. I should have done the same and spoken up at dinner. I'm sorry I didn't."

"Meli, anyone who speaks up against Kaye Borland risks life and limb. I'll never hold that against you."

"If you say so."

"I know so." He holds my eyes captive until I nod and believe him without a doubt.

"Why the list, Meli?" he asks.

I gingerly refold the napkin. "I was right. We ruined us for anyone else but each other."

"We should just marry again." He repeats my joke back to me.

"We should."

He goes very still. "Are you joking with me again?"

"No joke." I put aside the napkin and cup his face. "I've never been more sure about anything," I say, finally answering his question. "I love you, Aaron. I think I've loved you since the day I married you the first time."

Aaron inhales steadily, his eyes closing as he savors my declaration.

He fits both hands to my face. "Meli, I've loved you since I ran into you on the plane."

I grin. "When our hearts literally collided?"

His laugh vibrates low in his throat. "I couldn't have said it better myself." He smiles against my lips. Then he's kissing me.

I sigh with relief and gratitude, pure happiness and love. Throwing my arms around him, I squeeze my eyes shut and press my mouth against his. Aaron's arms draw around me and pull me in close. I want to kiss him all day, and I ache to push him back on the floor like I wanted to before my presentation, but I remember we aren't the only ones here. Someone is in the back room.

I press my forehead to his. "What do you say, Aaron? Will you be my partner?"

"'Bout time you asked. Yes, Melissa Hynes Borland. I will be your partner in business and in life."

The surname reminds me of something, and I lift my head, searching his eyes. "Our divorce. It isn't final. Should we file a dismissal?"

"Whatever you want." His fingers brush hair behind my ear, tenderly skimming my cheek. "We can let it proceed or stay married. Or even get married a third time. I really don't care as long as we're together. That's what matters to me."

"True partners."

"In every way."

"Fallon and your baby, Aaron. I'm okay with them being part of our lives, part of our family."

Aaron grimaces. "There is no kid. She called me with the DNA results an hour ago. It's not mine."

"Oh." Fallon was sleeping with someone else when she had been with him.

"Yeah."

"I'm sorry."

He shakes his head. "Not my problem anymore."

No, but I can tell he's hurting. For a good few weeks he thought he was going to be a dad. I fold my arms around his neck and press my lips to his temple.

"I would have loved that kid," he says into my shoulder.

He already did love it.

"I have no doubt you would have. And I would have loved your baby as if it were my own because he would have been yours, a part of you. I'm so sorry I ran out on you. I was scared, Aaron. I was so afraid that I couldn't balance it all and be a good parent at the same time and I'd only disappoint you. I didn't want you to come to resent me, so I left before any of that could happen. I should have known you'd never make me feel that way."

"I could never resent you, Meli. You're too important to me. I love you."

We're quiet for a bit, holding each other tightly, before Aaron releases a shuddering breath. He kisses me, then gets to his feet and helps me up.

"Come with me. I want to show you something."

He takes me to the workshop in back. At the sound of the heavy door swinging shut behind us, the table saw winds down and a head lifts up.

"Hiya, Meli!" Kidder waves.

"Kidder? What are you doing here?"

"Aaron gave me a job."

I look at Aaron and he shrugs. "If he was good enough for Artisant Designs, he's good enough for whatever we name this place. He's our full-time apprentice."

I am so pleased Kidder found work in the industry. He's talented and has great potential. He'll make a fine artisan one day.

Kidder moves around the table saw, separating the wood, and I notice the unfinished piece of furniture behind him.

"What's my dad's desk doing here?"

I walk over and glide my hand across the newly sanded surface. Sure enough, it's the same desk I helped him load onto Uncle Bear's truck yesterday evening.

Aaron comes to stand beside me. "It's here because I ordered it."

"I don't understand."

"I hired your dad to make you a desk. Sort of a wedding-slash-going-into-business-together gift."

All this time Dad was making the desk for me? It's the finest, most elegant piece he's ever crafted, something I thought long before I knew it was for me. So much love and care has gone into the artistry. For me.

I feel the burn of tears and a strong tightening in my chest rising up, forcing the tears to spill over. Aaron rests a comforting hand on my back.

Across the woodshop, a door slams. In walks Dad with a couple of brown bags from a local deli. He stops when he sees me, then hesitantly approaches.

"Sorry, Meli-pie. If I'd known you'd be here, I would have picked up a sandwich for you."

He unpacks the bags, tossing a wrapped baguette to Kidder.

"Thanks, Dean."

"You can have half of mine if you're hungry," Aaron offers.

I stare at him. I stare at each of them. "What are you doing here, Dad?"

"I work here."

"Since when?"

"Since this morning. Aaron offered me a job. I took it." He rips off a big bite of his sandwich.

"If that's okay with you," Aaron says to me. "It's your team."

If it's okay with me? Kidder is here. Dad's here. Aaron.

This is my family. *Our* family, I think, taking Aaron's hand.

"It's *our* team, and yes, it's okay for him to work here. Thank you for hiring him." With his record, he would have had a difficult time finding employment elsewhere.

I surprise Dad with a big hug. He pats my back.

"This mean you and Aaron are going into business together?" Dad asks, and I nod. Dad looks at Kidder, then Aaron. "All right. Who owes who?"

"What are you talking about?" I ask.

"We took a bet on how long you'd last at Stone & Bloom," Kidder explains. "What was it, half a day? An hour?"

"I didn't even make it to the showroom. I never clocked in. And you"—I point at Dad—"you aren't supposed to be gambling."

"It was a simple bet."

"I'm serious, or I'm firing you."

Dad holds up his hands. "It'll never happen again."

Aaron holds up his palm toward Dad. "Pay up first. I won."

"You?" I look at him, miffed.

Kidder smirks. "He bet you'd quit before you started."

"No faith." I playfully shove Aaron.

"I do love you, though."

"I know. Love you too. Now." I clap my hands. "Let's get to work. We have a business to build." I cup my hand behind Aaron's head and bring his mouth down to mine. "And a partnership to nurture," I say against his lips and kiss him.

Lucky in love at first collision, he kisses me back.

CHAPTER 29

GLUE, NAILS, AND SCREWS

Ten Months Later

"Three . . . two . . . one!"

Aaron tears off the paper we used to cover our new signage for today's open house, and the crowd cheers at the reveal. The double-layered dark-gray matte-acrylic sign with laser-cut lettering over a copper backplate looks gorgeous in its prominent space on the side of the building. *The Joinery.*

"Where luxury meets lumber," I announce, reading our slogan under the business name.

Joinery is the process of joining pieces of wood with glue, nails, screws, or any number of fasteners. Aaron and I thought the term perfectly summed up our partnership. A joining in work and in life.

After a hectic fall and busy winter, we are finally ready to officially celebrate our opening. Everyone is here: Charlie and Murphy; Uncle Bear and my parents, though they aren't here together. They circle around, avoiding one another. Their bowling team came, as did Graham and Oriana. Aaron was pleased they made it. So did Emi and others from the Chamber of Commerce. It's our official ribbon-cutting ceremony, and Shae and Tam, who embarked on their own a few months back to launch a video production company, are here to document the entire event.

Aaron swoops me into a hug, swinging me around. "I'm so proud of us."

"Me too."

We've had our share of ups and downs, but that comes with the territory when you launch a business; I see that now. I can also fully attest that I was right: finding a perfect balance between work and life is impossible. Plenty of times, we've been consumed with work. Plenty of nights and weekends, we haven't put each other first because our new venture demanded our attention. But when you share a teeter-totter with your person, the one you don't need but absolutely, wholeheartedly want to be with, you push off the ground when your partner is up there with their legs dangling. You reach out and grab their hand when they're spinning out. You check in when they're seriously stressed, take a temperature reading on the relationship. Then you remind them that you love them, and you tell them so because it comes from the heart. You truly become one another's center of gravity.

Sure, we aren't perfect. We bicker. And, holy moly, do we argue. Standing up to each other? We have that item on our list nailed down. But we also cherish, love, and adore. We admire and support. We stand up for one another. And we do so with kindness and respect.

Surprisingly, this long-term relationship we're in is a lot of fun. Life with Aaron is fun.

I kiss him to show how happy I am with him and with what we created together. Always together.

He puts me down, and we look at our sign.

"I love our sign," I say. "I love the name. I love our partnership. I love you."

"I'm just *in* love with you."

Our eyes meet and his palm cradles my cheek. "Love you," he whispers and I smile. We kiss again.

"Enough of that, you two." Shae interrupts the moment. "Plenty of time for that later. We need photos."

"Line up here, guys." Tam gestures at me, Aaron, the Chamber president, and a few other VIPs. "Everyone else, stand behind them."

Someone unrolls a thick red ribbon and hands me a giant pair of scissors.

"Would you like to do the honors?" I ask Aaron.

"We'll do it together."

He takes the bottom handle and we position the ribbon between the scissors' blades. At Shae's order, we smile for the camera. Someone counts down and when everyone shouts, "One!" Aaron and I cut the ribbon. More cheers go up.

The Joinery is far from the size of the Savant House. We don't have the name recognition, and it will take years before we have near the market share. But Aaron and I don't mind. We don't even want to directly compete with his family's business. This is our journey, and we'll find the perfect niche in a market that's right for us.

We invite everyone inside for champagne and cupcakes. Shae and Tam take more video and photos. Dad demonstrates to some of the other business owners in attendance how to plane wood and the steps that go into fabricating a piece of furniture. Emi gives our visitors a tour of the newly renovated front offices.

Yes, after much needling, I convinced her to join our team to lead our designers. We have a catalog of furniture to craft.

At some point, I find Uncle Bear leaning against the wall, watching the room, taking it all in.

"I'm proud of you, Melisaurus," he says when I join him. There's a sheen to his eyes, but I leave that alone and just smile. "You're right. I should have given you the shop. You would have done great things."

"Yes, I would have, but I'm glad you didn't. I wouldn't have created this." I needed to go out on my own, find my own way. "Thank you, though," I say, and a sense of contentment washes over me as I think of him and my parents, of Aaron and our love.

While my parents aren't together, they are civil toward one another. Mom visits our shop, and Dad and I have had some tentative conversations about the past. My relationship with my parents still has bridges to mend, but I can envision us, along with Uncle Bear and Aaron, and maybe even Graham and Oriana, enjoying Sunday dinners and celebrating the holidays as a family.

We aren't there yet, but I'm confident we'll get there. Someday soon.

Later, as the party dwindles to only a few stragglers, Aaron and I stand at a workbench and toast to a successful day. Kidder is across from us, peeling the wrapper off a cupcake.

"I've never figured it out," he says, biting off half the cupcake. "Are you guys married or what?"

Aaron and I look at each other and smile.

"Why don't you box up the rest of the cupcakes, Kidder, and take them home," Aaron says, changing the subject. He loops an arm around my shoulders and leads me away. The party is over and it's time to go home.

"Come on, guys," Kidder complains in a drawn-out whine.

I grin at him over my shoulder as we walk away. "We're partners, and that's what matters to us."

Outside, Aaron opens the passenger door for me. "Do we tell him?"

"Nah, let him wonder." They can all wonder.

"It was a good day, *wife*." He kisses me.

"A beautiful day, *husband*." I touch his cheek and settle into the front seat. I'm exhausted and ready to get home to where Blueberry waits in a house that will one day be as fully furnished from the Joinery's catalog as it will be full of life.

WHAT HAPPENED IN MAUI?

Curious as to what happened between Meli and Aaron during the five days they spent in Maui? Visit www.kerrylonsdale.com to download *The First Fall*, a free *Falling for You Again* companion novelette.

Acknowledgments

Ah, here we are, my novel's ending credits. Thank you to the entire Amazon Publishing production team, from my editors—Nancy Holmes, Jodi Warsaw, Karen Brown, Sarah Vostok, Rachel Norfleet, Angela Elson, and Darci Swanson—to art direction, marketing, publicity, and every department in between. I'm sure I missed someone, but please know I am grateful for your contribution to making this book shine. Thank you, Ploy Siripant, for the beautiful cover that tells as much of a story as the one between the pages. Thank you, Amanda Leigh Cobb, for your audio narration and giving Meli a voice. Thank you to my agent, Gordon Warnock, for sticking by my side since the beginning of my crazy yet rewarding publishing career.

To the team at Fuse Literary, who handles everything from literary to film rights, thank you for having my back. Thank you to my advance reader and influencer teams who helped me spread the word about everything that is good about this novel. Some of you have been with me since my debut. I feel blessed to have you on this journey with me. Thank you to my Facebook reader community, Kerry's Tiki Lounge. You put the *social* in *social media*. Thank you, Emily Bleeker, Camille Pagán, and Rochelle Weinstein for keeping the *sane* in *insanity* this past year (pretend there's an *e* in *insanity*); I love everything about our friendship. Thank you, Orly Konig: I won the writing partner lottery with you. Thank you to my family and loved ones for your boundless support. I am a better writer and person because of you.

And to you, dear reader: Thank you for reading my stories. There is nothing more rewarding as an author than witnessing the joy my books bring you.

About the Author

Photo © 2018 Chantelle Hartshorne

Kerry Lonsdale is the *Wall Street Journal, Washington Post,* and Amazon Charts bestselling author of more than ten novels. Her books have been Amazon Editors' picks, translated into twenty-seven languages, and sold over two million copies. She lives in Northern California with her husband and three former feral cats with an aversion to the spare human, and she is the lucky mother of two twentysomething-year-olds who will be—hopefully—successfully adulting by the time this book is published. You can learn more at www.kerrylonsdale.com. Follow her on Instagram: @kerrylonsdale.